Their eyes battled, absorbing each other.

Their noses were close, almost touching. Her breathing was loud, fanning his lips. God. She wanted him to kiss her, but she knew he wouldn't. He was too good for that. Too correct. He wouldn't do anything to her in this room. Even though she read the hunger in his eyes, he would hold back. He'd give her nothing. It was all about her doing things to him.

And God, she wanted to do things to him. She wanted to kiss him. She wanted to taste his wide mouth, nip his lips and suck on his tongue.

Pheromones raged through her, but she couldn't bring herself to do any of those things. It was up to her to do all the taking and she wouldn't take that kiss from him. Pride stopped her just short of that.

But she could wreck him in other ways. She could torment him all she liked.

By Sophie Jordan

BEAUTIFUL LAWMAN

A
DEVIL'S ROCK
NOVEL

SOPHIE JORDAN

AVONBOOKS
An Imprint of HarperCollinsPublishers

BEAUTIFUL LAWMAN. Copyright © 2018 by Sharie Kohler. All rights reserved. Printed in the United States of America. No part of this book may be used or reproduced in any manner whatsoever without written permission except in the case of brief quotations embodied in critical articles and reviews. For information, address HarperCollins Publishers, 195 Broadway, New York, NY 10007.

First Avon Books mass market printing: January 2018

Print Edition ISBN: 978-0-06-266656-7
Digital Edition ISBN: 978-0-06-266657-4

Cover design by Nadine Badalaty
Cover art by Steve Stone

FIRST EDITION

18 19 20 21 22   QGM   10 9 8 7 6 5 4 3 2 1

For Lindsay . . . for being there for me every single time.

BEAUTIFUL LAWMAN

ONE

*T*HE SECOND TIME Clive Lewis grabbed her ass, she was ready for him.

The first time he'd grabbed her, she politely warned him against such a move. She couldn't let a second time go unpunished.

Just like in high school, the former football player loved to harass her. And yet unlike high school, Piper wasn't the same five-foot-two, flat-chested, ninety-pounds-soaking-wet girl hugging the shadows in an attempt to avoid boys like him. She was a hundred and ten pounds now. Still short and mostly flat-chested, but she had learned to fight back. She had to. Even if she did work in a strip club where the general consensus among the female staff was to be amenable to grabby men.

She whirled around, colliding the tray she held directly into his face. To the casual observer it could have looked like an accidental move on her part. It *could*.

The edge met the middle of his nose with a crack, breaking the skin. He howled and cupped his nose as blood ran down its length. His friends hissed in empathy.

She made out his muffled words to be: "Jesus, Walsh!"

She glared down at him. "Oops. Sorry about that. Maybe you should keep your paws to yourself."

In high school he had been a muscle-bound behemoth. One of several that had prowled the halls. A jackal in the pack. Now all that muscle had gone to fat. His features had softened, too. Jowls gathered around his neck, making him look older than midtwenties.

"Piper!" Joe roared from across the bar.

Her gaze darted to her boss as he made his way between the small round tables toward her. *Great.* She would have to make a customer bleed when he was watching. He spent most of his time in his office with the blinds shut, occupying himself with any one of the girls who suppressed her bile enough to stomach his touch.

She lifted a hand, palm out in supplication, and spoke over the loud pump of "Gangnam Style" blaring from the stage speakers. "What? It was an accident. He startled me."

She knew her boss would accept that excuse more than the actual truth—that she was fed up of getting groped by customers.

From the way Joe charged toward her, his shiny face glaring hotly, she knew he didn't commiserate. She waitressed in a strip club. He'd told her on more than one occasion that a little grab-ass was part of the job . . . that it was even good for business.

"You have too many *accidents*!" He jabbed a finger toward the back of the club. "In my office. Now."

Setting her tray down on an unoccupied table, she marched a hard line toward the office, her Chucks smacking the ground hard in defiance. That was another point of contention with him— her choice of wardrobe. No stilettos and sexy attire for her, thank you very much.

Since Joe was too cheap to provide a uniform, she wore jeans and sneakers and the same Joe's Cabaret unisex T-shirt that the male bartenders, bouncers and DJ wore.

But really, she was a good waitress—when she wasn't hitting customers with trays.

She always got customers their drinks quickly,

and since that was half the bar's revenue, Joe let the matter slide about her conservative choice of wardrobe. She wasn't a dancer, after all. She didn't need to walk around with dental floss up her butt.

As she headed toward Joe's office, it was reminiscent of the many walks she had made to the principal's office as a kid. She felt the stares of several customers and staff. She almost expected to hear the old singsong, "Oooh, you're going to get it, Piper!"

Back in school, whenever anything went wrong—i.e., something was stolen, vandalized or someone just felt like making her life hell (more hell than it already was)—she was called before the principal. That's what happened when your last name was Walsh in this town. At least it had been that way for her. She was working hard so that it wasn't that way for Malia. Her sister deserved better and Piper was determined she get it. She owed that to her brother.

Joe waited until she passed through the threshold and then slammed the door so loud it rattled the thin wall. He pulled his pants up over his swollen midsection as he squared off in front of her.

"I just had to buy that table a round of drinks." He jabbed a fat sausage finger in her direction. The thick diamond band wrapped around that finger seemed to wink and jeer at her. It had to've cost a fortune. A fortune he made off the exploitation of women. "That's coming out of your pay."

She inhaled sharply, mentally calculating the cost of a round of drinks. "That's not fair, Joe!"

"You've used up all my goodwill, Piper. I only hired you because I thought you might change your mind and decide to dance." He looked her up and down appraisingly. "You got what it takes. You're small, barely got any tits, but you're pretty and lots of guys are into spinners. You could do a great Catholic schoolgirl—"

"Ew." She held up a hand. "Stop right there. I've already told you I'm not dancing. Besides. You need waitresses. You can barely serve all the tables you got." She motioned behind her, indicating the room on the other side of the bar. "All the girls are too busy taking private dances—"

"Because that's where the money is, sweetheart. If you want to bring home the green, then you need to do the same."

Yes. She knew that. But she was trying to cling to what dignity she had left. It was one thing to waitress at Joe's Cabaret and another thing to take to the stage or slink back into a private room for a lap dance. She knew more than lap dancing went on in those rooms.

She'd worked at Joe's for a little over a year and she'd seen enough to know how it worked here. It always started with dancing, but then that led to other things. She couldn't bring herself to take her clothes off for money.

She continued to apply for other jobs where she could earn what she did at Joe's, but no luck. Sweet Hill was a small town and the name Walsh was no good in these parts. Her job before this had been as a cashier at Brothers' Pantry. She'd worked there for almost two years when money went missing from the cash register. Of course Rick, the manager, told her he'd overlook it and she could keep her job if she gave him a hand job in one of the storage closets. Never mind the fact that she didn't take the money. He was convinced she had. She was a Walsh, after all.

After she told him to go screw himself, he'd fired her. Without a proper reference, the only other job she could land after that was Joe's Cabaret.

She couldn't lose this job, too.

For no other reason did she bite her tongue and forget about her dock in pay. She adopted a conciliatory tone. "I'm sorry, Joe. You need me. You know that. I get the drinks out fast and free up the girls so that they can work the stage and private rooms."

"I can get other waitresses to do that," he grumbled, his gaze flitting over her. "Ones who aren't nearly as pretty as you. We could make a lot of money together, Piper. The customers ask about you—"

Just then her phone started ringing in her back pocket.

Joe paused and scowled at her.

She forced herself to ignore it, resisting the urge to peek and reassure herself it wasn't her sister calling. Joe forbade phones at work, but because Malia stayed home alone while she worked, Piper hid it in her pocket.

She nodded as Joe kept talking, pretending to listen as her phone went silent.

Less than five seconds later, it started ringing again. She dove for it this time, unable to ignore it. "Sorry, Joe," she said, glancing down as she pulled her phone from her pocket, her stomach sinking at the name on the screen. "It's my little sister. I have to take it."

His face glowered, but she answered it, her fingers clutching the phone tightly as she spoke. "Malia? Everything okay?"

"Piper. I've been trying to get ahold of you for-ever."

Damn. She had missed her earlier calls. She must not have switched the phone to vibrate and the music must have been too loud on the floor.

Her sister's voice trembled as she continued. "I need you to come and get me."

"Where are you? You're supposed to be at home doing your homework." Or, given the hour, asleep in bed.

"Um, I went out with some friends."

Piper temporarily ignored the fact that her sister didn't have permission to go anywhere, instead seeking reassurance that her sister was safe. "Are you okay?" she asked anxiously.

"Yes. I'm fine. We're all fine. We were just walking around . . . doing nothing . . . and this cop picked us up and brought us to the station. He said we shouldn't be walking the streets so late and we had to call our parents to come and get us."

Of course a group of fifteen-year-olds shouldn't be roaming the streets at midnight. That was just a recipe for trouble.

Piper bowed her head and squeezed the bridge of her nose. Guilt stabbed at her. She should have been home looking after Malia instead of here.

And then how would you buy groceries? Or pay rent so they had a roof over their heads? To say nothing of Malia's soccer expenses. Those aren't insignificant.

Her sister continued. "I'm at the Sweet Hill Sheriff's Department. Can you come?"

"Of course. I'm on my way." She hung up and faced her boss. From his expression, he got the gist of what was happening and he looked as unhappy as she felt.

"Piper—"

"I have to go. It's a family emergency."

He waved a hand out toward the main floor of the club. "And what about all your tables? Who's gonna cover them?" Before she could answer him, he shook his head and continued. "Sorry, Piper. This isn't working out. If you leave, you're done. You can come by tomorrow to clean out your locker and get your last check."

"Joe, c'mon. You don't mean—"

"I mean it, Piper. I don't like being left in the lurch like this. I could hire a hundred more reliable girls—"

"I work hard for you and you know it. I hardly ever miss—"

"You walk out and you're done."

She held his unflinching gaze for a long moment before nodding slowly. "Okay, then."

He nodded back as though satisfied.

Turning, she called over her shoulder, "I'll pick up my last paycheck next week."

TWO

$\mathcal{T}$HE SWEET HILL County Sheriff's Department was on the opposite side of town. At least a dozen traffic lights slowed her down on her way to reach her sister.

Her stomach grumbled as she waited impatiently at yet another red light, reminding her that she hadn't eaten in a while. She'd been working since opening at 11 a.m. The only thing she'd managed to eat today was a bowl of Cheerios in the morning and the bar peanuts she'd filched.

She needed food and a bed, but unfortunately that wouldn't be happening for a good while yet. She had to handle this first.

Her baby sister. At a police station. The situation made her stomach twist in knots.

It was like déjà vu. She couldn't count the number of times the phone rang because her mother or brother or someone else in her family got arrested and was in jail. It wasn't supposed to happen anymore. Mom was dead. Her father was dead, and she didn't keep in touch with his side of the family anymore. She lived her life and they lived theirs. Her uncles and aunts and cousins might drift in and out of jail, but it had nothing to do with her. They might share a last name, but that was all they shared.

If her brother wasn't an inmate at Devil's Rock Penitentiary, she would have taken Malia and moved a long time ago, but she couldn't abandon Cruz.

Cruz had asked her to move away with Malia, but she couldn't leave him. Staying in Sweet Hill meant she got to see him at least every other week. If she left, who knew when she would manage to visit? She couldn't abandon him like that. Not after everything they had been through together.

Sweet Hill was the closest town to the prison. The next one was hours away. Out here, cities were remote like that. You could drive hours without even hitting a gas station. People actually traveled with fuel canisters.

Cruz would be released someday and then they could leave this godforsaken place and never look back. They had promised each other that. Now that he had quit trying to convince Piper to take Malia and move far away to some location where they could have a fresh start, he settled for looking ahead to the future they would all have when he was free. He worked on his degree and kept out of trouble while inside—at least, that's what he told Piper. Every time she visited and they talked via phone through soundproof glass he assured her he was okay.

She only had to hold it together until Cruz was paroled. It was her mantra that got her through . . . well, everything. All the visits to the prison when her brother showed up bearing the marks of a brawl. The nights when she couldn't sleep because she didn't know how she was going to pay the bills.

The light turned green and she charged ahead, careful not to speed. The last thing she needed was a ticket—especially considering she was out of work again. She winced at that reminder.

What had her sister done? Tonight had to be a mistake. It had to be. Malia was a good girl. She never got into trouble. That was the one bright light in Piper's life. Malia's goodness. She and Cruz had agreed they would do all they could to see that their sister had everything they never had. A good home. Guidance and love. College. A future.

Cruz sent what money he could and Piper worked every shift she could, especially since Malia was old enough to stay home alone now. *Especially* since her sister started high school and made the varsity soccer team. As a freshman, no less. The cost of soccer cleats alone was three days of tips, but she had talent. Piper and Cruz both agreed it was worth the sacrifice. Coach Chapman said she had a real shot of getting a scholarship.

"Malia," she grumbled, beating the steering wheel with the heel of her palm.

She thought school and soccer would keep her sister out of trouble. Hard to get into trouble when you didn't have an idle moment.

She thought back to the last time she spoke to Malia. Piper had called home on her break earlier and briefly talked to her. Malia had just gotten out of soccer practice. Dani's mom dropped her off. She said she had homework to do and then was going to bed. It was a tournament weekend so that meant an early game tomorrow.

So how did Malia end up at the sheriff's department when she was supposed to be at home in bed?

After hitting what felt like every red light in Sweet Hill, she finally pulled into the parking lot of the sheriff's department. Only a few cars occupied the asphalt lot, a testament to the lazy life of Sweet Hill. This wasn't a crime-riddled big city, which is why her family always stood out.

For a moment, her gaze focused on the bold black letters at the front of the white stucco building. She gnawed on her bottom lip, hesitating. Sweet Hill Sheriff's Department. *Sheriff.* As in Sheriff Hale Walters.

She'd finally met him a few months ago. She'd heard rumors that the new sheriff was a hottie, but she had never met him before then. They didn't exactly move in the same circles now and he was older than Piper so she never saw him in school. Plus, he went away to college or somewhere. Like all the kids from good families.

The image of him from their first meeting hadn't dulled. How could it? There weren't many hulking Thor look-alikes walking around town. He'd left a definite impression. Still, sheriff or not, he was decidedly un-Thor-like in character. Explaining why she'd dumped a pitcher of ice water in his lap.

He was surprisingly young for the role of sheriff, but then he had all the other criteria she associated with the role. Arrogance. Small-mindedness. The ability to rush to judgment. He was every misogynistic small-town sheriff she ever saw stereotyped on TV. And he'd deserved that pitcher in his lap.

Sighing, she climbed out of her car and headed up the walk, telling herself she wouldn't come face-to-face with him. He wouldn't be on duty this late. A big boss man like him had to have underlings. She would probably have to talk to the desk clerk or one of his deputies.

The first thing she noticed upon entering through the double glass doors was that the place smelled like cinnamon rolls. She stopped and blinked. Equally unexpected was the apple-cheeked gray-haired woman sitting behind a wide desk positioned in front of a dividing wall who gave her a cheerful wave.

The top half of the partition was glass so Piper had an open view into the building. There were several more desks beyond the divider and a couple doors that led (presumably) into offices or rooms. An opening spilled into a hallway. She couldn't see very far into the hall and she imagined this might lead to holding cells.

When her brother was arrested, he was taken to the City of Sweet Hill Police Department where they held jurisdiction over his crime. She had been eighteen at the time and went down in the hopes of bailing him out.

That never happened.

From day one of his arrest, her brother had never

been released. There was no bailing him out. The judge hadn't even offered it. That's what happened when you went to jail for killing a beloved member of the community.

She had never actually stepped inside the *county* sheriff's department before. Not that she imagined it would be very different from the city police department she knew so well. She assumed it would be like any other bureaucratic building full of stuffed shirts and eyes that judged her without really seeing her.

She knew those eyes. She'd felt them on her all her life, roaming her skin like ants crawling on a mound. She felt them whenever the police were called in for one of her mom's knock-down-drag-out fights with whatever guy she was dating. Or when her mom was pulled over for swerving all over the road and CPS had to come and get her, Malia and Cruz until their mom was later released and they were returned to her care. So many different occasions. When Cruz was arrested. When her mother died.

On the night Mom died the police had come to tell them she had crashed into a family of four. Because she was drunk. Again. Thankfully the family survived. One of the kids had been in a coma for a week and still suffered disabilities as a result, but thankfully Mom was the only fatality. That's what people actually said to her. *Thankfully your mom was the only one who died.*

When the deputy relayed the news, his eyes said just what he thought. Her mother got what she deserved. There was no pity for Piper or Cruz or Malia. They were simply Walshes and pity-exempt.

So when she entered through the double glass doors of the county sheriff, she did not expect a warm greeting by law enforcement. She most especially did not expect to be greeted by a grandmotherly type wearing blinged-out eyeglasses attached to her neck with a colorful beaded rope.

"Hello, sweetheart," the lady exclaimed. "Come in. Shut the door. You're letting all the cold air out. It might be night out, but it's still ungodly warm out there. Lud, this heat. It brings out the wild in folks. Phone been ringing off the hook all night. We've got every deputy out on calls right now." She shook her head. "We need more staff . . ."

Piper obeyed as she continued to prattle on, pulling the door shut behind her.

"What can I do for you?" the woman asked.

"Yes, I was called. I'm here to collect Malia Walsh."

"Ah. Yes. She's having a drink in the break room."

Piper straightened uncertainly as the woman stood and rounded her desk, revealing herself to be, rather impossibly, shorter than Piper. "She a sweet child, but ain't no good ever came of a bunch of teenagers wandering the streets at night." The desk clerk gave Piper a pointed look.

Piper tried not to squirm beneath the older woman's scolding stare. She succeeded only partly. The fact of the matter was she did feel guilty. Her sister shouldn't have been out wandering the streets at night. She should have been home in her bed with Piper home, too. Like the family they should be. In a perfect world that would have been the case. But then her world had never come close to perfect.

"I completely agree, ma'am."

The lady nodded, seemingly pleased with Piper's agreement. "Wait right here and I'll go fetch her."

She watched as she shuffled away, barely lifting her feet from the ground as she moved. She wasn't what Piper was expecting upon walking into the building, but the County of Sweet Hill was small and the city even smaller. Of course a grandmotherly type who looked like she should be home baking cookies would be working the front desk at the sheriff's department.

At least the place appeared to be void of Sheriff Hale Walters. There was that.

She shifted on her feet, her tennis shoes squeaking slightly on the tile as she tried not to feel anxious. Soon, they'd be out of this place that made her skin itch and feel too tight for her frame.

As the moments ticked, she started wondering if there was still that gallon of Coffee Toffee Bar Crunch in the freezer. Sinking into the creamy sweetness sounded like bliss right now after this day, but she had a feeling that she and Malia had polished it off, and there was no way she could bring herself to stop and pick up another gallon. Now was not the time to splurge on pricey ice cream. Not after losing her job. Right now everything had to be about necessities.

Voices drifted from the back. She thought she made out the sound of a softer feminine voice. Soon Malia emerged holding a can of orange soda, the dispatch trailing her with shuffling steps.

Her heart leapt at the sight of her sister, safe and smiling as though nothing were amiss. She would never *not* feel that searing relief. Not after losing both their parents. Not after losing Cruz. Every day when she parted ways with her sister she held her breath a little until she saw her again. Until Malia was back in front of her with all ten toes and ten fingers. Even watching her on the soccer field, her stomach clenched with worry every time a bigger girl, which was just about every player, bodychecked her sister.

"Malia," she breathed as her sister advanced. Her smile slipped as she noticed what her sister was wearing—or rather what she was *not* wearing. She was most decidedly not wearing the clothes she had left the house in today. No, she was wearing skinny jeans a size too small (even for skinny jeans) and a slinky tank top that refused to stay straight on her narrow shoulders. The scooped neckline dipped low, revealing cleavage she had never seen on her baby sister before. Mostly because her sister was built like her and lacking all cleavage. Malia didn't own a bra capable of creating cleavage like that. The only thing she ever wore were sports bras.

She doesn't own one, but you do.

"Is that my bra?" She leaned forward to hiss as her sister stopped before her.

Malia's brown eyes widened and she nodded and shook her head almost simultaneously, clearly unsure how to respond. Evidently admitting the truth terrified her. Piper didn't often get angry, but right now she was close to redlining.

"What has gotten into you?" she continued in a whisper.

Malia ducked her head, color burning her cheeks.

"Found her," the desk clerk trilled as though

Malia had been lost somewhere in the back—clearly oblivious to the tense undercurrent between them.

Piper grasped Malia by the elbow and tugged her close beside her. She pasted a smile on her face for the benefit of the older woman. "Thank you so much. Is there somewhere I have to sign her out? Or do you need to check my identification or—"

"Ah, yes." She clapped her hands lightly and scurried behind the broad desk again. "It's right here. The other parents already signed out their children . . ." She looked up and eyed Piper. "You hardly look old enough to be her parent."

"No, I'm her sister, but her legal guardian."

"Ahh. That explains it. You two are mirror images of each other. Cute as two kittens."

Malia giggled as the woman resumed searching through the clutter of her desk.

Piper reached deep for patience even though a part of her marveled at how this woman fared in emergencies where speed was required. She did work in a sheriff's department, after all. They had to have the occasional need for urgency.

Footsteps sounded, thudding deeply across the floor. Her nape prickled in awareness. She looked up just as a tall figure emerged from the hall, a big dark shape etched against the pale beige backdrop of the building's interior.

Her throat closed up at the sight of the deep blue uniform with its shiny brass bits. At first it was all she noticed. The only thing. It was familiar enough. As was her physical reaction to the sight of it. She supposed it was an unhealthy reaction. And abnormal. The sight of a policeman's uniform should provide comfort. But for her it never signified anything good to come.

Her gaze crawled over the uniform—and there was a considerable amount of it. Not just in breadth, but in height, too. The body that filled out the uniform was muscled and tightly built. Not an inch of fat anywhere on his bulk.

She dragged a breath in and forced her attention to his face as dread pooled in her stomach.

She knew what she would see. *Who* she would see. He was a tank of a man. There weren't many men built like him sporting a police uniform.

He would have to be on duty the one time she came here. She had feared coming face-to-face with him the moment she parked outside. Her brother's friend, North, had warned her that he was a powerful man, the implication being that she should give him due respect. Only she hadn't done that. Hopefully she wouldn't pay for it now.

She squared her shoulders, bracing herself for the moment he looked up and saw her. Maybe he wouldn't recognize her. He'd seen her just once, after all. In a darkened club, no less.

She stifled a snort. Wishful thinking. She doubted he had forgotten the first time they met. If that encounter in Joe's could even be called a meeting. The pitcher of ice water in his lap would have made a lasting impression.

Braced or not, when he looked up *she* was caught off guard.

Nothing could have steeled herself for the weight of those gray eyes. Somehow she had missed their magnitude in the dimness of Joe's, but she felt the intensity of them now. In one sweeping glance, he took in their trio before advancing in a long-legged stride.

"Ms. Walsh." He remembered her, all right. "Isn't it?"

Damn his voice was deep. Full of gravel. *It sounded like sex.*

The completely inappropriate thought hit her out of nowhere. For starters, she could hardly count herself as an expert on sex. And secondly . . . this was Hale Walters. A rude, arrogant cop quick to judge. He was everything she despised.

She'd heard him speak in Joe's but the music had been loud and she'd found him so offensive with his remarks that she hadn't absorbed the gritty drawl like she did now in the stark quiet of the sheriff's department.

"Sheriff," she greeted, the word escaping as a treacherous tremor.

As he drew closer she was only more painfully aware of his size. He'd been sitting that time in Joe's. She had no idea he was *this* big. *This* tall. He had to be pushing six-five.

She tugged her cardigan closer around her, feeling suddenly fragile in comparison, and she didn't like it. She didn't like feeling vulnerable.

His gaze drifted to Malia. "Your sister, I presume?"

She nodded.

"Appears she got into a bit of trouble tonight."

Her jaw clenched. The desk clerk had said as much, but she resisted nodding assent to him. Everything about him rubbed her the wrong way.

"Found it!" The older woman brandished a clipboard and abandoned her desk to offer it to Piper. "Just sign here."

The sheriff plucked it from her hands just as Piper was about to take it. "Thank you, Doris."

Doris beamed and turned for her desk again.

Piper stared at the sheriff expectantly, waiting for him to hand over the clipboard so she could be on her way.

Instead, he held it in his hands and looked in no hurry to pass it to her.

He and Piper stared at one another for an awkward stretch of silence. As the seconds ticked, her resentment grew. He couldn't just be linebacker big. No. He had to be hot as sin, too.

Malia looked back and forth between the two of them mildly, taking a slurping sip from her can of orange soda.

Piper lifted her chin a notch. "Are you gonna let me sign that? Or just keep me standing here? It's late."

Malia's eyes widened. Piper knew she was setting a bad example. She'd told her sister time and time again to always be respectful to authority figures. Even when it was hard. And here she was throwing sass at the county sheriff. She couldn't stop herself though.

The corner of his mouth kicked up. It was almost a smile. Only his eyes didn't smile. They stared coldly. "You know I thought my memory of you might have been wrong, Ms. Walsh."

She fought the urge to demand he explain himself, but that made it look like she cared what he thought of her . . . or that he thought of her at all.

"It wasn't though," he finished.

And she was quite certain that was an insult.

"You two know each other?" Malia asked.

"No," she snapped. "We don't know each other at all." She lifted her chin, making sure he understood that she didn't *want* to know him.

This time both corners of his mouth lifted in a full-blown smile. It was devastating. Unfairly, it made him even more attractive. She bet the women in this town threw themselves at him.

And that only annoyed her more.

THREE

*T*HE LAST TIME he saw Piper Walsh she poured a pitcher of water in his lap. Of course, he might have implied she was a bimbo. Fine. No "might" about it. He did say something to that effect.

It wasn't his finest moment, but his sister's involvement with North Callaghan had colored his behavior at the time. Could anyone blame him? He'd been pretty sure his sister was infatuated with the convicted killer living next door to her. Even worse, he suspected the convicted killer was taking advantage of her infatuation of him.

He'd gone to Joe's to simply question North Callaghan (and maybe intimidate him). As the sheriff. As a brother. Whatever worked.

When he'd seen Callaghan talking to Piper Walsh he had assumed the two of them had history. He even thought that maybe their history wasn't history and more like current events. Understandably he didn't like the idea of his sister getting played by a felon who kept a piece on the side.

So yeah. He and Piper Walsh might have gotten off on the wrong foot.

However, he was still a lawman. Most people respected a badge and what it represented. Not her though. In the flash of her dark eyes, that was instantly evident.

But then what could he expect? She had a brother in prison and a handful of uncles in lockup, too. Her old man had died in prison after getting five to ten for armed robbery. Repeat offender. And let's not forget the mother, who killed herself and almost killed a family of four when she decided to drive after boozing it up.

Yeah, he knew all about Piper Walsh. The day she dumped water on him, he made a point to find out her story. He told himself it was because, at the time, he distrusted North Callaghan. He knew the guy was getting close to his sister. Closer than he or his father liked, and he wanted to know everything he could about the guy—and that included his relationship with one trouble making stripper.

But he'd been wrong.

At least about Callaghan. It seemed the guy loved his sister, and Piper Walsh wasn't one of his playthings on the side. She and North were just friends, brought together by Piper's brother, who had served time with Callaghan.

He didn't think, however, he'd been wrong in his estimation of Piper.

She stared back at him with her eyes burning her dislike of him. Chin high. She didn't project the slightest deference as someone in her position might do . . . as someone *should* do.

She was a tiny pain-in-the-ass package of trouble.

Doris had called all the parents some time ago. Piper was the last to arrive to pick up her kid. Clearly she was a questionable role model for the girl. If that made him a judgy prick, so be it. He'd seen the pattern. His line of work gave him a bird's-eye view to it. First as an MP when he was in the Marines, then as a deputy under his father, and finally as sheriff. It always started at home.

He knew there were exceptions to every case, but considering he'd just picked up Malia Walsh traipsing through a rough part of town with kids who were already building a record for themselves? Yeah. The signs were there. She was headed for trouble.

He looked Piper up and down slowly, guessing

where she had just come from. The gray cardigan she wore failed to hide the Joe's Cabaret logo on her T-shirt. They'd interrupted her at work.

She felt his stare and pulled her cardigan tighter across the modest swells of breasts. As if she were shy.

"Do I sign her out somewhere?" She glanced around as though there was a form waiting for her to sign her kid out of gym class early.

"Are you her legal guardian?" He assumed she was, but his digging hadn't uncovered that detail.

"Yes." That chin went up higher, challenging him like she wasn't afraid of his authority.

He glanced from her to her sister. Piper Walsh was twenty-five. Another fact he remembered. He was good with details. Names, faces. It helped him do his job. It wasn't because she was a person of particular interest. Not then. Not now.

She was very young to be responsible for a fifteen-year-old girl. It would be hard on any twenty-five-year-old, but someone poor and without family support . . . he didn't know how she was managing it.

Except he did know. She was stripping at Joe's Cabaret. He grimaced, inexplicably not liking that idea. Couldn't she find a better job?

"Can I take her home?" she asked, her voice

strained, and for the first time he heard the anxiety there as he continued to keep the clipboard from her. She was worried. Which meant she was cognizant of his authority for all her lack of deference to him. He almost felt sorry for her . . . if there wasn't a child's welfare at stake.

Malia watched the exchange with wide eyes, picking up on the tension.

She was scared earlier when he'd hauled her in with her friends, but she had relaxed as her friends left one by one and Doris doted on her like she was some adorable puppy, feeding her brownies and soda. He winced. He hated to admit it, but it really was time for Doris to retire. She should have retired when his father did. She looked like someone's granny. Sometimes he wished he had someone with a little more steel in their eyes to be the first point of contact for his department.

"Piper?" Malia asked in a small voice.

As much as he thought a little fear was a good thing for a fifteen-year-old caught toeing the line, he didn't want to launch her into full-blown panic. The girl had been through a lot with both parents dead and a brother in prison. *And a sister stripping for a living.* Who knew what Piper Walsh exposed her to on a daily basis?

Did she bring men home?

He knew a lot of the girls at Joe's did tricks. It was a casualty of the trade. The thought that Piper might be one of them soured his stomach for some reason. He'd seen a lot of unsavory things in his career . . . but the possibility of Piper Walsh turning tricks and letting strange men climb over her body in the same house she shared with her little sister made him want to break something. One of his hands curled into a fist at his side.

Wrong thoughts, for sure. Too . . . *personal.* Where was his usual detachment?

He knew better than to get too involved. He knew how important it was to maintain a level of professionalism.

"Can I talk to you a moment, Ms. Walsh? Alone?"

Her lips pressed flat and for some reason he thought it was the Ms. Walsh designation that did it. There probably weren't a lot of people in this town to address her so formally. She probably thought he was mocking her.

Without waiting for her agreement, he set the clipboard down. Turning, he walked down the hall. There was a moment of silence before he heard her follow. The slight staccato slaps of her tennis shoes on the tile trailed behind him as he led her into the conference room they used primarily for meetings and interrogations. He held the door open for her and closed it after she passed through.

She crossed her arms over her chest, creating a ledge for her small breasts. Of course he looked. Even though he liked generous breasts on a woman (preferred them, even), he was a typical guy and what Piper had distracted him. They were small but well formed. Perfect for her frame.

He snapped his gaze back to her face and kept his eyes trained carefully above her neckline. He'd learned long ago to keep things professional with the females in his county. She watched him with a wary expression, her fine dark eyebrows knitting together.

"Are you aware that two of the other kids your sister was hanging out with tonight have been brought in before? One for drug possession? The other for assault?"

Alarm softened her gaze and made her appear vulnerable for the briefest moment before her expression returned to hard. She tucked a strand of dark hair behind her ear, clearly agitated. "Did any of them have drugs on them tonight?"

He took his time answering. Crossing his arms across his chest, he leaned back on the table, lowering himself almost to her height. "No."

"Did an assault take place?"

"No."

"Then I can take her home?" Her dark eyes narrowed on him expectantly.

He stared at her for several moments before answering. She shifted on her feet, clearly anxious to be on her way. It didn't take any great discernment to figure out she didn't care about what he was saying. He wondered if she was even going home or just going to head back to Joe's once she dropped her sister off at home. And then he wondered why he cared so much. People came and went out of this department every day. Some innocent. Some guilty. He couldn't afford to care too much and maintain his objectivity.

"I hope you will talk with your sister about the kinds of friends she chooses to associate with. These are the types of choices that can affect the rest of her life. One wrong decision—"

"Thank you for your concern."

He shook his head. She couldn't even be bothered to hear him out. He knew he should let it go. Let *her* go, but he heard himself asking, "Do you care about your sister, Ms. Walsh?"

Hot color flamed her cheeks. She uncrossed her arms and stabbed a finger in his direction. "You don't know anything about me or my family."

"Actions speak for themselves. You're in my station in the middle of the night because you can't keep tabs on your sister."

She flinched and then quickly recovered, her eyes like dark chips of obsidian as they fixed on him. "You won't be seeing me or my sister again, Sheriff Walters." She paused for breath. "I can promise you that."

"I hope you're right, Ms. Walsh."

"May I take her and go now?"

Still, he hesitated, which made him wonder. What else did he want to say? What *could* he say? He wasn't a social worker like his sister. It wasn't his job to reform anyone. "Yes." He waved her out of the room.

She stalked ahead of him and he followed, watching her storm off with more appreciation for her well-rounded ass than he should feel.

His gaze skimmed all of her. For someone so small, she radiated enough fury that she actually looked like she could level a small village. She seized the clipboard on Doris's desk and scrawled her signature.

"One moment," he called.

The sisters both froze, exchanging uneasy glances. He slipped his hand into his pocket and pulled out his wallet. Inside he fished out two business cards and handed one to Piper and then the other to Malia. "If y'all ever need to get ahold of me. My cell number's included there."

Malia looked from the card to her sister, her expression uncertain.

Piper Walsh glared at him with blazing eyes. She understood what he wasn't saying: *If either one of you are ever in trouble, you can call me.*

Her nostrils flared, clearly offended and he didn't know why. He gave his card out all the time. Especially to people in need. Especially to children living in questionable circumstances. He never wanted a kid to feel like there was no lifeline available for them.

"Thank you for your concern, Sheriff, but it's not necessary," Piper said again, her voice like ground glass. She thrust his card back at him, forcing him to take it. With a smile reserved for Doris, she took her sister by the hand and led her from the building without a backward glance at him.

He stared at the double doors through which they'd departed. Dark night pressed against the glass panes. Several moments passed and a flash of headlights streaked across the front doors, briefly filling the lobby as they exited the parking lot.

"Sweet girls," Doris commented.

He glanced down at the woman who served as dispatch for his father and now him. He had known her all his life. She was more than an employee. She was family. When he was a boy, she used to sneak him candy out of the top drawer of her desk.

"Trouble is more like it," he countered.

She grinned at him. "But who doesn't want a little bit of trouble in their life now and then? Makes for an interesting time." She paused a beat and then added, "That Piper sure is a pretty thing."

"I hadn't noticed," he lied.

Doris tossed back her silvery-haired head and laughed. "Oh, that's funny."

"What's so funny?"

She inched away from her desk. "You thinking I can't tell when you're fibbing. You forget I changed your diapers."

He ignored her—what he usually did when she mentioned the fact she changed his diapers. She mentioned it a little too often. "She's not my type."

"Oh, I know the type you usually cavort with, but *they're* not your type."

He knew he shouldn't, but he took the bait and called after her retreating figure. "Really? And what is my type, Doris?"

She didn't slow down and she didn't look back. "Oh, you'll find out someday soon, I warrant. And you won't need to ask me then."

He felt himself scowl as she disappeared into the break room wondering what the hell kind of answer that was.

FOUR

*T*HE NERVE OF that man. He thought she was some bit of filth under his shoe. Just like the night she had overhead him talking about her in Joe's. She'd known then he thought she was trash. Even if she hadn't overheard him say those words, she had seen it in his eyes, heard it in his tone. It shouldn't have stung. Others had thought it and said it to her face before. She'd developed a thick skin. It rarely bothered her anymore. And yet for some reason the sheriff being among their ranks affected her.

"You're very mad at me," Malia said quietly, interrupting the spin of her thoughts inside the car.

Piper took a shuddering breath. She was mad. Furious, even. Although one of the things she had learned after she became a parent, which she was essentially, was that when she was this angry she should wait before reacting. Wait and compose herself. Words spoken in anger led to regret.

And the thing was . . . right now she was mostly angry at the sheriff. The big jerk. She didn't want to take her temper out on Malia.

Sheriff Hale Walters thought he knew her, but he was wrong about her and it killed her that she couldn't convince him of that. And that, in turn, ate at her. Because why should she give a damn what he thought about her?

He didn't matter.

"Please. Say something. I can't take the silence, Piper."

Her mother had been one of those loud drunks. A real screamer. And considering she was intoxicated pretty much all the time, there was never a lot of silence in the Walsh household. Screaming was the only method of communication. Piper had vowed to live differently. She and Cruz said they'd be nothing like their parents.

Except he was in prison, which pretty much put him on the same path of every other male Walsh.

And she was raising their baby sister. Alone. While working in a strip club. Not exactly a stellar existence.

She sent Malia a quick glance before looking back at the road. Malia . . . their baby sister, who she just picked up from the sheriff's station. Clearly she wasn't doing a bang-up job parenting. She sighed and gave her head a slight shake.

"How mad are you?" Malia pressed.

Malia was a good kid. Ever since she was very little, she'd been an old soul who studied the world with wide, knowing eyes, taking it all in. A quiet observer, watching and learning. She was eons smarter than Piper could ever hope to be.

"I'm not mad." She inhaled, proud of her calm and even tone. There had to be an explanation for tonight's misadventure. Malia wasn't a bad kid. "At least, not *very* mad," she amended. "I'm just disappointed. Who were these kids you were hanging out with? The ones the sheriff said were trouble?"

"Just some kids from school. They're . . . popular. They invited me and I was . . . flattered."

Piper nodded. "They might be popular but they're not the kind of people you need to be around if they're going to get you into trouble like this. You're better than this, Malia."

Her voice was small and full of regret. "Claire said the same thing."

That only made her sigh. Claire was her friend

from soccer. Her mom helped get Malia to and from games when Piper couldn't. They were good people who made it possible for Malia to play soccer on a select team outside of school. "Then why don't you listen to Claire?"

Malia pressed her lips flat in petulant silence.

"Did you have a fight?"

Still no comment.

"Malia?" she pressed.

Finally she burst. "Because what else am I supposed to do? Claire is with Rafael now. She spends every spare minute she has with him. I only see her in history class and when we play soccer."

Piper flexed her hands around the steering wheel, her stomach knotting as she grasped the situation. "Claire has a boyfriend?" She was a freshman like Malia. God, she wasn't ready for her sister to start dating. She wanted her to stay little and innocent forever and—most importantly—never, ever get hurt.

"Yeah." Malia expelled a breath and there was a wealth of frustration in that sound. "Maybe I overreacted. I shouldn't have gone out with those kids. I knew I shouldn't . . . I knew you wouldn't approve. I don't know what I was thinking. I wasn't, I guess. I'll be more careful, Piper."

They exited the highway and passed a few fast food places, the lights of the buildings gleaming brightly even this late at night, like bright, watchful eyes in the dark, following them as they moved along the quiet highway. West Texas was always quiet. And endless. A place for secrets.

The farther they drove outside the city limits of Sweet Hill, the terrain turned rugged, an untamed land of extremes, whipped raw by wind and sun. Not that different from those spaghetti westerns from fifty years ago—minus Clint Eastwood.

Her stomach growled, reminding her that she had long neglected it.

"I'm hungry," Malia complained, as though she had heard Piper's stomach.

"I'll make you a grilled cheese when we get home." Mentally, she ran over what was in their fridge. It was pitifully meager. Hopefully they still had a couple of cheese slices.

Malia craned her neck, looking longingly at the hole-in-the-wall taco stand that served the best tacos this side of the Rio Grande.

They hardly ever ate out. Twenty dollars' worth of tips could buy groceries that lasted them for three days versus a single meal of fast food tacos.

She'd learned how to economize long ago when her mother forgot to feed them. She and Cruz would dig for change in the couch cushions and then walk to the corner store to buy a loaf of bread and cheese slices. Milk if they had enough. Cruz insisted milk was good for them and worth the splurge. Yes, in her world, milk was a splurge item.

"Guys come and go, you know," Piper volunteered as she turned off the feeder road, still thinking about Claire having a boyfriend. The fleetingness of love and relationships was one of many lessons courtesy of her mother. She had a lot of boyfriends after their father. They never stuck around. "Real friends last. They hang in there. Claire will come around again. A guy can't take the place of you. She'll figure that out."

Malia didn't comment and they fell silent for the rest of the drive home. From the slouch of Malia's small shoulders beside her, Piper knew she was feeling bad about tonight.

Tapping her fingers on the steering wheel, she resisted the urge to reach out and pat her arm. Comforting her and telling her everything was forgiven and all would be well would be counterproductive. If ever there was a time for a little tough love, it was now. Malia *should* feel guilty. It meant she still gave a shit. Apathy would be the end of everything. That she could feel regret, that she felt empathy at all, meant she was nothing like their mother. That had always been Piper's fear. That despite everything she did, she would fail to raise Malia right and she would turn out like their mom anyway.

Piper needed to be a parent now and not a friend. Not even a sister. Cruz had told her that when he went to prison. She'd only been eighteen at the time, but she remembered his words and the burden that had settled on her shoulders with them. *You're her mother now, Piper. She might not call you Mom but that's what you are. I know it's a lot to handle, but you'll do great. Better than our mom ever did.*

"Better than their mom" wasn't a high bar to hurdle, but she wondered what Cruz would think of her tonight. If he would think she was doing great.

Piper had lost her job. Malia had been hauled to jail . . . *kinda*. And they were flat broke. She felt like a failure.

She wanted to believe that Malia's shenanigans were just a one-time thing, natural growing pains that any other typical teen went through. But what if this was just the start of trouble? The beginning of the end?

If, if, if . . .

She shook her head and ordered herself to stop theorizing and playing the "what if" game. It wasn't helping. She flexed her suddenly sweating palms on the steering wheel. It only made her more neurotic than she already was. She wasn't screwing up Malia. Malia was a good person. She knew this.

To make matters worse tonight, that behemoth of a sheriff with his square-cut jaw and bedroom eyes had lectured her. His looks alone flustered her. The fact that he dispensed punishment to those he deemed deserving of it only made her skin itch and feet long to run in the opposite direction every time she saw him—which up until recently had been not at all. She needed to return to that "not at all" status ASAP.

Humiliation burned her cheeks as she remembered their conversation.

She'd had to deal with frequent visits from CPS when she first gained guardianship of Malia, but over the last few years those visits had dwindled. She had been lulled into a false sense of security that they were in the clear and no one would ever take Malia from her. Malia getting into trouble could change all that, however. All it would take was Sheriff Walters whispering to CPS and Piper could lose custody. It wasn't an unreasonable fear. It was obvious the sheriff thought she was unfit to care for Malia.

What if he was right?

She'd convinced herself they were doing just fine over the years—that *she* was doing fine raising her sister—but who was she kidding?

She was tired of eating ramen and tired of waitressing almost every night until her feet ached—and all for measly tips. It was hard, degrading work that took her long hours away from Malia.

Maybe the dancers were smarter than she was. At least they were well paid. If she danced, she'd be able to work less and feed them better. She could buy things for Malia and move them into a nicer place.

With all these fears whirling around in her head, she exited the highway and took the county road that led home, passing a few trailer parks and small houses that had been there since the turn of the century—weathered bits of clapboard sagging under the light of the moon.

She turned down a dirt road that led to her complex. Well, she wouldn't call it an apartment complex exactly. It was more like a cluster of efficiency housing. Single-room units that consisted of a bed she and Malia shared, a kitchen and a shower. It was a dump. Even more of a dump than the dump she had grown up in.

Piper pulled into the complex, Sunset Views. The building was at least forty years old with ancient air-conditioning units hanging off every window. A depressing stucco gray with mold stretching across the bottom half of the structure. Once upon a time that gray had probably been white. It was all flat lines and angles common from the nineteen seventies.

Even when Mom lived, they at least had two bedrooms in their trailer. Cruz slept on the pull-out sofa in the living room and shared her closet. His meager clothing didn't take up much space. When her mom would party and entertain friends, he would stay in Piper's room. They would lie in bed and talk late into the night. Over the sounds of partying they would make up names and pretend they were someone else, living somewhere else. Whoever Piper pretended to be, she always had a pool with a waterfall and huge birthday parties with a DJ and waiters carrying trays of food just like Shelley Rae Kramer. Not that she had ever been invited to one of her parties, but Piper had heard all about them. Everyone at school talked about them.

It was crazy how many of her fantasies centered on being like Shelley Rae.

They were dumb games, but they had kept their minds off what was happening in the trailer at the time.

She shut off the ignition and stepped out onto the broken asphalt of the lot. Malia, still subdued, followed her as she headed toward their unit. Piper fiddled with her keys, searching for her house key, when she noticed movement on her small stoop. Cacti and scrub crowded the stoop. She'd asked management to cut back the foliage. Unsurprisingly, her request had been ignored. Just like they had ignored her request to handle the rat problem. She could hear them scurrying in the walls, especially at night. Nocturnal bastards. They'd eaten through the back of the kitchen cabinets and gotten into the sugar and flour.

She'd had to break down and buy the traps herself with her own money. Either that or stay up all night guarding herself and Malia.

She peered through the dark toward her porch, her steps slowing. She'd recently replaced the porch light and could just barely make out a large shape at her door—a man with his back to her, a thin T-shirt stretched across his thick back. He fought with her lock and door handle, jiggling the hardware.

She stopped in her tracks, her hand flying to

grasp her sister's arm and keep her from moving forward.

She tightened her hand around her keys, finding the longest one and letting it jut out. A poor semblance of a blade, but it was all she had.

"Can I help you?" she asked loudly, forcing a deepness to her voice that didn't normally exist.

The man turned around, surprisingly quick for his size, and she immediately recognized the property manager, Raymond.

She relaxed only slightly because the guy always gave her the creeps. Ever since they moved in, her skin crawled in his presence. She had warned Malia never to let him inside their unit when she wasn't home. She'd even installed additional locks on the door, partly because of Raymond and partly for extra security in general. Actually, her brother's friend, North Callaghan, had installed the locks for her when he happened to stop by and caught her attempting to do it herself. An additional dead bolt on the inside and another on the outside of the door.

"What's this extra lock doing on the outside of your unit?" Raymond demanded, his face glowing with sweat beneath the yellow porch light. Apparently he noticed her additional lock.

She shrugged, striving for a light air. "We can never have too much security, can we?"

He scowled. "You didn't have permission for that."

"I wasn't aware I needed permission."

"Any changes to the structure of the unit need approval."

She fought the impulse to roll her eyes. It wasn't like she tore down a wall or did any other serious construction work. "It's a lock. What were you doing trying to get inside my unit anyway?" He couldn't possibly have meant to do any of the numerous requests she had requested over the last two years. At this time of night, no less.

He held up an air filter. "Changing the filters."

She stared. Was he for real? "This time of night?" He had never bothered with the task before. Or any task, as far as she knew. Any task other than spying on them from the window of his front unit or while he watered the small yard of near-dead plant life in front of the management office.

She held out a hand, clearly offering to take the filter from him. "I can see it installed. Thank you." Actually, North had changed their filters a few times for them, insisting it would help with Malia's allergies. Not that she felt like explaining that to him. She just wanted him gone.

He looked across the distance at her, his small eyes inscrutable beneath the gleam of his glass lenses.

He'd always been too interested in his female tenants. She hadn't missed that fact when she first moved in with Malia, but he'd had a wife that kept him on a pretty tight leash. That had given her some comfort. Up until recently. Marsha had run off with a truck driver about three months ago. Since then, Raymond always found some reason to knock on their door or stop them outside for conversation. This was the first time, however, that he had ever attempted to enter their home.

He huffed out the round barrel of his chest a little and glanced back at the lock. Clearly he wasn't ready to let the subject go. "I can understand a pair of young girls like you wanting a little extra protection." His voice softened to a slithering ribbon on the air. "What you need is a man around to look out for you." His gaze roved over Piper as he made this declaration.

Malia snorted behind her and Piper gave her hand a warning squeeze. She knew that belittling this guy wasn't the way to handle him. She needed to mollify and appease him until they managed to move out of this dump. Until she'd lost her job, she was hoping to do that soon. "I appreciate your concern. It's very kind of you, Raymond."

Funny she had not handled Sheriff Hale Walters with the same kid gloves. It would have been wise, she supposed, to be more deferential to a lawman, but there was something about him that prevented her from doing that. She could probably blame it on her genetics. No Walsh ever got along with law enforcement. It wasn't possible.

"Well, I do have a boyfriend," she blurted. The lie was instinctive. She told a lot of her patrons who got too frisky and asked her out on dates that she had a boyfriend. It was easier than crushing them with a rejection and kissing any hope for a tip good-bye. Only as soon as the words left her mouth, she realized that her lie might be easily verified when she never had a guy show up at her place.

"You do, huh?"

She nodded, detecting a thread of skepticism in his voice.

"Yes," she insisted. Maybe she could get North to pretend he was her boyfriend. He'd done that at Joe's to scare off customers that were getting too handsy. Although if she told North that Raymond was giving her a hard time, he might just resort to kicking the man's ass, and that wouldn't be a good thing for anyone. Kicking someone's ass was most definitely a parole violation . . . and something told her it would also get her kicked out of Sunset Views.

He dragged his eyes off her and looked back at her door with its additional lock. "Not sure about the lock," he grumbled. "I'll have to look at your lease agreement."

This time she softened her voice. "It's just one little lock."

He hooked his thumbs inside his waistband and hefted his pants higher over his huge stomach that spilled over his waistline. "I'll check with the management. They frown on structural modifications . . . but maybe I can put a word in for you."

"Or don't mention it at all . . ." She let her voice fade suggestively.

His gaze went back to crawling over her body. He actually ran his tongue along his lower lip. She'd noticed his fleshy lips before. They were very red. Almost like he'd been perpetually sucking on a lollipop. "Mebbe I can do that. You've always been a model tenant . . . would hate to lose you." He placed a wealth of meaning into his words and that urge to submerge herself in a Clorox bath surfaced again.

Quelling the rise of bile in her throat, she clung to her smile.

Why, she wondered, did she always feel like she was surrounded by predators? Was this poverty? Because God knew she'd lived most of her life hovering on that brink. Did poverty make victims out of people or was she just special?

Not you. You're not a victim.

She knew how to fight. Backed into a corner, she would come out swinging. History had shown her that.

She nodded. "I'd be grateful."

"You would." It was half statement and half question. He let it hang between them.

"Of course." She nodded. At the moment she would say anything to get both she and Malia inside her house and close the door on his face.

He stepped off her stoop, giving her enough room to pass. She edged around him, keeping herself between him and Malia.

She took the filter from him.

He gestured at the square. "Now you sure you know how to—"

"Yes. I've done it before."

"Because I'm happy to help." His beady eyes blinked through the lenses of his glasses. He pushed the frames up the moist line of his nose.

"We're fine . . . but thank you." *Sound nice, Piper.*

"Just doing my job." He held her gaze for a lingering moment, pinning her to the spot. Would he ever leave? "Let me know if I can do anything at all for you girls."

She backed up closer to the door, pushing her sister until she was practically backed into the cacti. She turned to stick her key in the first lock, glancing over her shoulder. "Will do."

"I'll let you know about the additional lock. If it's okay."

She murmured something noncommittal. With the second lock free, she shoved her sister forward and plunged them both inside. Flipping on the light switch, she released a breath as she shut the door behind them. Turning, she looked through the peephole to see Raymond still standing there, staring at the door with his head cocked at a contemplative angle. She could swear he was staring at the lock—the lock that he didn't possess the key to . . . that barred him from entering their apartment. *That's right, you bastard. Stay away.*

"God, he's creepy," Malia muttered.

Nodding, Piper turned back around and dropped her bag on the small table beside the door.

Sighing, she shook off thoughts of Raymond the Creep. The day had been endless and she was ready to put it to bed. "Get ready for bed while I make you something to eat."

Malia nodded, her face once again contrite. She started to move away, and then paused. "I'm really sorry, Piper."

"I know you are, but you have to be better than this. Other kids can mess up, but you can't. Understand? We don't have that luxury."

Malia nodded, her velvety brown eyes deep and sorrowful, and that hurt. A fifteen-year-old shouldn't have such sad eyes. Piper had worked hard to keep sadness from her sister's eyes, but she supposed she couldn't protect her from all pain.

"Good. Are Claire and her mom still picking you up tomorrow?"

"Yes. Six-thirty."

"Okay, good. Hurry up now. Six-thirty is gonna come early."

Malia hurried forward and gave her a hug. Tough love or not, Piper hugged her back, inhaling the apple scent of her hair.

"I love you, Piper," she murmured. "Someday

things will be better. I'll go to college and get a good job. You'll see. We won't live like this forever. We'll have a nice house and nice things. I promise."

"I know, Malia. And I love you, too, sweetie." She watched as her sister disappeared into the bathroom and then turned to the fridge. Fortunately, there were two slices of American cheese left. She grabbed the butter and bread she kept in the fridge (so that it would last longer) and quickly slathered two slices. Heating a skillet, she starting cooking the sandwich. She put both slices of cheese in her sister's sandwich. She was a growing girl and burned countless calories on the soccer field. She needed the nutrients.

Once the grilled cheese was finished, she set it on a plate and grabbed a box of crackers. Sinking down on a chair at the kitchen table, she opened her laptop where she left it on the table earlier today. North had given the device to her a year ago when he got himself a new one. It was an improvement from the ancient one she'd owned before. This one was faster. It took almost no time at all to open up a search engine for jobs in Sweet Hill, Texas.

Rubbing her tired eyes, she munched on a cracker and reached for her notepad to start jotting down possibilities.

She hadn't gone job hunting in a while. Maybe

it wouldn't be as bad as last time. Maybe people would give her a chance now. Maybe her employer wouldn't mind that her last job was at Joe's Cabaret—or that her last name was Walsh.

It wasn't impossible.

FIVE

IT WAS IMPOSSIBLE. No one would hire her.

Piper made it to the Sweet Hill City Park by 4 p.m., just in time for Malia's final game of the day and after she had been rebuffed from five restaurants around town. They never outright rejected her; they simply told her they'd be in touch, but she could always tell they were lying. They'd never be in touch. One look into their eyes and she knew that.

A few of them had seemed interested enough until they discovered where she last worked. One of the hostesses at a popular barbecue place had even refused to give her an application for employment. She'd remembered Piper from high school. She'd actually been a cheerleader with Shelley Rae. The moment Piper walked through the double doors, the hostess's ready smile had melted off her face to be replaced by a scornful smirk.

She could almost hear Cruz's voice in her head, encouraging her to take Malia and move to another town. In moments like that it was tempting.

She'd stuck it out this long, staying in Sweet Hill ever since her brother's incarceration, but if she couldn't find work soon, she was afraid she would have to move whether she wanted to or not. And she hated knowing that. It felt like she was failing Cruz even if he was the one telling her to leave.

Parking was crazy. She spent fifteen minutes driving up and down rows before swerving into a spot just after a car vacated it. Grabbing her purse, she jumped out and grabbed her folded lawn chair from the backseat.

With her work schedule, she didn't often get to see Malia's games. This was about the only bonus of losing her job. Malia was going to be surprised, too. Other than North, who occasionally came to watch her play, she didn't usually have any family or friends there to cheer her on at games.

Slinging the strap of her lawn chair over her shoulder, she took off in the direction of field eight. It was hot as hell and she was still wearing her interview clothes—a simple skirt and blouse that stuck to her shoulder blades like a second skin. Her wedge heels weren't ideal for rushing across concrete and cutting through the sticker-riddled grass. The sticker burrs stabbed at her toes peeking out of her shoes. Wincing and muttering curses, she pushed on.

Multiple soccer and baseball games were happening in the vast expanse of park. Shouts and cheers went up from every direction. Additionally, amateur basketball games were being played on nearby courts. She hurried past one court, eyeing the grown men who were a far cry from NBA players.

Well, except that one. Her steps slowed as she appreciated the sight of him. Lean, muscled and over six feet, he was a blur as he moved. She watched, her chair bumping her side as she walked. The shirtless player drove the ball right through the other players, dodging left and right, the ball moving from hand to hand with ease as he dribbled. Her steps paused as he slammed the ball through the net. His body seemed to hang in the air, suspended for a moment, the hard lines of his body glistening. His washboard abs were something out of a Calvin Klein ad.

The rest of the guys looked like a bunch of Homer Simpsons beside him. She couldn't help gawking. His teammates slapped his back as he came down from the shot—and that was when she recognized him. *Holy hell. Not him.*

Out of uniform, out of his shirt, he was totally drool-worthy.

She shook her head. A physique like that was wasted on an arrogant cop. *Arrogant* was a mild word for him. He probably didn't blink an eye when he arrested people and threw them in a cold jail cell. No, he probably got off on it. He probably only saw the world in black and white. No consideration for the gray where people like her existed. All she knew was that area in between black and white, right and wrong. She'd lived in that stretch of gray for her entire life.

Suddenly he was staring back at her. His eyes locked on her and she stumbled, catching herself right before she fell. She forced her gaze forward, cursing her lack of grace and the sticker burr wedged deeply in the tip of her big toe. Bending, she quickly plucked the thorn out of her skin.

"Hey!" a deep voice called. "Ms. Walsh!"

Straightening, she kept walking, moving stiffly like a robot on high speed, fervently wishing her ears were playing tricks on her and Hale Walters wasn't calling her name.

"Piper!"

As though she could mistake that growling baritone. His voice was closer now. *Fabulous.* A bare-chested Sheriff Walters was chasing her down through the park. She couldn't imagine why he wanted to talk to her unless it was to continue lecturing her about what a horrible guardian she was. Already been there. Done that. She didn't care for a repeat.

"Piper."

He wasn't going to quit.

Sighing, she turned around, sending the chair hanging off her shoulder swinging wide. The strap slid down her arm. She fumbled for it and pulled it back on her shoulder, feeling like ten kinds of idiot.

"Yes. Sheriff. How are you?" Her voice came out breathless and a tad too loudly. He looked her up and down. It was the slow assessment he'd subjected her to before, but it felt a world different coming from him like this—with *both* of them out of uniform.

She tried not to stare, but he was standing in front of her in sneakers and athletic shorts and nothing else. God, his torso was bigger than she was. Holy hell, was that an eight-pack? And his waist was narrow. A faint hint of his briefs peeked out from the waistband of his shorts and her traitor eyes strayed there.

Clearly this man didn't spend his time in a doughnut shop. Throw that stereotype out of the window. Her skin flushed hot and her tongue felt thick and clumsy in her mouth.

Instead of waiting for him to answer, she rambled on. "Am I trespassing? Did I park illegally?"

He blinked at her aggressive question, and she cringed inside. Did the words out of her mouth have to be so antagonizing?

Clearly her bitchiness was a defense. Just not a very smart one. Even she recognized that.

"I was going to see if your sister is doing okay. After last night?"

She eyed him closely, trying to read him for sincerity. He was Faith Walters's brother. There had to be something redeeming about him if he was related to North's fiancée. That penetrated for a moment. This was sweet, generous, never-judge-a-book-by-its-cover Faith's brother. That had to make him at least partially decent. The badge on his chest might not offer her that same assurance but his family tree gave her pause.

"She's fine," she responded, her tone somewhat conciliatory.

"Good." He glanced around her and in his next question she understood why. "I don't see her with you."

Because she *should* be with Piper. Because a girl that was hauled into the police station last night shouldn't be left to her own devices. That's what Piper heard in his words. Judgment. The same thing she'd faced all her life. Did she really think this guy might be as decent as his sister? What did he think? That she was out here cavorting at the city park while her sister was off snorting lines with her delinquent friends?

"That's because she's on field eight playing a soccer game."

He looked in the distance of field eight as if he could spot her. "Soccer?"

"Yeah. You know, that game with the ball where you kick it."

He stared down at her with a frown. She wasn't sure if it was because of her sarcasm or that he was still grappling with the fact that her sister played a team sport. Most delinquents shied from organized sports. Too demanding of dedication, time and responsibility. Malia was probably the first Walsh to ever play for a school team, much less a competitive select team.

"I know what soccer is."

"I see you're having difficulty wrapping your head around the fact that my *delinquent* sister is disciplined enough to play on a soccer team."

"I didn't say that."

"You didn't have to." She readjusted her hand around her strap. "You don't know me, Sheriff Walters."

He inhaled and the motion lifted his enticing chest, drawing her gaze down, down . . . the way the waistband of his briefs hugged his tight waist mesmerized her. "Just following up when I see an opportunity, Ms. Walsh. It's my job."

Why did the sound of him addressing her as *Miz* Walsh make her want to sock him in the mouth? She wasn't a violent person. Really. He brought it out in her.

"And I'm sure you're great at your job." She waved her fingers in a little circle in his direction, coming dangerously close to touching his chest. She told herself that wasn't deliberate. "You just don't need to do your job so much with us. We're fine. Concentrate your efforts elsewhere." God, she could practically feel the heat radiating from his body.

She dropped her hand at her side and curled it into a fist.

He propped his hands on his hips. "I'll try to remember that, Ms. Walsh, but my job isn't the kind that can be turned off just because you tell me not to worry. There are some people that demand worry."

Because he had a stick up his ass and he was unbendable like that and only saw things as wrong or right. He judged things in absolutes.

It didn't occur to her that he might actually be concerned for her—despite what he said. So few people cared about her, she couldn't believe this of him. Maybe that made her a hardened cynic, but so be it. Life made her this way. Trust no one. Let no one in. Take care of yourself.

Clearly he saw her as only one thing. And that filled her with all sorts of helpless rage. A man like him, a man who was supposed to be a conduit for justice, should serve all. He should see her for what she was. A woman who was simply trying to get by.

"You know what you are, Sheriff?" she hissed.

His eyes widened slightly and she tried to ignore how lovely a gray they were. "What's that, Ms. Walsh?"

"You're a bully." She'd been enduring them all her life. She would know. "A bully with a badge."

Tension feathered the skin across his jaw so she knew she had hit a nerve. It satisfied her but also sent a pulse of guilt through her that maybe she had hurt his feelings. *As if she could hurt this big arrogant hulk.*

And so what if she had? He deserved it . . . living his overprivileged life and judging her when he didn't know her from Adam.

"That a fact?"

"That's a fact. And I'd appreciate it if you would butt out of my life."

"As long as you keep your sister and yourself out of my jail, that won't be a problem. I can do that."

"Good," she snapped.

"Good," he returned.

Suddenly she realized how close they were standing. How had that happened? They had started out this conversation with a healthy distance between them. She took a hasty step back, marveling at the way the pulse in her throat felt like it was about to burst free from her skin.

She felt his gaze, a palpable trail of heat as it moved over her face. It was hard to explain but she felt pinned under that gaze, desperate to move and turn away, but unable to. She held herself still. Confused . . . but waiting for something to happen. Wanting it to.

Oh. My. God. This was attraction. She was *attracted* to him. She still thought he was an arrogant jerk with a stick up his ass, but she wanted him right down to the marrow of her bones.

It was horrifying, but the awareness also released something inside her. A pulsing tightness pulled low in her belly as she stood there gawking at him.

"Hey!" the guys on the basketball court behind them started hollering.

She jumped slightly, startled. Spell broken. Good.

He glanced back at his friends.

She nodded at them and waved in their direction. "You're holding up the game. Better get back to it, Sheriff."

His friends continued to call for him.

Yeah. Go. Get out of here so she could examine her brain and try to figure out how she broke it and then how to repair it. His face and body might be the stuff of dreams but this man, Sheriff Hale Walters, was the stuff of her nightmares. She could almost hear Cruz's voice. *Run, Pied Piper. Don't look back. Get the hell away from him as fast as you can.*

The sheriff nodded slowly. The fading sunlight hit his hair, gilding the brown strands gold in some places. "Take care, Ms. Walsh."

He kept his gaze trained on her, walking backward several steps before turning and jogging toward the court, giving her a perfect view of his backside—and the sight of that was simply ridiculous. She had never been the kind of woman to gawk at a guy's ass, but *this* man and *this* ass demanded its due.

Too bad he was such a jerk. And too bad she didn't have time for men in her life.

The last thing she needed in her life right now was a man to complicate things. Things were already complicated enough.

Forcing herself around, she turned and started toward field eight, and couldn't help wondering what it would be like for a man like Hale Walters— barring his jerk qualities—to look out for her, to turn his protective instincts on her and to genuinely care about her. Not because it was his job. Because he wanted to.

What would it feel like to be wanted by a man like that?

The list of people who gave a damn about her was pitiably short. She had her brother in jail and then North Callaghan—and the only reason she had him was because her brother tasked him with looking out for her. It was rather embarrassing when she thought about it. North was living his own life now and on the verge of getting married. His visits and looking after her made her feel like a burden. She'd started attempting to distance herself from him without being rude—not that that kept North and Faith out of her life. They had a way of popping in uninvited. She just didn't want anyone in her life there purely out of obligation or pity.

She believed in that kind of love and happiness even though she had witnessed so little of it in her life. And then she remembered. That kind of fairy tale existence wasn't for her. She didn't deserve it.

She'd lost the right to that kind of life a long time ago.

AS SOON AS Hale reached the basketball court, he glanced back to check Piper Walsh's progress across the expanse of sun-withered grass. She was the only human out here in a skirt and blouse. She looked like she just came from the office—even if her clothes weren't anything fancy and actually looked cheap and ill-fitting on her small frame. She reminded him of a little girl playing dress up in her mother's clothes. Whatever the case, looking at her now, she didn't resemble a girl who worked at Joe's.

At least, not until she'd opened her mouth and reminded him that she was that same prickly, smart-mouthed girl.

"Who's that?" Baker, one of his buddies from

high school, stepped up beside him. He was a firefighter, married with three kids and definitely enjoying the domestic life. He weighed thirty pounds more than when they were in high school with all the weight concentrated in his stomach. A veritable beer gut, but Baker didn't seem to mind. Nor did his wife. He loved his life.

"No one."

"Really? So you were just talking to no one for a few minutes."

"I talk to lots of people. It's part of my job."

"Talking to her is part of your job, huh?" He glanced back to where Piper was a shrinking figure. "I'm thinking I went into the wrong line of work."

He shot his friend a quick frown. "You're a happily married man. Amber would kick your ass to hear you talk like that."

He held up both hands. "Hey. I love my wife. I'd never stray, but that doesn't mean I'm not a red-blooded man and I don't have functioning eyes in my head."

"Like I said. It was work related." He looked back at her fast-fading figure. She was part of the job. Her little sister getting hauled into his department had established that last night.

"Yeah. And everyone knows you don't mix business and pleasure. You're much too disciplined for that," Baker murmured. "She's not your type anyway."

He snapped his gaze back to Baker. "What do you mean?"

"You know. Like your Miz Alpine. What is she? Double D? Legs up to her chin. Bottle blonde. Amber tried to get her hair that color once. Came out orange." He snickered.

He didn't bother correcting Baker. He wasn't far off from the truth. Only Annabelle didn't get anything out of a bottle herself. She worked for the biggest accounting firm in Alpine. Gordon and Fitzmichel happened to be based out of Dallas with satellite firms all over the country. Her salary was double Hale's and he made a decent living. At least he always knew she wasn't after him for his money. But then, he knew what she wanted from him. Annabelle had never disguised that fact.

He knew she would only go to the most expensive salons to get her hair that shade of white-blond. She demanded the best for herself and she worked hard to get it.

Every few weeks Hale visited her. Spent a night. Spent himself in her willing body. It was easy. No strings. They both had a good time and parted ways until the next time.

Only lately . . .

Well, they were overdue. That was probably it. He hadn't seen her in almost a month and he wasn't sure why. She'd been texting him about hooking up. He'd had some free time. He just hadn't taken her up on any of her offers.

He studied Baker. "I'm not so predictable. I don't have an exclusive type."

"Riiiight. I've known you since high school, man. You have a type and Miz Alpine fits it."

At this point he didn't want to argue because it would be like insisting that Piper Walsh was his type. Tiny things with dark hair and dark eyes had never been his choice female.

Baker continued. "A little variety would be a good thing for you but that one is probably too young for an old man like you."

"Who you calling an old man?"

Baker ignored him. "You need to be working on that family. Doubt you'll get that with that Disney princess you were talking to."

He shook his head. "Man, you don't know what you're talking about. I'm not into Piper Walsh—"

"Walsh?" Baker said abruptly. "As in of *the* Walshes? Well, forget that. Steer clear of her."

His hackles rose higher, but he couldn't say why. Baker wasn't saying anything Hale himself hadn't already thought. Still, he felt a surge of protectiveness. He didn't like Baker thinking about her like she was some lesser grade of human.

"Hey, you girls gonna keep gossiping or play?" Dan, another firefighter friend, called as he bounced the ball, looking ridiculous with his bright red sweatband around his head.

Hale responded by jogging forward and stealing the ball from him. Dan shouted an obscenity, but he didn't care. He just dove back into the game, making a mental note to answer Annabelle's text waiting on his phone. She sent it yesterday and he hadn't responded yet.

He was off next weekend. It was time to make a trip to Alpine.

SIX

*B*Y THURSDAY, THE panic set in, sinking deep. She could feel her heart hard and heavy in her chest, like a stone weighing her down.

For days now the terrible sensation had grown. Their fridge was nearly empty, the pantry was getting low and her bank account was floating on fumes.

She was running out of options . . . if she ever really had any.

She'd tried everything. Applied—or tried to apply—for employment at every restaurant in Sweet Hill and surrounding areas. She knew better than to aspire for anything beyond waitressing. Since high school, her resume only consisted of wait-ressing jobs.

The cold reality of her situation pressed in on her like a wall closing in. She was going to have to ask Joe for her job back. Who was she kidding? She was going to have to beg him.

Friday morning after seeing Malia off to school, she headed out of town for Devil's Rock Penitentiary after scrounging fourteen dollars and seventy-two cents in change from the bucket of coins she kept in the closet. The cashier at the gas station had glared at her as she counted out her change. Yes, she'd filled up her car with precisely fourteen dollars and seventy-two *cents*. She'd glared back at the attendant. Money was money even if it was all coins.

It was over an hour's drive and she wanted to be on time. She didn't want to miss a moment of the precious allotted visitation time allowed. Seeing her brother always grounded her and always reminded her of what she needed to do.

She didn't have to wait long before he joined her in the visitor's room. They'd sat together in this very room for years now. At least once a month. She'd watched her brother change and grow into the man behind the glass barrier separating them. He was lean and muscled and tall, topping off at six feet. Surprising considering they shared the same gene pool. He looked dangerous. The scar bisecting his eyebrow and ending in his cheek (a souvenir from a fight when he first entered Devil's Rock) added to his threatening appearance. He was lucky it hadn't gone deep enough to take his eye.

There were a few other visitors in the room, focused on the inmate they had come to visit. Just as they paid her little attention, she barely spared them a glance. She leaned forward in her chair eagerly as her brother picked up the phone on the other side of the glass.

His dark eyes settled on her, looking her over. "Hey, Pied Piper," he greeted, using the nickname he always used. Not very original, but then he'd been calling her that since she was two years old. He claimed their father had called her that once and it just stuck in his mind. Long after Dad had abandoned them and got sent away to prison when he killed a man in some drunken bar fight outside of Lubbock. She was her brother's Pied Piper.

"Hey, bub." She pressed a hand against the glass. He placed his hand there, the broad palm of his hand flattening as if they were making actual contact. It was as much as they could have until the day he was released and they could actually hug each other.

Her brother was a good man despite what everyone said—despite what a jury of twelve thought. It was a miracle, she supposed, that someone as good and noble as he could be the product of their parents—and he'd been under their influence practically all the formative years of his life. Malia was good, but she couldn't even remember Mom or Dad. Lucky for her. It was maybe the thing that saved her.

"You look thin," he said right away.

"You always say that."

"You always look it," he countered, lifting that dark eyebrow broken by that scar.

She shrugged and deliberately didn't tell him she'd eaten ramen for dinner the last three nights in a row. "I'm bigger than I was in high school."

"Well, yeah. You were just a girl in high school. You're twenty-five now. You *should* have more meat on your bones."

"Says the guy who looks like he could use a hamburger himself." She eyed the hard lines of her brother's face. He reminded her of a wolf, all hungry and lean. His hair was closely cropped to his head and only added to his fierce demeanor. "Seriously. Are they feeding you well?"

"Three squares. It was more than we got growing up." The corner of his mouth lifted.

She nodded. That was the truth.

"How's Malia?" Here was the part where she

could tell him what happened last weekend—how her sister got dragged into the sheriff's station and Piper lost her job as a result. And watch him lose his shit? Thank you, but no thanks.

She knew that's what got to him the most. What ate at him like a disease.

Not that he was in jail.

Not that he was stuck in here for several more years.

Not that he couldn't walk into a Starbucks and order a five-dollar cup of coffee.

No. It ate him up that he couldn't protect them from behind these bars.

"She's great. Scored three goals yesterday." She shrugged. "Well, in the first two games anyway. They won the first two and lost the last one. Zero to four."

"Ouch." His gaze drilled into her. He always got that earnest look when she talked to him about Malia. He hung on every word as though it was everything to him. And she supposed it was. She and Malia were the only people he had outside of this prison. "But she did great? Her coach? What did he say? He still thinks she looks good? She's still on track to play in college?"

She almost wished she had never told him about that. Last year, Malia had tried out for a select club and made the top team. Her new coach had pulled Piper aside after a couple weeks and told her that Malia was on track to play in college . . . full ride, no less, if she kept developing her skills. It was practically all Cruz could talk about. Malia, the first Walsh to go to college . . . to break the curse of their name.

"Yes, Cruz. Her coach says she's coming along great."

"Good. Good." He nodded, looking relieved. He worried. It was all he could do behind these bars. Worry about them. "And her grades are still strong?"

"Yeah. I mean, she's passed me up in about everything. Math? Forget about it."

He snorted. "I don't believe that. You were always so smart. You should have gone to college."

Should have. She'd lived all her days in a continuous state of "should have."

"It's true," she insisted with a chuckle, shaking her head. "I'm no help to her. But it doesn't appear to hurt her."

They fell into silence for a moment. Then he found his voice again. "How's work?" The hated question but he forced himself to ask it. Every time.

He hated where she worked and he had never disguised that fact. He stomached it because he knew she only ever waitressed there and her options elsewhere were nil. She had to take what she could get. He understood that. Plus, he had North.

North kept an eye on her for Cruz. That gave him some comfort. Even though she knew he had to know North couldn't cover her every moment, it gave him some peace of mind. And considering he was stuck in here, she wanted him to have that measure of peace, however false it was.

"It's fine." She shrugged. "Work, you know . . ." She hated lying to him, but she definitely didn't want to tell him the truth of it. She couldn't bear to put this on him. He worried enough and worrying about her when he was in here and could do nothing was pointless.

She'd come to see him because she needed to see him.

She needed to look at his face. So that she could fortify herself. So she could convince herself that going back to Joe's was the only solution.

She stared at him, absorbing his large hands knotted around the phone, his prominent knuckles crisscrossed with the battle scars of this place.

It put everything in perspective and made any sacrifice on her part small and insignificant.

She glanced down at her hand splayed flat on the cold surface of the table, feeling her shoulders dip from an invisible weight. "This isn't right, Cruz. You're not supposed to be in here—"

"Piper, don't. We've gone over this and we're not going to talk about it anymore." His gaze slid left and right as though verifying no one was paying attention to them. "The subject is closed, understand?"

"North is engaged, you know."

He nodded once. "Yeah. I know."

An awkward pause fell and she wondered if her brother was thinking about his future. If he believed there could be happiness ahead of him when he got out of here. Just like North found. He deserved it and she wanted him to believe it could be his, too. For herself, selfishly, she needed him to believe that.

She moistened her lips. "His fiancée is a social worker. Her father is the retired sheriff of Sweet Hill. Her brother is the current sheriff. They're an influential family in these parts."

He stared at her, waiting for her to get to her point.

She paused, knowing she was ignoring her brother's request by taking the conversation in this direction, but she had to do it. "She's a good person, Cruz."

"I'm sure if she's marrying North she is a good

person." He meant because she could overlook the crimes of his past.

"I could talk to Faith . . . tell her about Shelley Rae. Maybe she would have some insight. Maybe she could help you—"

"No." He slammed a hand down on the table, jarring her.

A guard near the door took a step forward and called out a warning. Cruz leaned back in his chair, appearing relaxed, but his eyes glared at her in warning. "You can't tell anyone, Piper. We made a promise. We can't risk it. Don't go messing things up."

Piper lowered her gaze and stared at her hands knotted on the table in front of her. Her knuckles had gone white. "As opposed to the way things are now? Because they're already pretty messed up."

He laughed darkly. "You have no idea. Things can always be worse. And they will be if you go talking to people you shouldn't." People like Faith Walters and the members of her family.

It was strange thinking that things could get worse than her brother sitting in prison for a crime he didn't commit.

SEVEN

"**H**I. IT'S ME." She flexed her hand around her cell phone. She'd put off this call as long as she could. For hours today she had been gathering the nerve to do it. "Piper," she clarified, in case he didn't recognize her voice.

Joe started laughing and then the sound twisted into a hacking cough. He really should lay off the cigarettes. After a moment he caught his breath and asked, "Called to beg for your job back, huh? That didn't take long."

"I've been thinking." She glanced toward the closed door of the room she shared with her sister, afraid that Malia would finish her shower before she finished her call. She didn't want her to walk in on her and hear this conversation.

"Don't matter none. I told you no second chances."

"Just hear me out." She inhaled, bracing herself

for the words to come. The words she had called to say.

They were merely words . . . sounds that passed her lips, but it felt as though she were lifting long-rooted boulders out from her depths.

She had wanted to break the mold fashioned by her family. She'd wanted to be a better person for her sister. A role model. But then maybe that chance had long ago deserted her and she simply needed to accept that.

"I'm not ready to go onstage yet," she began. Hopefully that could be avoided altogether. Taking off her clothes to a room full of men shouting filth at her was something she'd vowed never to do.

Taking off your clothes for men doesn't make you a bad person. Plenty of good women strip for a living and aren't too proud to do it. It was the mantra she had been telling herself all week.

Besides. It wouldn't matter what kind of person she was when she couldn't afford to buy groceries and she had to send her sister to bed hungry. At that point nothing else would matter. She'd sell her soul to keep her sister from starving.

She released a pent-up breath and added, "But I can do private dances. I—I can do a couple of those a night . . . but I get to choose. I say yes or no to the client." She reminded herself that it was better than being on stage before a house full of rowdy men. She wouldn't feel so on display then . . . so like a piece of meat to be slavered over. Not only was the money better if she did private dances, but the prospect of a bouncer standing watch in the corner made her feel more secure.

"Huh. And how picky you plan on being?"

"Not too much," she reassured.

The image of Clive Lewis flashed before her. His face and others like it, boys she'd gone to high school with—the bullies who'd tormented her and called her trash because her last name was Walsh. She could never dance for them.

"If I do that, will I still have a job?" she pressed.

He took a long moment before replying. "Sure, Piper. If you start doing private dances, you'll still have a job." He chuckled lightly. "I guess you all have to start somewhere."

She winced, hoping that wasn't true, that this wasn't the start of her heading down a dark path.

EIGHT

"*So* YOU'RE *NOT* going to Evan's bachelor party tonight?"

Hale couldn't hide his grimace at his sister's question before ducking back inside his mother's musty-smelling closet for another box.

They were in their parents' bedroom, hauling boxes out and sorting through them. Unfortunately, their mother had never thought to label any of them.

The room had changed very little since their mother's death years ago. The entire house had changed very little, in fact, but nowhere less than this room.

Their father had left everything virtually untouched. Her clothes still hung in the closet. The book she had been reading still sat on her nightstand beside a tiny jewelry dish that held her wedding ring. It's like that band was still waiting for her to return it to her finger. The sight of it all made him uncomfortable—always had.

The idea of loving someone and losing her and then never fully recovering from that loss . . . never truly being whole again? No thanks. He wanted to avoid anything permanently scarring like that. Besides. He liked his life the way it was.

Hale was thirty-one years old and had never been in a relationship that lasted longer than six months. There was a reason for that. He chose to keep relationships short. He was okay with that. He saw no reason to change that pattern.

He emerged from the closet holding another box. Faith pointed where she wanted him to put it. She'd asked him to come over and help her today on his lunch break. She knew better than to ask Dad. These kinds of chores got him emotional.

Faith was on the hunt for their mother's box of wedding things. Now that he could face the fact that his sister was marrying North Callaghan without wanting to hurl something through a wall, he'd agreed to help her.

North was out of town delivering some of his welding pieces to a buyer in Oklahoma City. He preferred to deliver his work personally, assuring that it arrived safely and that he had face time with buyers and gallery owners. The guy was actually making a living off his welding. Faith had bragged that his last piece sold for five thousand dollars. Just another reason he should feel relief. His sister wasn't marrying a deadbeat that planned on mooching off her meager salary.

"Hello? Did you hear me? Are you going to Evan's bachelor party?"

"Uh. No." He shook his head. "What makes you think I would go to that?"

His sister made a face. He knew that face. It reminded him of their mother. She had made that face, too, whenever their dad tracked mud in the house. Or when he and his brother horsed around and knocked over some piece of furniture. Man, he and Tucker could do some damage.

"What's with the look?" he prodded. "I didn't think you were a huge proponent of strip clubs. What did you used to call them? Dens of exploitation? When you were fifteen didn't you make a stink? Insisting Dad shut Joe's Cabaret down?"

She nodded grudgingly. "Yeah, but Evan is our cousin."

"Is he really?" He squinted and looked sideways as if contemplating that fact.

"Fine. Second cousin," she allowed. "But it's

not as though we have a ton of family in this town. Mom always wanted us to be closer to him."

He sighed. She had a point. Family was family. His mother had always invited her cousin and his family to every holiday. Thanksgiving. Christmas. Easter. When Hale and his brother played football in the yard, Evan would watch from the porch in his perfectly starched shirt and pressed chinos, sullen because his parents had forced him outside and wouldn't let him play video games inside the house.

Evan was the only child of their mother's cousin, Sam. Sam and his wife had retired years ago to Florida, so now Evan ran his father's concrete business. Although that didn't mean that Evan actually worked for a living. He left everything in the hands of his office manager so he could play golf, doing little more than collecting a fat salary every month.

The guy was an asshole, plain and simple, but that asshole was his family . . . whether he liked it or not.

Hale met his sister's gaze. "Gotta pull out the Mom-would-have-wanted-you-to card, huh?"

"Works every time, right?"

"Right," he grumbled as he opened up another box and peered inside. Just old albums. No wedding stuff. "Fine. I'll go. But I'm not going to what's-his-name's bachelor party."

His sister's pretty features twisted into a scowl at his reference to North. "You know his name."

He made a noncommittal sound.

"North," she reminded him sharply.

"Yeah, yeah." He'd come to terms with the idea of North Callaghan and his sister. Together. A couple. *Engaged.* But that didn't mean he didn't like giving his sister a hard time. As a brother, it was his job. He'd never think any man was good enough for his little sister. Much less a man like North Callaghan. Convicted and imprisoned for twelve years, he most assuredly wasn't good enough for Faith. Unfortunately, she was in love with him. And at the risk of losing his sister, Hale accepted that and supported her.

That didn't mean Hale wouldn't kill him the first time he hurt her. He winced as the irony hit him. North Callaghan went to prison for killing the man who had raped his cousin. A rape that had ultimately pushed her to suicide. Hale might be a lawman who believed in the system meting out justice, but if he'd been in Callaghan's shoes . . . he wasn't certain what he would have done.

"North has no interest in having a bachelor

party. I've already asked him. And Joe's isn't really his thing anyway."

Hale was hard-pressed not to remind her that her husband-to-be had spent plenty of his time at Joe's Cabaret before they met. But then, *before* her, Callaghan had done many things and none of those things seemed to make a difference to her now.

"You mean he doesn't like to hang out at Joe's in his free time? Well, that's a relief. You know, considering you're getting married."

"Ha." She closed a box back up and slid it to the side. "Trust me. He doesn't go to Joe's anymore."

Except when he goes there to see Piper Walsh.

He sucked in a breath at that thought. He'd been having one too many thoughts about Piper since seeing her. He didn't know why. It wasn't as though any of their exchanges had been friendly. They could hardly even be called civil.

It was unsettling. He wasn't one of those guys that liked women who played hard to get. He didn't like prickly women and he didn't get his rocks off fighting with a woman. He liked women who liked him. Women with soft smiles and soft words. He saw enough fireworks when he was on the job. When it came to his personal life, he wanted peace and ease. Like Annabelle in Alpine.

There was never any drama with her. Just good sex and good times.

"He doesn't even go there to check on Piper Walsh anymore?"

She looked up, startled. "How do you know about Piper Walsh?"

"I know things."

"Of course. 'Cause it's your job," she said sharply, but the judgment was there. He knew that growing up she hadn't loved having an overprotective brother working in law enforcement. What little sister would? There wasn't a guy she dated that he hadn't run a background check on. At least, once he became a deputy for his father. Before that, his father ran the background checks.

He shrugged. "And I'm your brother."

"Before you get any ideas about him and Piper, let me assure you they're just friends." Yeah. He already knew that. "North and her brother go way back—"

"Her brother is in prison for murder."

"And so was North," she reminded. "Try not to be so judgy, Hale."

"You trying to say Walsh and North are alike?" He shook his head. There was a huge difference in their crimes. "Cruz Walsh killed a girl. An innocent high school girl. Not a rapist."

She inhaled. "Why are we even talking about Piper's brother? Whatever he did has nothing to do with her." Her expression turned speculative, eyes narrowing slightly on him. "Why are we even talking about *Piper*? You like her or something?"

He snorted and opened another box, averting his eyes.

Her eyes widened. "You *do* like her! When did this happen? *How?*" She dropped down on the bed. The ancient springs squeaked in protest.

"Watch your mouth, Faithy. Get that out of your head. I don't like her. She's just a kid."

"A kid?" She shook her head. "She's not *that* young."

"Whatever." He shrugged. "I don't even know her," he repeated. She couldn't stop staring at him. It was almost like he had something on his face. "What?" he demanded.

"Piper is great—"

"Stop right there." He pointed a warning finger at her. "I don't need you playing matchmaker with us."

She pulled back, clearly affronted. "What's that supposed to mean? You think you're better than her or something?"

"I didn't say that. I'm not looking for any—"

"Let me tell you something about Piper. A lesser woman would have broken under the kind of pressure she's had to live with. I see it all the time in my job—"

"So do I," he bit out. "I'm aware that's she been dealt a rough hand, Faith. That doesn't mean I'm a dick if I don't want to date her." He didn't date *anyone*. His sister knew that. He doubted Faith would appreciate it if he entered into a casual sex-only relationship with Piper Walsh.

Not that that was even a possibility. Piper didn't respond to him the way most women did. "Besides. She doesn't like me either." And that, for some reason, bothered him. Maybe that's even why he was so antagonistic with her.

She tapped her chin. "Now I'm just going out on a limb here . . . but could it be because you're a prick to her?"

He shrugged. Maybe. But Piper gave as good as she got.

She gave her head a slight shake. It looked as though she wanted to say something more, but instead she pressed her mouth into a flat line. The lawman in him stirred to life. How many times had he faced a perp and knew when there was something they weren't saying. If not outright lying, they were withholding information at the very least. Plus, this was Faith. He knew all her mannerisms. He especially knew when she was hiding something from him.

He decided to let it go though. Sometimes it was better not to dig too deeply in Faith's mind. Especially if she actually believed he might *like* Piper Walsh. She needed to get that idea out of her head.

He went back to rummaging through boxes. "Here we go," he announced, lifting one lid and looking inside. Inside was his mother's wedding veil, wrapped in protective plastic. He handed it to Faith. Underneath there was more. A handkerchief trimmed in blue. Other things that he didn't even know what they were called, but they all looked decidedly wedding-ish.

"Ah." Faith sighed as she opened the plastic and pulled the veil from its packaging. Standing, she held it over her head and moved to stand in front of the mirror, examining herself from multiple angles.

He watched her with a growing tightness in his chest. When had his sister gotten old enough to marry someone?

"So you are going to put in an appearance. Right?" Faith asked, rotating until she stopped before him.

He shook his head, confused. "What are you talking—"

"Evan. His bachelor party?"

He groaned. Apparently she wasn't forgetting about that.

An *appearance.* That didn't sound too bad. He'd have a beer, toast the groom and be out the door before Evan and his buddies became too unbearable.

"Yeah. Sure. I'll put in an appearance at Joe's."

NINE

$\mathcal{T}$HE ASSHOLES AT tables three, four and five were unbearable.

But then she supposed that was the nature of assholes everywhere. They were unbearable or they wouldn't be assholes. It didn't help that there were so many of them, all clamoring for more drinks and more girls like they were children at a candy store.

She reminded herself that she'd dealt with *unbearable* before. A lifetime of it, in fact. Rowdy drunks flashing dollar bills as though that gave them a right to do everything. *Anything.* She knew their type even before she came to work in a place like this. They didn't rattle her. She'd faced them and worse. Only tonight she would be facing them as Joe's newest entertainer. If not a dancer onstage, she was still available for private performances. Still for sale.

She lurked in the back, near the front door, watching them, these thoughts gnawing at her and making her stomach churn. She'd been inside the building for almost ten minutes, observing from the shadows, when Joe spotted her. He made a beeline for her. Stopping in front of her, he cut right to the point.

"I've already told Marty you'll be taking on clients tonight." He mopped his ever-present handkerchief against his glistening forehead, his gaze pinned to her expectantly. Expectant because he didn't think she would actually go through with it? After all this time of refusing he was probably waiting for her to chicken out.

"Sounds good. I still get to pick them though," she'd reminded him with a lift of her chin. She needed to keep some control and Joe needed to remember that. If she didn't like the guy, she wasn't taking her clothes off for him.

His lip curled in a smirk. "Right."

Ignoring his clear skepticism, she stepped around her boss and headed for the employee dressing room. A couple of the girls were already there, getting prepped for the night. She stood before her locker and hung her bag on the hook.

Unzipping the bag, she slid the dress she brought

out of the vinyl bag, giving it a slight shake in hopes of tossing out any wrinkles. It used to belong to Malia, before she grew and passed up Piper in height. Unfortunately that made the minidress entirely too short for Piper to wear out in the real world. But then Joe's wasn't the real world. She wouldn't be caught dead wearing it in public . . . which was the point. Her chest wasn't much to brag about, so she was counting on showing a lot of leg in the hopes of gaining attention—and customers—that way.

The garment was a definite change from her usual jeans and Joe's Cabaret T-shirt, but she knew she needed to look the part of someone willing to entertain in the back room tonight.

Not only had she brought the dress, but she'd also splurged on lingerie. She was already wearing some of it—a white lacy thong and strapless push-up bra. The delicate fabric felt different on her skin. It made *her* feel different altogether, which she supposed was okay since she doubted she would be the same Piper Walsh when she departed this place today.

She'd spent more than she could afford on the new items. It was a far cry from the simple cotton panties and bras she usually got for herself at Wal-Mart. She winced when she'd slapped her credit card down on the counter of Angelina's Boutique, but she told herself it was a necessity. She would more than make up for the expenditure. She could hardly strip off her dress to reveal serviceable cotton panties and bra. That wouldn't get her any tips. She needed a bra that actually made it look like she had breasts. As for the panties . . . she hoped she would get used to them. Plenty of women wore G-strings.

Sliding off her jeans and T-shirt, she reached for the simple shift dress. It was black and would serve as a contrast to the lingerie hiding underneath.

She'd gone with white because everyone else wore the obvious bold colors: red, black and varying shades of pink. She could honestly say she had never seen white on any of the girls inside these walls. Hopefully she would stand out and that would get her a lot of requests for private dances—a lot of requests that she could then cull from and choose.

Serena whistled. "Are those bare-ass cheeks there, Piper? Girl you got some sweeeet junk in the trunk."

Piper's face burned as she slid the dress over her head, glad for the cover.

She shrugged at the dancer, and tried not to appear as self-conscious as she felt. Serena only worked a couple nights a week. She didn't need to work more than that. She was that good—a favorite among the customers.

Piper cleared her throat. "I thought I might give a few private dances. Earn a little extra money."

Serena stared at her hard before speaking. "Joe bully you into this?"

"No. I need the money."

Serena snorted. "We all need the money, sweetie. That's how it all starts."

"I'm sure. Why else would anyone want to do this?"

A corner of Serena's mouth lifted. "Oh, don't fool yourself. There's a certain thrill . . . it can be a power trip. You'll see."

Piper shook her head, rejecting that. "I don't see that ever happening."

Serena smiled, the fine lines around her eyes crinkling. Piper had never noticed those before. She wondered if Serena had a plan for the future or was this it? Stripping at Joe's until she was forty? Fifty?

Serena had to be in her early thirties. She graduated from high school with North Callaghan. And yet she was looking older than her years. That's what this life did to you. And it was the life Piper was taking for herself.

She watched as Serena rotated in front of the mirror, adjusting the tiny strings of her underwear that wrapped around her hips. Her skin was still smooth and taut there. No sign of the age that her face revealed. She guessed in a darkened club no one noticed the signs either.

She'd been told before that a girl could pocket fifty or a hundred dollars per private dance—and that was even after giving Joe his cut. She supposed if anyone would know, Serena would. She was one of the most popular girls here. It wouldn't hurt to ask about that and glean any other information that could help. If Piper was going to do this, she wanted it to be worth it. "How much you think I can make a dance? Fifty? More?"

"Ah, honey. Aiming high for your first night, huh? You must think the innocent schoolgirl look is gonna be a big hit."

She shrugged, feeling suddenly foolish. She didn't think she was anything special. She knew, even with her wardrobe change, her looks weren't very flashy and that's what you needed in a place like this. Flat-chested, dark hair, brown eyes. It definitely wasn't the description of a centerfold.

Serena continued. "Well, it depends how much you rev his engine." She turned back to study herself in the mirror, adjusting her large breasts inside her demicups.

"You don't actually have to get naked, do you? Not all the way?" She would feel naked enough with her bottom popping out of her G-string. She had a generous backside, and wearing a G-string made her feel almost obscene. But then she guessed this whole situation could qualify as obscene.

She was about to dance naked for strangers. She was going to expose her breasts for men whom she knew nothing about. It didn't get much more obscene than that.

Serena snorted and rolled her eyes. "You really are a babe in the woods. Still. Even after working here."

She shrugged. The last guy to see her boobs had been Rex Smithy in the eleventh grade and she had been so disappointed in herself for that. Actually, for everything that went down between them. All the dry humping and feeling each other up and coming so close with him was one big ball of regret when it turned out he was a lowlife. Little better than Colby Mathers and that boy loved to torment her through high school. She blamed herself for not figuring that out sooner about Rex.

He turned out to be like all the rest of the guys

in her high school and after only one thing when it came to her. Other girls got asked to prom and introduced to parents. Piper Walsh was a dirty secret you kept on the side, the girl from the wrong side of the tracks good enough for screwing in the back of your truck, but that was it. Get her some Dairy Queen, drive her to the bluffs and call it a date.

And she'd come so close with Rex. For weeks, they had worked up to it, doing everything except IT. And then she caught him bragging to his friends that he'd been fucking her nonstop (douchebag!) but was about to dump her since prom was close and no way could he take a Walsh to prom. His parents were expecting him to take a girl that went to their church.

The timing couldn't have been better, she supposed. She had overheard him, incidentally, the night before she had planned on going all the way with him. She'd finally decided she was done with all the dry humping and ready for the real thing. She thought she loved him. She thought he loved her. She thought together they would graduate and leave Sweet Hill behind and move to a city where they could get great jobs, marry and start a family. Yeah. Delusional. But she thought that because he had told her that. All lies.

Her mother had always warned her that men

lied. Usually this was when she was high or drunk and just broke up with some loser. Since her mother was usually wrong about everything in the world, Piper had dismissed her advice. Apparently Mom had been right about something, after all.

It might have been seven years since Rex, but she'd given men and relationships a wide berth since then. It was too risky when you didn't know whom to trust. And you had another life to support. She wasn't responsible for just herself so she couldn't afford to make those kinds of mistakes. She wouldn't.

She cleared her throat. "Um, you don't *do* things to the men—" Piper knew girls did tricks on the side. She refused to do that. Prostitution was an absolute line she wouldn't cross, but she didn't think she could bring herself to touch and be touched either. At least, nothing more than a cursory pat or brush of hands.

Serena swiveled around. "Look. You take it as far as you want to. If you're into it, then fine."

Piper made a sound of disgust and Serena rolled her eyes. "Okay, Sister Teresa. It's not like a man hasn't ever seen you naked before." Her hands seized her own breasts and squeezed them over her demicups. "They're tits. Yours might not be big but trust me . . . they'll want to see them." She let go and turned back to the mirror to practice her pouty face. "At least here, you get paid for your time and no one breaks your heart."

Piper nodded, thinking about that room positioned in the corner of the bar where she would soon perform private dances for strange men. She'd been curious enough to enter it once before. In the daylight when no one was using it. It was dark. Not very large. A leather love seat—red, of course—was positioned against a far wall. A small table beside it and nothing more.

"You do what you want. But just one piece of advice if you're hoping to make any actual money doing this?" Serena's voice softened. "It helps to be a little into it. Otherwise you better be a great actress."

Her stomach turned. "I don't think I can . . ."

Serena stepped forward and patted her shoulder. "You'd be surprised. It's not as hard as you think. Well, maybe the first dance, but after that?" An expression came over her face that was faintly wistful. "Just don't be surprised if there comes a time you get your rocks off with a client. That's all I'm saying. I wish someone had warned me so I didn't feel so guilty." She blew out a breath. "There. That's my favor to you. If you can enjoy it a little, it will come across and you'll make more money. Don't blame yourself when it does. You're only human."

Her stomach knotted. "What if the guy gets it into his head that he wants more and I don't?"

"Marty is just inside the room. One word from you and he puts an end to it."

She nodded. She knew that, but it was a useful reminder. She wished it alleviated her quaking nerves.

She'd never be alone in the room. Never be unprotected.

And yet she still felt vulnerable. Every moment she was in that room, baring herself to strange men, she would feel exposed.

After this, after she made enough money, she would never put herself in a position where she felt vulnerable and weak again.

TEN

𝓔VAN AND HIS friends had rented one of those obscene stretch limos for the night. Despite his in-
sistence that Hale accompany them in the limo,
Hale drove himself and met the group at Joe's
Cabaret. Now he wouldn't be trapped. He could
leave whenever he wanted. Which wouldn't be too
much longer than when he arrived.

He'd come up with an excuse to meet them there.
As county sheriff, he was never really off duty. If
a catastrophe occurred, rare though that may be
for a county as sparsely populated as Sweet Hill,
he would need to be available. At least, that's how
he viewed the job. The same way his father had.
The sheriff of Sweet Hill never really clocked out.

When he stepped inside the building, he blinked,
adjusting to the dim lighting. He scanned the room,
assessing it all in a sweeping glance. Of course, it

wasn't the first time he'd visited the establishment. Aside from the time he'd been here to check out North and Piper dumped water on him, he'd been called in a couple times over the years for minor infractions.

He scanned the room for her now. It was instinctive. Think of her. Look for her.

He didn't see her working. Maybe she took his advice and quit this place.

Although nothing about his last encounter with Piper in the park indicated she respected his advice. On the contrary. She looked like she wanted to stab him.

Evan spotted him, lifting partially from his chair as he waved him over. The dozen or so men in his group occupied three tables closest to the stage. Of course. They appeared to be having a very good time if the number of pitchers and shot glasses on their tables was any indication. They were also the rowdiest group in the bar. And that was saying something for a Friday night.

Evan stood and clapped him on the back. "Hey, cuz! Glad you made it." He turned to his group. "Hey, everyone! Hale made it," he called out as though they were all good friends.

Hale couldn't recall knowing any of them, but evidently they knew who he was. Which only annoyed him more. He didn't enjoy pretense—people pretending to be something they weren't. In this case, he wasn't friendly with any of his cousin's friends. Didn't even know them. Why fake like he gave a shit about any of them?

"Awesome! Now we can break whatever law we want and not get in trouble!" a guy sitting at Evan's table proclaimed, his face flushed bright red either from beer, the warmth of the room or a sunburn.

"Doesn't quite work that way." Hale sank into the chair Evan dragged over from another table.

Hale didn't break rules for his actual friends. Why would he break them for these pricks?

Evan chuckled and tossed a balled-up cocktail napkin at his friend. "Yeah, tough luck for *you*, Clive. He's my cousin. I'm the only one who gets favors."

Hale stomped back on the impulse to tell Evan it wouldn't work that way for him either—cousin or not, groom-to-be or not. He'd never given Evan favors before. When he was a teenager he would come to Hale about his speeding tickets, hoping Hale could get his dad to take care of it. Hale had refused. He doubted Evan had forgotten that. He was merely showing off. Pretending they were something they weren't.

Just one hour. That's what he had promised Faith. He only had to suffer these assholes one hour and then he could leave. He had tomorrow off and he'd already made plans.

He was going to get out of Sweet Hill and head to the springs to fish in the morning. He couldn't remember the last time he went fishing. It had always cleared his head. There was something about the solitude of it. The simple act of casting his line in the water and listening to the subtle slap of waves. For some reason, he found himself craving that. Peace and quiet to settle the unease that had been plaguing him lately.

Following a morning of fishing, he'd drive to Alpine. He had texted Annabelle last night and she texted back right away. Yes, she was down for hooking up. She promised to cook him dinner, rattling off some wine that paired beautifully with buttered salmon and asparagus. She was always treating him to expensive wines, which he liked well enough but a beer and burger would suit him just fine.

Really, he didn't need to drink or eat at all when he went to see her but he couldn't be a complete dick and just fuck her and bail.

He just had to get through tonight and tomorrow he'd get a long overdue day off. A little fishing and he'd get laid by the kind of woman most men only admired in the pages of *Penthouse*.

Thankfully the music was loud enough that conversation with Evan and his friends didn't seem required. They hooted and hollered at the girls on the stage like adolescent boys and high-fived when the dancer awarded them with attention—as though they had somehow earned it through any merit on their part and it wasn't her job to pay attention to them.

"You gonna get a lap dance tonight, Hale?" Evan shouted across the table. "My treat."

"No, you're the man of the hour," he declined. "The lap dances are all yours, buddy." He lifted his beer in salute and took a swallow. It tasted bitter going down.

"Forget about it." Suddenly there was a wad of money in his cousin's hand and he was motioning to someone across the room before looking back at Hale. "You know who I'm marrying, right? Ol' Don Webster's daughter." At Hale's blank look, he added, "The guy in all the car commercials? About four hundred pounds? Looks like he's one breath away from a heart attack?"

"Yeah. I know him." He'd actually brought Don in for a DUI a couple years back. He'd been weaving all over the road, a known prostitute in the front seat with him. The guy's pants had been unzipped, so that, in addition to the alcohol, might have had something to do with his erratic driving.

The businessman had not been happy, blustering about who he was and how his team of lawyers was going to sue the department for wrongful arrest. He vowed to have Hale's badge.

"Yeah, of course you do." Evan beamed. "Well, my little bride-to-be is an only child."

One of the guys at the table guffawed. "Little. That's a good one."

Evan did not appear to mind the insult to his fiancée. He continued. "Don's already talking about retiring and letting me take over the dealerships." His chest swelled. "Can you fucking believe it?"

Last Hale knew Don Webster owned three car dealerships in the Sweet Hill area. If Evan was going to inherit that he was about to get a whole lot richer.

Hale couldn't help feeling a stab of disgust. There were a lot of poor people in Sweet Hill. They had a strong migrant community working the ranches and outlying areas. Too bad some of that wealth couldn't be spread throughout the community to help others instead of all going to line the pockets of the asshole beside him.

Hale took another swig from his beer. "Congratulations," he muttered, his tone decidedly unimpressed, but his cousin did not appear to pick up on that.

"So drinks and lap dances for all are on me," Evan proclaimed. The guys at the table cheered. "And, Hale," he said, clicking his tongue and pointing at him. "You get the first lap dance of the night. I insist. Any girl you want."

Hale waved off the offer and glanced at the time on his phone. Only forty minutes to go and he would take a call. Say it was an emergency and bail.

"Hey, Evan, here comes your girl."

Hale looked to where Clive pointed and instantly tensed as he recognized her. *Piper.* So she was working tonight. And apparently she was his cousin's *girl*? His stomach turned to think of that prick touching her. Was he one of her clients? And what did that even entail? Did she dance for him in the back room where private performances were conducted? How far did those *performances* go?

The idea that Piper Walsh fucked his cousin made him want to lose his lunch. And following that, he wanted to punch Evan square in the nuts.

Piper hadn't noticed him yet. Which was just as well. He probably looked as sick as he felt. She headed their way bearing a fresh tray of pitchers, the beer sloshing dangerously close to the rims. She kept her eyes trained on the beer, careful not to lose her precious cargo.

He took the time to assess her. He couldn't help himself. His eyes ran over her. Up and down, then back up again.

She looked different than the last time he saw her. No attempt to look respectable tonight. She wasn't wearing the standard Joe's T-shirt and jeans. No, she was wearing a dress that was little more than a scrap of black fabric. It was short, fluttering around the middle of her thighs. Too fucking short. It wouldn't take anything for a man to slide his hands underneath and explore that sweet ass.

And she didn't look so young anymore either. His sister was right. Not *too* young. He gave himself a swift mental shake. Just because she was legal didn't mean she was old enough for this . . . for these men. For *him*.

Her dark hair was pulled up on top of her head in a pile of loose waves, accentuating the delicate line of her throat. She wore more make-up than he'd ever seen on her face. Those Disney princess eyes, already big and dark in her face, didn't look so innocent anymore. The effect of eye shadow, liner and mascara made her look like a woman ready for bad things. She looked like a woman who would get on her knees and not worry about getting her dress dirty. Now she actually looked like a girl who worked at Joe's. A girl that reveled in doing dirty-good things.

Her mouth . . .

Jesus, that mouth.

He'd noticed those lips before, of course. Full and pouty. Always void of lipstick. Tonight they were deep crimson. Fitting. A striking contrast to the olive of her skin. The lipstick wasn't glossy or shining. No, this red looked permanently coated on. Like it could take anything and wouldn't smear no matter what.

He couldn't look away from it.

Couldn't stop himself from imagining what that mouth might look like wrapped around his cock, a suction of red moving up and down over his shaft, slicking him wet.

Christ.

He had no business thinking such a thing. Even if she wasn't a Walsh. And wasn't young. And wasn't a stripper.

And she was the opposite of everything he liked in a woman. From her looks to her personality to her background. She was difficult. He didn't do difficult women.

She wove with ease through tables, dodging men and more than one groping hand.

"Damn," Evan groaned, and sat back in his chair, his hand dropping to his crotch to adjust his dick. "I love a fucking spinner."

She wore a pair of strappy black heels that made her legs look endless even though he knew the top of her head didn't reach his chin.

"Your girl?" He couldn't stop himself from asking. "Thought you were getting married."

Clive elbowed him. "Yeah, he is, but that doesn't mean he wouldn't like a taste of that one. He's been trying to get her on her back ever since she started working here."

So she hadn't slept with Evan. That bit of information simultaneously satisfied him and pissed him off. He was glad she hadn't slept with his cousin, but he was pissed that she was even here where his cousin and his friends could salivate and manhandle her. It didn't make any sense. He shouldn't give a shit. She worked in a place like this. Of course guys manhandled her. It was her job. That and probably more.

He released a breath. None of his business. *She* was none of his business.

And yet as she stopped at their table and lifted her gaze to collide with his, it was hard to remember that. Those fuck-me dark eyes of hers widened as they rested on him and for a moment it was as though it were just the two of them again, exchanging words that felt like knives.

He gave her the slightest nod of acknowledgment.

Color stained her cheeks, and she looked away clumsily as though she didn't know where to stare now. With a little shake of her head, she turned her focus to setting the pitchers on the table, deftly slapping Clive's hand as it slid up her thigh. Clive chuckled and made another play, forcing her to move two steps to the side.

Tension wrapped around his chest and he had to stop himself from grabbing Clive's wrist and snapping it back.

"How's your brother, Walsh?" one of the guys asked. Laughter rang out all around the group. Of course in a group this size, someone would know Cruz Walsh.

She set her last pitcher down and straightened. "Serving his eight to fifteen. I'll tell him you said hello, Rawlins."

That brought forth more laughter. "Yeah," Rawlins replied. "Doubtful he'll remember me from high school. We ran in different crowds."

"Yeah." Evan shook his head, his eyes brimming with mirth. "You ran in different crowds, all right, but that didn't stop him from banging your girlfriend."

The table exploded in laughter.

Piper's expression didn't crack as they continued to make jokes about her brother. She endured it with stoicism. Like an untouchable royal, looking down her nose at the unsavory rabble. Ironic considering she worked in a place where being touchable was a requisite of the job.

Just when he thought he had Piper Walsh figured out, he realized he didn't know her at all. He had met her a total of four times—counting tonight— but he had naïvely thought he had her figured out. Probably like everyone else—especially these jackholes at this bachelor party. And the idea that he had anything in common with these assholes rubbed him wrong.

He watched her as she bent to clean the mess the men had made on the three tables as the conversation carried on around them. Her bare shoulders looked sleek and smooth to the touch, the olive skin touched with a bronze hue that he doubted she got from a tanning bed. He somehow doubted she gave in to such an indulgence.

"Sure I can't treat you to a lap dance, cuz?" Evan asked him, his loud voice carrying over the din.

He flicked an annoyed glance at Evan before looking back at Piper. She met his gaze for a moment before ducking her head and looking away. She gathered up the wadded balls of napkins where these assholes had spilled their beer. "Not my thing," he finally replied.

"Having a hot woman rub all over you?" Clive snorted. "What about that isn't your thing? You gay?"

He didn't bother glancing at Clive. Simply continued to watch Piper as though she were the most fascinating thing in this place. *Because she was.*

"Paying for it isn't my thing," he clarified even as he wondered why he bothered explaining anything to the asshole.

"But you wouldn't be paying for it," Evan reminded. "I would. It's my treat."

"I don't want it." At this point he didn't even sound polite. Faith would be disappointed, but he didn't care. His cousin and present company were the dregs of humanity.

"Evan, man, you didn't say your cousin was such a fucking Boy Scout."

His fingers tightened around his beer, but not from Clive's words. No. Piper's lips had twitched like she wanted to laugh.

"Strippers don't do it for me." He looked squarely

at her as the words fell on the air. It was a lie, of course. At least in reference to her. The woman definitely did it for him. Too damn much.

Her eyes shot to his. She dropped the last wadded-up cocktail napkin on her tray and cut him a cold look before whirling away from their tables and stalking away in high fume, her glorious ass swaying with the pound of her feet. *Glorious?* Another word he didn't need to think in relation to any part of her.

"Are you serious?" a guy in a pink-on-pink plaid shirt beside Hale asked.

"Have you seen the girl your cousin is marrying?" Clive demanded, lifting his cup to his mouth, lifting his eyebrows. "Evan is gonna be spending even more time with strippers once he's married. Trust me."

Instead of being offended at the insult to his bride, Evan nodded morosely. "I'm definitely earning my father-in-law's business marrying his little princess."

"Only she ain't little!" Clive chimed, chortling like a hyena.

Evan nodded in agreement. "Well, I always have Joe's girls to look forward to."

Hale shouldn't have looked but he couldn't help himself. His gaze tracked Piper across the club.

She was at the bar, gathering more drinks and setting them on her tray.

"Sounds like you're really looking forward to a
promising future," he murmured.

"Oh, I am. I'm going to have more money than
I know what to do with. I'll send my wife on long
vacations with her friends and stay back here and
do whatever the fuck I want with who I want."

Hale looked back at his cousin, marveling that
they came from the same gene pool. Evan lifted
his arm and motioned for someone. Hale followed
his gaze, watching as Joe himself crossed the room.
The heavyset man waddled over, weaving between
tables. When he reached Evan they shook hands
like long lost friends, only confirming how often
Evan frequented the place.

"Congratulations," the proprietor declared through
wheezing breaths. "I hope this doesn't mean we will be
seeing you any less?"

"Of course not. I could never give up your girls,"
he declared.

Just then Joe caught Hale's eye. "Ah, Sheriff. We
don't get to see you nearly enough in here. Welcome, welcome." He clapped him on the back.

Hale nodded tightly. The only time he ever
stepped foot in here was work-related. To follow
up on a complaint or investigate a person of interest

or suspect sighted within this establishment. Just a few times over the years. He'd long suspected Joe offered prostitution services, but he had no hard proof of that. And his department didn't exactly have the resources to conduct a sting operation. Whether the women here offered illicit services on the side independently or it was something that ran through Joe, he didn't know. But he wasn't fool enough to think it wasn't happening.

"We're going to need some private dances tonight, Joe. Only your best girls."

"Of course." Immediately Joe started glancing around the room as though to check on the availability of his dancers.

"Any chance Piper is free for half an hour?" Evan asked.

Joe's face suddenly broke into a wide smile. "As a matter of fact, she is."

For some reason, Evan looked startled. Like Piper Walsh giving lap dances was an unusual thing. She worked in a strip club. That's where things like lap dances occurred.

"Now you been coming here long enough to know that Piper is somewhat of a diva. At least in her own head." He leaned in as though to impart something conspiratorially. "She's been working here for over a year now. Usually I have girls broken in by then, but she's taken a little longer to bring to heel. She's finally coming around."

Hale had never wanted to hit a man so badly in his life. His hand curled into a fist under the table. The man had done nothing illegal. There was no crime in being a despicable person. Sadly, society tolerated and even celebrated men like him. Hell, more times than not they even got elected to office.

Sweet Hill was like any other place. It had its fair share of corruption. Hale worked hard to keep his department clean and uphold his office with integrity, but right now he was tempted to throw all that away and commit assault.

"So I can have her?" Evan asked, his tone anxious, eyes somewhat glassy at the prospect.

Hale flinched at the words. *Have her.* Like she was a piece of property. He'd seen bad things as sheriff. Sweet Hill might not be the murder capital of the world, and the majority of their calls might come from old Mrs. Ryan about the raccoons in her attic, but ugly things happened here, too. He shouldn't be so offended. Joe's and Evan's words were hardly the worst thing he'd ever heard and yet everything inside him rebelled at the idea of Piper dancing for the likes of his cousin.

And would it end at a dance?

The image of his cousin's pale, soft hands touching Piper, fondling her and groping her because he paid for that right, was all kinds of messed up. Evan with his fancy car and nice clothes and fat house in Sweet Hill's single upscale gated community wasn't fit to touch her.

That thought made him sit up a little straighter. He had been telling himself he didn't have an unhealthy interest in Piper. That looking out for members of this community was his job. It's what he did. But maybe that wasn't entirely true.

Let's face it. She was a mess. She needed someone to look out for her, and if that someone happened to be him, wasn't it okay? He put on this badge to protect and serve, after all.

He almost laughed out loud at his logic. He was attempting to justify his interest in her.

Joe nodded. "Sure, sure. Just let me go and send her to the room. You go on in there whenever you're ready." Turning, he left to fetch her.

Evan took his glass of Scotch and downed it. Slapping the glass back down on the table, he rubbed his hands together in a self-satisfied manner. "This bachelor party is definitely the best part of getting married, gentlemen. Gonna go get a piece of—"

"I'll go," Hale suddenly declared. "I'll take that lap dance."

His voice sounded disembodied even to his ears.

Like it was coming from somewhere else faraway . . . from someone else. He was no saint, by any means. But no part of himself as a man, as a lawman, could have conceived of a moment where he would pay a woman to dance naked and rub up on him.

Maybe it was wrapped up more in his ego than morals for him. He knew women liked his face and body. He didn't need to pay for it. But no way in hell could he sit here while his cousin paid for it. While his cousin paid *her* for it. Fuck that.

Everyone looked at him with startled expressions, almost as though they had forgotten his presence among them. And why not? He was hardly participating. He wasn't thrusting money at any of the women on the stage or circling their tables. He'd made it clear he wasn't interested in having a lap dance.

Evan shook his head, his mouth working.

"You said I could have a lap dance. Your treat. Any girl I want," Hale reminded him, keeping his voice casual and revealing none of his tension. He shrugged like it was no big deal. Like he wasn't trying to save Piper from his cousin.

"Y-yeah," Evan hedged, glancing toward the back of the club. "Sure. You can take it."

"Thanks." Standing, he headed to the back room to wait for Piper Walsh.

ELEVEN

PIPER WORKED WITH determined focus all night, falling into her old waitress routine and delivering drink order after drink order. Her changed appearance didn't go without notice. The tips were better. There were roaming hands and pinches, wherever they could reach. Requests came for private dances. She shook her head when Marty approached her with the requests, not ready even though she knew she needed to be. She was going to have to say yes eventually. And eventually needed to come tonight.

She caught Joe glaring at her from across the room. At one point, he tapped his watch, clearly reminding her that the hour was growing late and she had yet to make him any money in the back. She wouldn't escape tonight without doing it. Not if she still wanted her job.

She just needed to do it. Rip the Band-Aid off and say yes no matter who the guy was. None of them were going to be right because nothing about this felt right to her. Maybe if she closed her eyes, she could forget where she was. Maybe she could convince herself she was just dancing alone in her apartment.

"Extra ice in the Scotch," she directed to the bartender. She waited as he added a few more cubes. "Thanks." Lifting the tray, she turned and ran nearly smack into Joe. She staggered back against the bar, clutching the tray to keep from losing it.

"Piper," he growled.

And she knew. The time had come. The moment of truth. The hour of reckoning. All those horrible clichés. That. Them. Those.

"Joe," she returned. From the moment she had let him know she was agreeable to taking lap dances— even wanted them—she had been barreling toward this.

Joe jerked his thumb to the bachelor party going on behind him. Despicable men and Sheriff Walters. Well, Walters wasn't despicable. He was many other things but not that.

She couldn't even understand why he was with those guys. They didn't fit him. *This* place didn't fit him. By his own admission, he didn't do strippers.

And that stung. She wasn't an actual stripper—yet—but he assumed she was a veteran and to him that made her beneath him. Like she was something dirty.

She supposed she could have told him. Explained that she only worked as a waitress all this time at Joe's. She could have done that days ago, but pride stopped her and the fact that she owed him nothing, least of all an explanation. Stripping wasn't illegal. It was a living and right now the only one she had.

True, she didn't grow up wishing for this career, but who did? Serena and the others worked hard, but even they had plans, goals, for a life after this. For now, they were doing their best. Just like she was.

"You got another request."

Heavy stress on the word *another*. He wanted to remind her that she'd refused her other requests so far tonight . . . that she wasn't living up to expectations.

She followed Joe's gaze to the bachelor party where Evan Sanders sat as the man of the hour. Hard to believe some poor girl was marrying that letch. She felt her lip curl. Of course the request came from Evan. He had been one of her more ardent and persistent admirers. She suspected it was because she was one of the only women in this place who hadn't taken her clothes off for him. He viewed her as a challenge. Him and his stupid friends.

Or at least she used to be the only one. That was about to change.

She sucked in a heavy breath and expelled it. "Yeah. Okay."

Joe blinked. "Okay?"

She nodded. "Okay."

"Okay, you'll do it?" he repeated, clearly needing clarification.

"I said I would, didn't I? That's why I came back."

"Well. Yeah." Now he eyed her suspiciously.

"I'll just drop off these drinks."

"Okay, then." He smiled and looked her up and down. "You're going be very popular, Piper."

She frowned. "I just want to make some money."

"Oh, you'll do that, girlie. You'll do that."

She walked past him with her tray, trying to feel glad about that . . . and not like she was about to lose a little bit of her soul.

PIPER TRIED TO move with confidence even though she felt as sturdy as a leaf. She whispered encouraging words under her breath as she lifted one foot after another. *You'll be fine. Everything will be fine.*

Lap dances happened all the time in this place. She wasn't the first girl who ever had to give one to a disgusting pig.

She'd get in, dance for a little bit, twist, turn, shake, and then show the girls and get the hell out the second the song ended—money in hand. Simple. Just like she had imagined in her head. All that, and Marty would be there in the corner.

How bad could it be?

Taking a final, deep breath, Piper walked into the room, ready to face Sanders, taking comfort in the bouncer, tall and terrifying in the corner by the door, arms folded across his chest. She nodded at him, and he grunted at her in return. Typical. Marty wasn't exactly a talker.

Only two recessed lights illuminated the room. Half the room anyway. The other half was cast in darkness. She imagined this was a deliberate move. Customers could sit in the shadows and do whatever it was they did while enjoying naked women dancing for their personal gratification. Her lip curled, trying not to imagine that grossness.

She walked through the lit portion of the room— the part of the room where she would be dancing. A single chair stood off to the side. She knew some girls used it while they danced. It gave them something to hold on to as they worked their moves.

She tried to walk in an appealing way, giving her hips a little sway. It felt silly. She knew she was shaped like a boy, oversized ass notwithstanding. Her breasts barely filled a B cup.

She moved with determination toward the couch backed against the wall.

He was sitting there. Sanders. And she was going to strip for him.

She swallowed back the swell of bile rising in her throat. Vomiting on her first customer wasn't likely to get her future ones.

She stopped a few feet from the couch. She could get closer, but she didn't want to see his face. She didn't want to have to think about him as she did her thing. And she didn't want to be so close that he could reach out and touch her. Even with Marty just inside the room, she was still a big ol' coward about that.

His body was a vague shape. Denim-clad legs were visible, jutting out from the chair. That gave her a moment of pause. She didn't think Sanders was a casual kind of guy. She'd only ever seen him in slacks. He was a polo-and-blazer-wearing kind of guy.

Lifting her chin, Piper straightened her shoulders and let her eyes adjust to the dim lights, focusing on the man seated on the low couch on the other side of the room. He was big. That made her frown. Sanders wasn't that big . . .

Recognition flared.

How *bad* could it be? Bad.

It could be really bad.

Several beats passed before she found her voice and the only thing she could choke out was: "*You.*"

He didn't reply right away. She stood there, not sure whether to bolt or step forward and punch him. Was this some kind of joke? The guy that sneered at this place, at *her* . . . was in this room as her first client? It didn't make sense. The sheriff she knew—the sheriff she *thought* she knew—wouldn't even think about stepping foot in this room. Not him. Not Mr. Stick-Up-His-Ass. He didn't do strippers. His words. *Jerk*.

"My cousin insisted that I take a lap dance," he finally said. She froze at that deep voice, goose bumps breaking over her skin as the gravel of his words rolled over her.

Nightmare confirmed. It was him. He was doing this. He was sitting there. It was happening. She had to take off her clothes and dance for him.

Heat flared inside her. It was anger. That was it. Nothing more. The fact that it was him in all his hotness did not affect her libido at all.

"Your cousin?" she asked.

"Evan Sanders."

"That jackass is your cousin?" She made a sound of disgust. "I should have guessed the connection."

"Really?" He angled his head. "Should people judge people based off family connections?"

She sucked in a breath. That arrow was aimed directly for her. "You're a lawman. Can you even be in here? Doesn't this break some ethical code?"

"There's nothing illegal about me being here. You're just dancing."

"And taking off my clothes," she flung at him.

He settled his big hands on the tops of his thighs. His fingers were blunt tipped, the nails trimmed and clean. He was quiet for a moment before that dark voice of his agreed. "And taking off your clothes."

Her skin shivered. She couldn't move. She felt like the clichéd deer caught in the crosshairs. She shifted her weight. "Well. You paid for half an hour."

"That long?"

"Thirty minutes is the minimum."

"Then by all means." He fluttered a hand. "Do your thing."

Right. *Do your thing.*

She squared her feet apart and focused, for the first time, on the music being piped in from the speakers overhead. It was classic rock. She closed her eyes and let it fill her.

She rolled her head slightly and let her hips move, hands coming to her sides. Her palms drifted up over her abdomen and rib cage. She tried not to think of him, but she couldn't help it. She could actually feel his eyes on her, his gaze crawling all over her.

The same pulsing tightness she had felt in her stomach when they talked at the park returned. Just like that. A match catching fire. She was turned on knowing he was watching her as she touched herself. It was so messed up.

She let her hands move of their own accord, dragging them across her breasts. She gave in to temptation and opened her eyes and met his gaze.

And there was nothing. He watched her blankly. No reaction.

Damn it. This was humiliating. Her movements stalled and she heard his arrogant voice in her head again. *I don't do strippers.* She felt foolish. All her efforts were wasted on him because he didn't want this. His cousin insisted he take a lap dance. That's why he was here.

A loud commotion sounded from outside the room. She turned and looked toward the door. The door opened and one of the girls stuck her head in. "Marty! We need you!"

Marty hesitated and glanced back at them.

Piper shrugged. "Go on. I'm fine." She wasn't in danger with the sheriff. The guy was a block of ice. Marty didn't need to worry about leaving them alone.

The bouncer glanced at the sheriff. Clearly Marty knew who he was. Satisfied she was in safe hands with the lawman, he nodded and hurried out of the room. She turned back to face Walters.

"You sure about that?" he asked.

"Being alone with you in here?" She snorted. "Yeah, I'm sure it's fine."

He wasn't going to pounce on her. He looked more interested in a nap than watching her take off her clothes. And that bugged her. Perversely, she knew, but she wanted this guy to be . . . affected.

"Should I be worried?" she asked, her fingers curling around the hem of her dress, inching it up just a little.

"You work at Joe's. You should always be on your guard."

"Such a very correct answer, Sheriff Walters." She stepped forward, moving into the shadows with him. "But why should I be worried about you? You don't *do* strippers, remember?"

His gray eyes fixed on her face, but he didn't answer.

In one move, she pulled her dress over her head. It whispered on the air before it dropped on the floor behind her.

She stood there in her heels. Chill air skated over her and her nipples puckered and tightened inside her bra.

"You're a cop," she murmured. "If I'm not safe with you . . ." She let her voice fade suggestively.

His eyes were still fixed on hers, but there was an intensity there now. His jaw was locked, face frozen as though he couldn't look anywhere except at her eyes. As though he wouldn't allow himself to look anywhere else but her face. Such a masochist.

And she wasn't having that.

She ran her hands over her front, dragging them over her demicups and down the slope of her stomach. She arrowed her fingers over the tiny swatch of fabric covering her sex, sliding her fingertips sensuously against the silk.

Still, he did not look anywhere except her face. Ugh. Stubborn man. "What's the matter? You knew I was going to strip. You don't want to look?"

Something ignited inside her at the challenge

he presented. He was a block of ice but she would crack him.

With a growl of frustration she backed up several steps, offering him a wider view. She moved slightly with the music, letting it pump through her. She wanted him to want her.

She needed him to.

She fanned her fingers over her face, keeping them parted so she could still peer out at him. Her goal was to start where he was fixated—on her face—and work her way down, bringing him with her.

As her fingers reached her lips, she let impulse guide her and sucked a finger into her mouth.

And there it was. Something flickered in his gaze, cracking the frosty gray.

It was all the validation she needed.

She popped a wet finger out of her mouth and trailed it downward between her breasts. His gaze followed. Triumph sizzled through her and the blood pumped hot in her veins. *Yesss.*

She brushed the front clasp of her bra. Again, impulse pushed her and she sprang the clasp, turning around as it popped open so he couldn't view her breasts. Yet.

She heard him suck in a breath over the pound of music and she knew he was feasting on the sight of her ass. Her ass, the bane of her existence for so long. Now it was working for her.

She bent slightly at the waist, her hands gliding down her thighs to her ankles, letting him have more of the view. She snuck a glance over her shoulder and the look on his face made her stomach dip to her toes.

Blazing hot desire. The hands on his thighs were white-knuckled and clenched tight.

Straightening, she turned slowly, provocatively, her hands cupping her breasts, shielding them. She moved toward him again, not stopping until she was standing between his spread legs. Then, slowly, she let her hands fall away.

His eyes were all over her now, but he didn't move. Didn't reach for her. His hands balled into fists and fell to his sides.

She placed a knee on one side of his hip and then followed suit with the other until she was straddling him. She settled her hands on the back of the couch, steadying herself. Very deliberately, she let the tips of her breasts brush the crisp shirt covering his chest as she slowly lowered her weight down on him. His body was a furnace, singeing her everywhere they touched.

"What are you doing?" he rasped in that voice that made her think naughty thoughts.

"Just dancing," she echoed his earlier words, and rolled her hips a little as though to confirm this. "And taking off my clothes. Nothing illegal, remember?"

"It's more than that." He sounded angry. Furious, even.

She laughed breathlessly. It was more. He was right. At least for her it was, but he didn't need the satisfaction of knowing that.

"Is this what you do for all your clients?" he growled.

"You're so annoying," she bit out, and then gasped as she felt the hard ridge of his cock under her. She arched her spine and shifted, sliding into a better position so that his erection was directly aligned with the seam of her.

A breath hissed out from him.

"Are lap dances still not your thing, Sheriff?" she whispered, leaning down and letting her mouth brush the whorls of his ear. God. He smelled amazing.

"I haven't decided yet. You would be my first, Ms. Walsh." His voice rolled out of him and got lost in the messy pile of her hair.

Part of her wanted to tell him this would be her first, too, but he wouldn't believe her so why bother?

She pulled back until they were face-to-face. "Then I'll do my best and try to make it good."

Their eyes battled, absorbing each other. Their noses were close, almost touching. Her breathing was loud, fanning his lips. God. She wanted him to kiss her, but she knew he wouldn't. He was too good for that. Too correct. He wouldn't do anything to her in this room. Even though she read the hunger in his eyes, he would hold back. He'd give her nothing. It was all about her doing things to him.

And God, she wanted to do things to him. She wanted to kiss him. She wanted to taste his wide mouth, nip his lips and suck on his tongue.

Pheromones raged through her, but she couldn't bring herself to do any of those things. It was up to her to do all the taking and she wouldn't take that kiss from him. Pride stopped her just short of that.

But she could wreck him in other ways. She could torment him all she liked.

She rocked against his cock in time with the music. Flexing her hands on the back of the couch, she lifted her breasts and dragged the hard tips down the front of his chest.

His breathing grew as labored as her own. The

blazing hot desire she read in his face echoed through her and that was scary.

Serena's words ricocheted through her. It was already happening. Her first time giving a lap dance and she was getting her rocks off on it.

Was this what she was? Who she was now?

No. It's him. Hale Walters.

There'd been something there from the start. Chemistry. She might have spent the last year working at Joe's but she'd been living like a nun and she was one giant ball of suppressed desire.

She knew she should stop. She knew it was wicked and definitely sending the wrong message . . . probably confirming every bad thing he thought about her, but she couldn't stop herself.

Her body didn't belong to her anymore. It was his. Whether he knew it or not. Whether he wanted it or not.

She lifted her hips slightly and went for his belt. Her fingers were surprisingly nimble as she unbuckled him and snapped open his jeans. Probably only confirmed his assumption that she was a pro. She dragged down his zipper and slipped her hand inside. It had been a long time, but she still remembered how to do this.

It took a moment to gain access, but then her

fingers were wrapped around the considerable width of him. Silk on steel.

She felt her eyes widen. "Oh. My." She didn't remember everything, after all. Not *that*. He was big. She shouldn't have been surprised, she supposed. As big as he was it made sense that he was big all over. She pumped her hand over the hard length of him, imagining taking all of him into her body. Her belly clenched at the prospect. It would be a tight fit.

"Is this part of a lap dance?" he asked through gritted teeth, body unmoving, hands still balled-up fists at his sides.

She rolled her thumb over the plump head of him, rubbing the wet drop of semen all around his crown. She'd given oral sex before, but it had never been her favorite. Now her mouth watered at the idea of bending down and bringing this man's cock into her mouth.

In that moment, she faced the glaring truth and accepted it. She had it bad for the sheriff of Sweet Hill. Her libido took one look at him and gave a resounding, "YES, THIS MAN CAN PLAY IN YOUR GARDEN." Who was she to fight the demands of her heretofore dormant libido?

"For you it is," she gasped as she freed him.

Her hands resumed their grip on the back of the couch and she ground down against his naked cock, only the thin silk of her panties offering any barrier. And that wasn't much.

She felt every inch of his length, the hard ridge gliding against her barely covered sex. It was wondrous.

And then she was lost.

She went to work, grinding on him in a simulation of sex. It was like she was a teenager again, making out in the back of Rex's truck. Her panties were soaked with her juices and it only made his cock move faster, sliding wetly along her seam, the head of him bumping her sensitive clit.

She was making all kinds of embarrassing sounds, but she didn't care.

He didn't say anything, but his breathing increased, and his body tensed under her like a tightly wound coil, ready to snap. Spring. Attack.

She hoped he did. She wanted that. Wanted the unyielding sheriff's resistance to break at last.

Her hands moved from the couch to his shoulders. She clung to the bands of muscle, whimpering and crying out as she writhed wildly on top of him.

Suddenly he came up off the couch, taking her with him. "Fuck this."

She squeaked and clung to him. The mountain was moving.

Wait . . . *he* was moving?

"What are you—"

"We're not doing this where you've had other men," he growled as he spun her around and pinned her against a wall.

Fury spiked through her. He was the worst. He thought she was no better than a prostitute.

Even burning outrage didn't stop her though because now he was fully participating, pumping his hips and rubbing his huge cock against her, bumping into the opening of her sex, the tip of him slightly prodding her soaking panties and pushing in slightly. Just the tip of him.

"Oh my God." She didn't even recognize her voice. It sounded like she was dying.

It would only take a small tug to push that scrap of fabric aside. She could have him impaled deep inside her then.

If he did it, she wouldn't care. She wouldn't try to stop him.

"I'm close," she choked, pushing into his driving cock, frustrated because as good as this was, it wasn't enough. She wanted more.

As though he could read her mind, he pulled them from the wall and relocated to the chair.

He sat down with her on his lap. But when she moved to close the distance between them and continue riding him, he stopped her. Kept her at arm's length.

His gaze dropped to her crotch. His hand followed, moving in quickly. He didn't ask, simply pulled the white strip of her underwear aside and bared her. He rubbed his fingers, soaking the tips in her wetness. "Fucking hot."

She whimpered, a shudder racking her at this man—a man she had thought so cold and emotionless—touching her and playing with her sex like it was his new favorite toy.

"Pretty pussy," he husked, driving a finger deep into her channel, giving her the *more* she craved. "Christ, you're tight, sweetheart."

She bit her lip, a fine edge of pain bordering the pleasure. *And this was just his finger.* What would it be like to have him inside her?

He pulled out and drove deep again, curling his finger up in a move that brushed against some hidden part of her and sent her careening over an edge. Moisture rushed between her legs as a violent orgasm crashed through her. She screamed and his mouth was suddenly there giving her the kiss she had craved, smothering the sound.

In the far back of her mind, she knew he was

trying to silence the cry, but she didn't care. She was starved, her body far too horny, too hungry for this thing she'd been missing. She was a twenty-five-year-old virgin who needed sex.

She kissed him back, hungry and desperate and not nearly done with him. She continued to ride out her orgasm as her tongue tangled with his.

Seeking another one, she rode his hand, using that finger still wedged inside her. She pumped her hips forcefully, pushing toward her goal, feeling it hovering there close again. He rubbed at that spot again. God, how did he know just where to touch? She was going to have a second orgasm. The man was amazing.

A loud burst of music spilled into the room from the outside as the door opened. She squeaked and flattened against him, stilling all movement.

"Out," he growled. "Give us a minute."

She snuck a glance over her shoulder to see Marty scowling.

"It's fine," she promised in a shaky voice.

The bouncer hovered for a moment before turning and leaving the room.

She sat back for a moment and stared at the sheriff's face. The *sheriff*. She should probably start thinking of him by his name after . . . everything.

Hale.

Heat burned her face as she realized his finger was still buried deep inside her. It was shockingly intimate in this moment of cold reality.

She pulled away, extricating herself from him. Standing on her feet, she hurried to snatch her bra off the floor. In her effort to prove to him that he wasn't too good for a lap dance from the likes of her, she had lost control.

She needed to take it back.

"Thanks, Sheriff. Not every dance I give is that . . . pleasant."

"Piper—"

"Half hour is up," she said, snapping her bra into place and turning to face him again.

He was holding out her dress. She took it from him and slipped it over her head, trying to act normal. Like she did this all the time. It's what he thought, after all.

"Piper—"

"Be sure to leave your money with Joe. Unless you want to buy more time." She dipped her gaze, noting his pronounced erection pressing against his jeans. "Looks like you could benefit from that. We could finish . . . things." She held her breath at the outrageous offer, hoping he refused. Hoping he just left her alone.

She couldn't bear another moment of this. She

was shaken and rattled and needed to hide in a closet somewhere so she could start the process of forgetting about tonight. Because she and the sheriff—*the sheriff damn-it-to-hell!*—could not be a thing. It would never work. It was doomed from the start. Even before the start. There was more than the problem of her last name between them. So much more.

The heat in his eyes extinguished. "No. I'm fine. I got more than I paid for, after all."

She flinched. If his intention was to make her feel like a whore, he had succeeded. But then, she guessed that had been her intention, too. She'd wanted to cheapen the moment and push him away. Because that's what she had to do. It was the only smart thing in this situation. She'd made enough mistakes for one night.

"Good night, Sheriff. Enjoy the rest of the bachelor party."

With those parting words, she presented him with her back and exited the room.

TWELVE

AFTER FINDING JOE and pulling him aside for a brief exchange that involved Hale emptying his wallet, he returned to his seat, his heart still racing and his dick still aching from his thirty minutes with Piper. Thirty minutes and his world had been blown to bits.

How had this happened?

How had he *let* this happen?

He only knew he had lost control. He'd gone inside that room with the best of intentions and ended up with his cock out and his hand buried between her legs.

He'd lived in this town all his life. Even as a teenager, he'd never played around much. When your father was the sheriff there were expectations. It wasn't okay for him to fuck around with girls in the back of his truck. In fact, he hadn't gotten laid until he'd entered the Marines. He'd been eighteen years old, but then he'd sown oats, enjoying sex finally and frequently. For the first time, he had been his own man and not the sheriff's son, not a high school football star, not the town's golden boy.

When he returned to Sweet Hill and took office as sheriff, he'd returned to his self-restrained ways, never taking the bait as women flirted and threw themselves at him. Getting entangled with women in the community he served was one complication he wished to avoid when he had no intention to settle down and marry any of them. He could do without the drama. That's why he reserved his hookups for out of town.

Tonight he had not been self-restrained. He'd been the opposite of that.

In one night, he'd cast his principles aside and caved like a house of cards. He'd been one minute from driving his cock inside her tight heat. In a back room of a strip club, no less. Yeah, it sounded seedy, but it had been the singularly hottest and most gratifying encounter he'd ever had with a woman.

And then she'd coolly dismissed him with the reminder of payment. Unless he wanted to *buy* more time with her. She'd offered that with no shame.

Like she was something to be purchased . . . a bit of horseflesh. It's like she wanted to drive a wedge between them. She wanted him to view her as a prostitute. Damn her.

"Hey, Hale! How was she?" Evan asked upon his return.

He grunted a response and scowled, not about to share a word about the encounter with his prick cousin.

Evan looked concerned for a moment. "That bad, huh?" Then he shook off his disappointment. "I'm sure it wasn't that bad." He rose from his chair. "Well. My turn."

Hale turned on him with a snarl. Grabbing his shoulder, Hale shoved him back down in his chair and leaned over him. "If you or any of your other friends take one step near her, I'm going to fuck you up. Understand? She's off-limits."

Evan's eyes bulged in his face.

"Understand?" Hale pressed.

Evan nodded once. "Yeah. Understood."

"Good." Then, even though he had stayed well over an hour and he had been fantasizing about escaping this place all night, he dropped back down in a chair and scanned the room, searching for her.

Clearly he was out of his mind.

He couldn't get the sensation of her skin against his hands out of his mind. He couldn't forget how tight her pussy had felt. Her scent. Her taste. That one searing kiss they shared was imprinted on his brain like a brand.

They'd just had that one kiss, he realized with a stab of regret. Not enough.

He shook his head at that unacceptable thought.

All of it was unacceptable. Getting embroiled with Piper Walsh might be the dumbest move on his part. Yeah. Time to get out of Dodge. Tomorrow couldn't come soon enough. He needed to get out of Sweet Hill.

Except not right now.

Right now he wasn't moving from this chair for the rest of the night. Right now he had to make sure no one bothered her and she stayed out of that back room.

"WHAT'S THIS?" PIPER looked down at the cash in her palm. It was the end of the night, the place was empty except for employees and she was dead on her feet. She blamed the shoes. She didn't know how the other girls managed it. Three-inch heels were not for sissies. Right now she just wanted to kick off these shoes, take a shower and slide into bed beside Malia.

"Can't you count? Four hundred dollars. It's your cut."

"I just did the one lap dance." She shook her head in confusion.

After the half hour in the room with Hale, she couldn't bring herself to go back into that room with anyone.

She'd told Joe she was done for the night the instant she had emerged, and she didn't regret it despite Joe's scowl.

"I'll do more tomorrow," she had promised.

"You better have done a good job and given him his money's worth." He'd wagged his sausage finger at her. "That's the first lap dance the sheriff ever took in here. We want him on our good side."

She squared her shoulders. Given that she had just stopped short of having sex with him, she was pretty sure he'd got his money's worth.

Now she was holding more cash than she'd ever held at once in her hand and she didn't know why. "I don't understand. What's this for?"

"Sorry I doubted you." He chucked her under the chin. "You must have done a good job with the sheriff tonight." Joe waggled his eyebrows suggestively. "Marty said he thought you two might have gotten . . . uh, carried away."

Her face went from hot to scalding. "Nothing happened. Just a lap dance." And an orgasm. She had used his body to get herself off . . . just like Serena warned her could happen.

At least that would never happen again. Hale had been the key component. She couldn't imagine letting anyone else touch her like that. Revulsion skated across her skin at the mere idea.

"Well, whatever you did, keep it up."

She looked down at the money in her hand, knowing she needed it, but still feeling sick. Maybe it would get easier.

When had life ever been easy?

Shaking off the dismal thoughts, she went to get her things from the back. Serena was there changing clothes. "Hey, how'd it go?"

Piper forced a smile. "I survived."

"Of course you did." She fished a piece of candy out of her giant bag and tossed it into her mouth. "And it will get easier. You'll see." She offered a piece of hard candy to Piper.

Piper took it and popped it in her mouth. She didn't know if that was true . . . or if she even wanted that. She didn't want this to become normal for her.

"What are you doing now?" Serena asked. "How about you come back to my place? I've got leftover pizza in the fridge, plenty of beer and the last two episodes of *The Voice* on DVR."

"That sounds great, but my sister is home alone. I need to get back to her."

Serena nodded. "Okay. Another time, then."

"Yes, I'd like that." And she meant it. She was always so busy working to stay afloat she didn't have a lot of downtime, but it would be nice to just have pizza and watch TV with a friend. Maybe now that she was making more money, she could afford to do that.

When she emerged from the club, there was just the bartender and one of the waitresses cleaning up at the bar. All the other dancers were gone. Serena had hightailed it out of there, claiming she had a hot date.

Piper waved at the employees and pushed through the door, heading into the parking lot. There were only a few cars there, but she was almost to her car when she noticed the Bronco and the man sitting inside the driver's seat. Hale.

Her heart skittered before picking up a hard beat. Swinging her tote bag around her shoulder, she stalked over to where he was parked. She knocked hard on the glass, waiting as he rolled down the window.

"What are you doing? Stalking me?"

"It's late. You shouldn't be out here alone. I'm just making sure you got to your car."

She processed that, clinging to her indignation even though she felt some of it slipping away. "I can take care of myself. I've been working here a long time and no one ever worried about me getting to my car before."

All the girls walked to their cars on their own. Joe wasn't exactly someone that worried about the safety of his female employees and had them escorted out at night.

"It's not safe."

She cocked her head. "You're really taking that protect-and-serve thing far, huh? Thanks for the gesture, but you can't do this every night, can you?"

He stared at her a long moment. A gnat buzzed by her ear and she swatted it away. He leaned forward, one strong arm draped over the steering wheel. "You could quit. You shouldn't be doing this job, Piper."

He was the worst. Still judging her even though he had been quite complicit in that back room with her.

She held his gaze for a moment as a brittle smile took hold of her lips. "You didn't seem to have any objections to my job earlier. I think you appreciated my talents."

His nostrils flared and eyes sparked and she recognized the heat in there again. The same heat she had seen from him in that room. Her belly tightened in response. She crossed her arms over her chest, needing a buffer between them. Suddenly the space separating them wasn't enough.

"You can't like this job—"

"Well, no shit," she exploded. "I hate it." Stupid, frustrated tears pricked her eyes.

"Then why do you—"

"You think I want to work here? I don't have any choice. I can't get any other job in this town. Who's going to hire Piper Walsh? Cruz Walsh's sister? Dominic Walsh's daughter? Nina Walsh's daughter? Want me to keep going? The reasons people have *not* to hire me are pretty endless."

"Then has it occurred to you that maybe you should make it easier on yourself and move to a different town?"

The fact that he sounded like her brother only pissed her off more. She tilted her head back and looked up at the night stars for a moment before lowering her gaze to him again. "You sanctimonious ass. You think you have all the answers."

He shrugged. "Just a suggestion."

"You don't know the first thing about me. There's a reason I've stayed in Sweet Hill."

"Let me guess? It has to do with your proximity to Devil's Rock Penitentiary?"

She jerked back a fraction. Okay. Maybe he did know a *little* about her motivations. Not that it made her like him more for that. He still didn't know the biggest motivation to drive her. He knew nothing of her guilt.

She spread her arms wide. "You think I want this. You were my first lap dance. Not that you'll believe me, but you were. I was just a waitress up until tonight, but I need the money. You think I would have done the things I did with *you*, with *anyone*, that I didn't feel—" She stopped abruptly, compressing her lips as horror washed over her.

She'd almost said it. Almost let him know exactly how much she liked him. How attracted she was. She was one breath from revealing her perfect idiocy. Piper Walsh had a crush on the town sheriff.

It was so sad it was almost funny. He wasn't for her. She didn't get nice things. Men like him went for the good girls of the world who went to college and took yoga classes and were raised by loving parents. Not girls who woke in the middle of the night from nightmares because the past could never release its grip.

"What?" he demanded, his gray eyes oddly intense.

She shook her head and took a step back.

He opened the door to his Bronco abruptly and hopped out, towering over her. She retreated several more steps, her feet shuffling hastily over the asphalt.

"Piper," he growled, his voice all gravel and grit. "Finish your words. Anyone that you didn't feel . . . *what*? What do you feel about me?"

Her fight-or-flight instinct kicked in. Turning, she fled.

She dug her hand in her purse, fishing out her keys. She didn't look back.

Keys in hand, she unlocked her car and dove into the driver's seat. With air crashing from her lips, she stared out her dirty windshield.

He remained motionless beside his Bronco, staring across the distance at her. She started the car and pulled out of her parking slot, turning her gaze away from him. She pulled out of the lot and didn't look back.

She'd be back in this place tomorrow. Because her life was a never-ending cycle of "have to." She'd be back in this place, but he wouldn't be. He wouldn't be here because his life was better than this place. Because he was better than her.

THIRTEEN

*H*ALE THREW HIS fishing gear in the back of the Bronco and headed to his place for a shower. He smelled of the outdoors and he knew he couldn't show up on Annabelle's doorstep like this. She always smelled like lilacs. She wouldn't want him near her until he smelled of soap.

He walked through his house, yanking his shirt over his head as he moved. He showered, hands splayed on the tiled wall as he let the water beat down on him. He only took off the last Saturday and Sunday of every month. Saturdays were busy nights. Nights when people drank and partied and generally got into trouble.

He had a good deputy and could probably trust him with more than one weekend a month, but he liked to be on duty. Doris claimed it was because he was a control freak. She also claimed he needed a woman to come home to and then maybe he wouldn't work so many hours.

Immediately Piper filled his mind. She hadn't been far from his thoughts. Last night he'd dreamed of her and woke humping a pillow. She'd gotten under his skin. Had she meant what she said? Was he really her first lap dance?

He wanted to believe her with a desperation that annoyed him.

He thought about how she'd danced for him, how she rubbed her pert tits over him and took his cock out so she could ride him in her barely-there panties. How she'd let him play with her pussy and finger-fuck her. She'd been so responsive . . . wild for him. No way had she faked that. And he knew. Not just because he wanted to believe her either. She was telling the truth. She'd never taken a man into that back room before. He was the first.

He told himself it didn't matter either way. What happened between them was wrong. It could be considered an abuse of power. He expected better of himself. It couldn't happen again or anything remotely close to it.

Despite his stern thoughts, his hand moved to his dick. Head bowed, one hand braced on the slick tile wall, he masturbated to thoughts of Piper in that white thong. That hallelujah ass and those sinful lips and that hot pussy. He came hard and swift, spilling his seed in the shower. Gasping, he lifted his face to the spray of water.

He needed to get laid. Something that he would rectify tonight. Then he wouldn't get so fucking hard every time he thought about Piper.

It was almost six when he climbed back into his Bronco.

Two hours later he pulled in front of Annabelle's house in her upscale subdivision in Alpine. He plucked the bottle of wine off the passenger floorboard. He was by no means a wine connoisseur but his mother always insisted you never go empty-handed to someone's house.

Annabelle greeted him in a cloud of perfume, her white-blonde hair falling in sleek, straight lines around her, angled perfectly with her jawline. She pressed a kiss near his mouth in a clear attempt not to muss her lipstick. "Hale. I've missed you." She took the wine from him with a murmured thank-you, although her nose wrinkled as she read the label.

"You look beautiful." And she did. She was stunning in a black figure-hugging dress. She was his age. Professional. Sophisticated. With her own money. He should count himself lucky.

She led him into the living room where a tray waited with carefully arranged cheese and fruit. "Chardonnay?" She offered him a glass.

He took it and sipped, looking around her immaculate house. She sank down on the leather sofa and patted beside her. "Notice anything different?" She smiled and tipped her head coyly.

He sank down beside her. "Um. Did you change your hair?"

"Well, yes, of course, but that's not what I meant." She slapped him playfully. "With the house."

He looked around. "Uhh."

"I got new floors."

He glanced down at the hardwood. "Oh. Was something wrong with the previous flooring?"

"I just got bored with it. It was so dark. It cost fifteen grand, but it was worth it. I wanted to lighten the place up so I thought this blond wood would look so much cleaner . . ." Her voice continued in his ear, but he zoned out, nodding as though he were listening, but wondering if she had always been this boring.

He stood suddenly. The movement caught her off guard, upsetting her wine glass and sloshing it over her fingers. "Hale!" she cried out.

"Sorry." He ran a hand through his hair and set his wine down on the coffee table. "I have to go."

"Go? Where? You just got here. We haven't even had dinner yet—"

"Annabelle, I'm sorry I wasted your time tonight. This isn't working out anymore. And if you were honest with yourself, you'd agree. You deserve something better than what we've been doing here." He motioned between them.

She stared at him, gaping. "You've got to be kidding. You're walking out on me? We haven't even had sex yet."

He winced, stopping just short of saying he didn't want to have sex with her. He didn't want to be unnecessarily cruel, but she must have read something to that degree in his face.

Her mouth dropped. "Oh. My. God. You don't want to have sex with me?" She glanced down at herself as though verifying that her ample breasts were still present and on display.

He stared at her, unable to deny that.

She continued, charging ahead. "There's someone else. You want to fuck someone else. Exclusively, I'm guessing."

He didn't know about exclusively, but Annabelle was right. He did want to fuck someone else.

She shook her head with a disgusted air. "Oh, Hale, I thought you and I were alike. I thought you were smart."

"I guess not."

She clucked her tongue, looking him up and down. "I'm going to miss that body. Such a shame. Who knew you could fall?"

"I haven't fallen," he denied.

He might have Piper on the brain and have a serious hard-on for her right now, but after last night, who wouldn't? There was no *falling* involved. This was about lust . . . and sitting here with Annabelle felt about as wrong as anything ever felt.

"Yeah. Right." She laughed harshly and reached for the bottle to add more wine to her glass. "Well, go on. No sense wasting time here, is there? Not when there is some sweet little girl in Sweet Hill waiting for the big sheriff to come and plunder her garden. Just don't get her knocked up. You know these small-town girls . . ."

Everything in him rebelled against this entire conversation. Was Annabelle actually giving him relationship advice? Terrible advice, no less.

Still, her words produced an image of Piper, her belly round with child. *His* child. The vision didn't make him shudder as it should have and that had him cursing under his breath. What. The. Hell.

Annabelle heard his epithet and laughed.

"I gotta go." He shrugged awkwardly and moved for the door, wondering if Piper Walsh had cast some spell on him.

The moment he climbed into his vehicle and pulled out of the driveway, the tension eased from his chest. Instantly, he felt better and relieved.

He wasn't going to wonder why he couldn't shake loose thoughts of Piper Walsh anymore. He was simply going to follow his instincts and see where it took him. Because really. Was there any other choice when everything inside him demanded he find her and make her his?

SATURDAY NIGHTS WERE always rowdy at Joe's but there was something about tonight . . . a sharp, bitter edge to the air. She felt it the instant Marcy went onstage in her new nun's habit get-up and started to strip. Aside of the fact that it was just wrong to see a nun dancing with a rosary between her lips, a patron jumped onstage and flung her over his shoulder caveman-style to the wild cheers of the crowd. That was actually unusual behavior. It never happened. It took Marty and two other bouncers to get him down.

"Full moon," Serena announced beside her.

Piper turned to look at her. "Is that it?"

"Yep." The other dancer winked at her. "Be careful out there."

Piper watched her move away, weaving between tables before she went to pick up her next tray of drinks waiting at the bar. She worked steadily for another half hour, getting the drinks out on the floor and dodging grabby hands.

A guy sitting alone at table three had requested a lap dance. He looked harmless enough. Small build. Clean-shaven. Weak-chinned but this wasn't a prospective date, so what did she care? He just needed not to creep her out. He'd been polite all night. Never touching her unlike the other Neanderthals of the night.

If she had to do it, she might as well start with him. Because he would technically be her first. She couldn't count last night. Last night was about free will and desire and need. She might have gotten paid for it, but what she did with Hale was something else. Something rare. A precious bit of memory she would take out at night and hold close, reflecting on it when lying in the dark of her bedroom.

She'd directed the guy to Marty to make arrangements. The place was crowded and she knew there was a line ahead of her waiting on the back room. It was almost ten o'clock before the room was available. Mr. No-Chin was already waiting in the room when she arrived—and so was Marty, his presence a comforting factor.

She inhaled and tried not to think about being in this room last night with Hale. Was that only last night? It seemed long ago already.

She positioned the chair in the middle of the lit portion, determined to use it throughout her dance and avoid the customer directly until the very end of the half hour. She danced in her dress for a few minutes, playing with the hem, giving him peeks of her upper thighs. She was about to cast all her inhibitions aside, right along with her dignity, and pull the dress over her head when the door burst open.

Everyone froze—even Marty—as a crazed woman flew into the room. The door smacked the wall as it flung open. "Anthony!" she screamed. "I knew it! I knew you were here!"

The man jumped from the couch and moved into the light. "Beth! What are you doing here?"

"Me? What am *I* doing here? Of all the nerve. What are *you* doing here? You were supposed to be working late at work! Lying pig! Is this what you want? To hang out with whores?"

Nice. Deciding this was her cue to leave before she felt inclined to defend herself against the insults of an enraged wife, she inched toward the door. But her movements only made Beth notice her.

The wife spun around. "Where are you going, *whore*? Is this what you do? Take off your clothes for strangers?" Piper held up her hands as though to ward off the woman's verbal onslaught.

The woman thrust her perspiring face into Piper's. "Answer me, whore, *whore, whore*!"

Well, clearly the woman thought she was a whore.

Piper tried to exit the room, but the woman stepped in front of her and blocked her escape. "'If she profanes herself by harlotry, she shall be burned with fire.'"

"Please let me pass," she said, desperate to leave the room and escape the fanatical gleam in the woman's eyes. She looked over her shoulder at Marty for help. He lifted both hands palms up as though he didn't know how to deal with one irate wife. He was used to handling brawling men.

The husband approached his wife, reaching for her arm. "Beth, honey, let's go home and talk about this."

"Don't touch me!" Beth twisted her arm free and, before Piper realized her intent, slapped Piper solidly across the face, sending her head snapping back.

"Hey!" Marty stepped forward and grabbed the woman's arm.

At that point, Beth started screaming, "Take your mitts off me!"

Her husband jumped to action and hurled himself on Marty's back.

For a moment Piper could only watch, fingering her burning cheek, awestruck as the smaller man clung to Marty's back like a monkey, pounding on his giant shoulders with his fists.

"What are you staring at, whore?" the irate wife demanded as she came at her again.

With a yelp, Piper dodged her, putting the chair between them, but the woman kept coming at her, swinging her fists.

"Stop it," Piper warned, but still the madwoman charged after her until she was forced to do something. Not about to be slapped again, she shot out her fist and punched her in the nose, just like her brother had taught her to do before he went to prison. The lady went down like a sack of bricks, howling like some kind of jungle animal.

Bodies crowded into the room to see the commotion. Joe pushed his big frame between them. He paused and took stock of the scene, a scowl forming on his face. A scowl, she couldn't help noticing, that seemed directly centered on her. What was he so unhappy with her about? She was the one that just got bitch-slapped and had to defend herself against a crazed wife.

"I want her arrested! I'm going to sue this place," she screamed, blood pouring out between her fingers.

"Piper!" Joe roared her name.

She lifted her chin and held his gaze. She hadn't done anything wrong.

He settled his hands on the sides of his barrel waist and continued to glare at her. A bubble of unease grew in the pit of her stomach. She was used to his bluster and threats, but she saw something in his eyes that she hadn't seen before.

"The police are here!" someone shouted.

"Great," she muttered, already seeing how this would be going down. As with all other Walshes, she was going to be held at fault for this.

Then Hale pushed through the doors.

Her chest lifted on a huge exhalation. She didn't know why, but she felt suddenly buoyed. Elated. She had convinced herself last night was the final time she would see him and that it would be for the best. For a moment she forgot that she was in the center of all this crazy drama. She could only see *him*. Drink him in—so big and strong and tall. His gray eyes like a stormy sky. His face so beautiful.

His eyes immediately found hers. He looked her up and down. It was a different kind of perusal— one assessing for damage. His gaze hovered on her face where she still felt the sting from the woman's blow. He strode across the room, ignoring everyone else. He touched her chin, lifting her face. The tips of his fingers lightly grazed where her cheek throbbed.

"Who did this?"

"The woman." She nodded once in her direction. "She slapped me when . . ."

She stalled, for some reason reluctant to give voice to her next words even though she had no reason to be. She was doing nothing criminal and she owed him nothing. No loyalty certainly. So he had her first lap dance . . . and then some. That didn't mean he had an exclusive on her lap dances—*on her*. She was free to shake her ass anywhere. She had to make a living and he could go to hell if he didn't like it. Confessing to being in this room was not a betrayal to him. *So why does it feel like it?*

She tore her chin from his grasp and finished her words. "She slapped me when she came in here and found me with her husband."

There. She'd said it.

From the cold shutter that fell over his eyes, he understood the situation perfectly. He sent the wailing woman another glance. Currently, her husband and Joe surrounded her. Both were arguing with each other.

"You hit her back." It was more statement than fact.

"When she came at me again, yes. I didn't particularly want to be slapped again." Indignation heightened her words. He stared at her for a long moment, indifferent to the arguing still going on around them.

"Wait here." He moved away from her and called out to the room in a booming voice. "Everyone out of here except the parties involved!"

Grumbling, everyone filed out of the room except the husband, wife, Marty and Joe.

Hale moved away from her and pulled Joe aside.

Marty moved in front of her and eyed her cheek, wincing a little. "Sorry about that. Didn't think she would hit you."

"It's okay," she mumbled, still watching Hale with Joe.

"Should ice it," Marty offered. "Might bruise."

"I'll be fine," she said hollowly, watching as

Hale moved to speak to the married couple. Then Joe was in front of her.

"You're done here, Piper." That's what she had seen in his eyes earlier. He was done. Truly finished with her this time. His words just made her feel . . . *tired*. Buried somewhere deep inside, a little sigh of relief whispered through her soul.

She wouldn't have to do this thing she hated anymore.

But she would have to move. Leave Sweet Hill.

Joe was making the choice for her, but now she knew what needed to be done. She and Malia would be starting over somewhere else.

Joe continued. "It's not working out. Some girls just aren't cut out for this line of work. The sheriff agrees—"

"Wait, what? *He* told you that you should *fire* me!" Instantly, the numbness.

Joe looked uneasy. "Now, Piper, he's just looking out for your best interests."

"Unbelievable!" She dragged in several breaths, trying to calm herself when what she really wanted to do was storm across the room and slap *him* across the face.

She shot an accusing glare at Hale where he stood, oblivious to her. Was the man out to ruin her life? First he gave her a taste of what she could never have last night in his arms . . . and then he got her fired from the job she desperately needed.

"This wasn't my fault," she insisted.

He shrugged. "Trouble always seems to follow you." He shook his head. "Probably should have known when I hired a Walsh. Your daddy, for all his ways, I considered a friend. Liked to think I was doing him a solid by giving you work."

She stared at him numbly. "Yeah? Well, now you're not."

He shrugged. "You can come by and pick up your last paycheck next week. Good luck to you."

It was on the tip of her tongue to shout at him that this wasn't fair, but that would be pointless. Life wasn't fair. She had long ago learned that lesson. Crying about it didn't get you anywhere.

He left the room, and she turned her attention back to Hale and the other couple. The wife, Beth, wasn't covering her nose anymore but blood dribbled down her chin to stain her shirt. For the first time, Piper noticed her T-shirt. In big block letters, it read GOD PUT THE AWE IN AWE-SOME. Piper wondered if God approved of her attacking another woman.

Beth was still irate, throwing her hands up in the

air as she talked. Every other word was "whore" and "arrest."

The deep rumble of Hale's voice carried across the room, but Piper couldn't make out any of the words. Finally he looked at her and there was a grimness in his eyes that sent an uneasy tremor through her.

He left them and approached her. The couple watched, the wife crossing her arms over her bloodied shirt, a smug tilt to her lips.

"Ms. Walsh." She started. It was Ms. Walsh again now?

"Yes?"

"I'm going to have to take you in."

FOURTEEN

THE ASSHOLE WAS arresting her.

As they walked through the club, all eyes fixed on them and mortification swept through her. Her face burned and it had nothing to do with an irate wife slapping her. She wasn't in handcuffs, but everyone knew. She might as well be wearing steel bracelets. Piper Walsh was going to jail.

There was a time when she thought this would ultimately be her fate. Turned out, she was right. She might not be going to jail for a heinous crime, but she was headed there nonetheless.

She held her chin high and tried to look dignified, even though she was trailing after Hale like a scolded child. She tried to look composed even though her feet were killing her in her stilettos.

Suddenly Serena was in front of Hale. Hands

on her hips, she glared at him. "You've got to be kidding? What did she do?"

"Please step aside," he said evenly, politely, voice void of emotion. It was his cop voice, she realized, and more often than not he didn't use that voice on her. She wondered what that meant.

Serena's eyes sought hers over his shoulder. She shook her head in obvious disgust and reached around Hale to hand her a small card. "This is my lawyer. He's a good guy. For a lawyer. Tell him I referred you."

Piper took the card, grateful for the gesture if nothing else. She wasn't completely without people who cared about her. "Thanks."

"Call me," Serena said loudly as they continued through the club.

Outside, he walked her to his Bronco, leading her to the passenger side.

Facing him, she held out her hands, wrists close together. "Go ahead," she invited, her voice ripe with challenge. She knew she could have a more deferential air at this point, but she was pissed and raring for a fight.

"What?" he asked, looking genuinely confused, and that only infuriated her more.

"Cuff me."

Something danced in his eyes and she felt its echo deep inside her belly, a snap of heat that curled and bloomed. Damn him. Why did he have this effect on her?

She shook her wrists. "Go on. Do it."

The barest chuckle escaped him, but it was mirthless and grated across her quickly fraying nerves.

"Nothing about this is funny," she bit out, her temper spiking. "Believe it or not, I've never actually been to jail."

"I know," he said matter-of-factly.

"Of course you do," she sneered. One click of the keyboard and he could pull up everything on one Piper Walsh of Sweet Hill, Texas.

Almost as though he read her mind and knew it annoyed her, he said smugly, "I know everything about you, Piper Walsh."

Not everything.

"You don't know *anything* about me," she countered, leaning in close and stabbing a finger in his rock-solid chest.

He stepped closer, reaching for the door handle, very deliberately brushing his chest against hers. She took a sudden step back, but didn't get far. Her back collided with the wall of the Bronco.

He was so close she could actually feel his breath

on her cheek. Could actually see the striations of navy blue in his gray eyes. "Get in." That crazy hot voice of his rolled through her.

She splayed her hands on the cold metal of the vehicle. "Shouldn't I get in the backseat?"

"Piper, get in." His words came out clipped. She was clearly trying his patience.

"I don't want special treatment. Don't think because of what went down between us you need to give me special treatment. Treat me like any other criminal."

"God, you're fucking stubborn. Just get in the damn car." He took her arm and practically lifted her up into the seat.

He closed the door after her, sealing her in. She watched as he walked around, his strides angry and hard. Once in the driver's seat, he started the car and pulled out of the parking lot. She crossed her arms and fumed beside him.

"Why are *you* so angry?" She was the one who should be mad.

"It always pisses me off when a person lands herself in a stupid situation."

A *person*? She was just a *person* to him? He got mad at everyone he arrested, then? "You must get pissed a lot, then, given your line of work is to put stupid people in jail."

"You could have been hurt," he accused, sending her a sharp glance. "It could have been worse than a slap across the face."

So it was because she'd put herself at risk? That's why he was mad?

She shook her head and turned to stare out the window. She didn't buy it. He couldn't be too concerned for her welfare. He was dragging her to jail, after all.

After a few moments of staring out the window, she quickly realized he wasn't taking her to the sheriff's department. "Where are we going?" She looked back at him, studying his stern profile.

"I'm taking you home," he replied without taking his gaze off the road.

She processed that, turning it over in her head. He was taking her home. Not to jail. *Home.*

Of course he knew where she lived. He claimed to know everything about her. And while she knew that wasn't true, thankfully, she knew her address would be an easy enough piece of information for him to access. After several moments, she found her voice. "Why?"

He slid her a look, his gray eyes piercing. "You really think I was going to arrest you?"

She frowned. Well. Yeah. He'd said so. To do

anything else seemed too *nice* for him. "I don't understand."

"That lunatic back at the club wasn't going to shut up until I agreed to arrest you." He shrugged. "It got you out of there. She thinks she got her way. She'll go home with her husband. It's done. All's well."

She stared straight ahead, blinking at this news. He wasn't hauling her to jail. He had lied for her. Only one person in her life had lied for her before and that was her brother. Cruz did it because he loved her.

She didn't know why Hale had done it.

She should probably thank him. Any other cop would have arrested her, and then she'd be up to her neck in trouble. She didn't have the money for a lawyer. She'd have to rely on a court-appointed attorney to defend her in a town where the name Walsh was mud. No one would believe she was struck first and it was self-defense on her part. Something told Piper that that lady had the re-sources and good name to win. It would be a losing battle.

Then she remembered that she had lost her job tonight. Because of him. He wasn't totally a hero here.

"I guess all's well except that you got me fired," she reminded him.

"That wasn't *all* on me. Joe—"

"No, but you certainly didn't help matters, did you?"

He adjusted his grip around the steering wheel, and she took that as an admission of guilt. "You didn't want to work there," he countered.

"I *had* to work there, but you lead too privileged a life to understand anything about anyone having to do something they hate in order to get by."

He made a growling sound and quickly pulled the Bronco over onto the shoulder of the road. He turned in his seat in a swift move, his eyes blazing, incinerating her where she sat. "Maybe I was trying to help you."

"By getting me fired? Wow. Such a good friend."

"Maybe I am."

"You're *not* my friend," she shot out with a brittle laugh.

Something passed over his face and then he nodded slowly as though coming to a realization. "You're right. I'm not your friend."

That gave her pause. It actually stung a little, and she didn't know why since he was just agreeing with her. Piper Walsh and Sheriff Hale Walters *friends*? Uh, not likely. Not smart.

"Okay," she mumbled, looking down at her lap where she twisted her fingers. "Glad we agree on that."

"I don't do this to women I'm friends with."

Alarmed, she looked up just as he reached for her. She caught a flash of those blazing eyes a second before he wrapped a hand behind her neck and pulled her to him.

She would like to say she shoved him away. Slapped him. Called him a jerk. Something. But she wasn't as strong as that. Or as smart.

Their mouths crashed together like two bullet trains meeting head-on. He hauled her into his lap, forcing her to straddle his bigger body. Their mouths devoured each other, lips and tongues mating in wild fury.

The steering wheel was right against her back so she could only sit leaning forward with her breasts mashed into his chest. One of her knees was wedged uncomfortably against the armrest of the door, but she didn't care. It was a small discomfort when she had *him*.

His delicious mouth.

His big hands sliding under her dress to grip her bare cheeks.

He groaned into her mouth, his hands flexing and squeezing her bottom. "Your ass is a wet dream."

She moaned, her sex clenching in pulsing contractions searching for something, searching for *him*. She was desperate to be filled. To have him deep inside her where she'd had no man before. Her body might be untried, but it knew. It recognized what it wanted.

She sucked on his tongue and pulled back slightly to speak against his mouth, her voice an unrecognizable purr to her ears. "Do you dream about me, Sheriff Walters?"

"God, yes. I can't close my eyes without seeing you."

A whimper escaped her at this confession.

She buried her hands in his hair, scraping her nails against his scalp. Her hair fell around them in a dark veil as she kissed him harder, deeper, loving that she was sitting up high over him. She felt powerful. Like she held this big, strong man and his desire in the palm of her hand.

She tried to rock against him, but movement was limited in the cramped space. She could only growl in frustration and rub her breasts against his chest as they continued to kiss like two teenagers who finally figured how to use their mouths.

She made wild sounds as he continued to massage the plump mounds of her ass, her desire growing to a desperate, feverish pitch.

"I dream about taking you like this. With you riding me and my hands cupping your ass, guiding you just how hard to fuck."

Ohh. Those words. That voice. The hands kneading her. She was five seconds from climax. Who knew the town's golden-boy sheriff had a dirty mouth and dirtier mind? The residents of Sweet Hill would be horrified. *She* should be horrified and running as fast as she could to get away. Instead, she was galloping straight toward an orgasm.

He squeezed her cheeks and then released one, giving it a sharp slap that made her sex twist so tightly it edged pain. Oh. My. God.

She cried out as that twisting tightness snapped and pleasure knifed through her. Her body convulsed as she came in a blinding rush. A rush of moisture dampened her panties. She ground down on him as much as she could, riding it out.

"Damn. That gets you off? You really do need to be fucked, don't you, sweetheart?" he growled. "You're aching for it."

She nodded mindlessly, lost as the aftermath of her climax rippled through her.

Then his hands were gone from her ass and she could have wept. She made a keening sound of disappointment at the loss. Her displeasure was short-lived because then his big hands moved to her breasts, fondling them through her dress just shy of too rough. It was like he knew just how to touch her.

She gasped, shooting up straight, the throb between her legs back again, clenching and demanding fulfillment.

"You like everything, don't you, sweetheart?" he rasped, watching her face as he played with her breasts, his thumb brushing over her nipples, back and forth, back and forth, each swipe making her shake.

Like? Her long-neglected body *loved* this. Loved everything he did.

She nodded. "Everything . . . you do . . . to me," she panted.

He added his forefinger then, pinching and rolling the hard tips.

"Hale!"

"That's it. Say my name." He pinched her nipples harder and pleasure speared straight from the arrow-hard tips of her breasts to her core.

Dimly, she realized it was the first time she had called him by his first name. She opened her eyes and feasted on his face. His beautiful face with its gray eyes and luscious lips, the bottom almost too full for a man. "Hale," she breathed, saying his name slowly, savoring it, gratified when she watched his eyes grow more hooded . . . when she felt his cock swell under her.

With a curse, he dipped his head and closed his mouth over one breast, sucking the pebble-hard nipple deep, even through the material of her bra and dress.

Then he bit.

She gave a sharp gasp, but killed it, biting her lip. Other embarrassing little noises fought to break free as she arched atop him, thrusting her breast closer, but she bit herself harder to contain them, not even caring when she tasted the copper of blood.

"Don't," he commanded. "I want to hear every sound you make."

She released her bottom lip on a shriek, obeying him, letting the sound out. God help her. This man could do anything to her. *Everything.* She wanted him to. She wanted him to take her and use her body until she couldn't walk.

Suddenly lights flashed and a siren chirped. Her eyes flew to the rear window. "Oh my God! It's the police."

"Sweetheart, I am the police," he said dryly, moving her off him and depositing her in her seat.

She smoothed her hands over her hair, tugged her dress from where it clung to her chest and caught him watching her. The hunger in his expression brought her to a halt. She'd never seen a man look at her with such need. For her. And she stoutly believed that it was strictly *her* he wanted, not simply a vessel to slake his lust. In his eyes, she read his desire for her. For her and no other.

"Wait here," he grumbled, his deep voice all kinds of disgruntled.

Opening the door, he hopped out. She released a pent-up breath, glad for the momentary reprieve from him. The distance. He was too much. Too much man who made her feel too many things.

She turned and watched as he moved to greet the deputy. They shook hands and talked for a moment. Hale laughed lightly, the sound casual and not at all like the intense beast of a man who had been unraveling her in the front seat moments ago. Then he was turning back for the truck and the deputy was walking away. She whipped her gaze straight ahead.

He climbed in and settled his weight in the seat beside her. Her nostrils flared at his closeness, at the heady musk of him. Her body was still aching, yearning.

"Everything okay?" she asked, her voice regrettably breathless.

"He was just checking. Thought I might have car trouble."

She nodded jerkily.

Hale sighed and she wondered what that sound meant. What was he thinking? Was he thinking what she was? That it was a good thing they were interrupted before things went any further?

"Please take me home now."

He turned, staring at her from hooded eyes. Nodding, he faced forward again and put the Bronco into drive and pulled onto the highway. They didn't talk the rest of the way home. When he pulled up in front of her unit, she flung open the door and hurried to her apartment without saying goodnight.

The moment she reached the door, she realized she had left everything at the club. She didn't have her key. Hale had discombobulated her that much. She'd left it all behind, too flipped out that she was being arrested.

Great. She was going to have to knock on the door for Malia and explain why she didn't have her keys or her car. Claire was spending the night, too. The two of them had planned on watching movies and eating frozen pizza. Thanks to Hale's generous payment last night, she had been able to buy groceries.

She was on the verge of knocking when footsteps sounded behind her. Whirling around, she faced Hale. "What are you doing?" she demanded, already suspicious. Did he think she was going to invite him in so they could pick up where they left off in his front seat?

"Walking you to your door."

"Oh." Somewhat mollified, she crossed her arms over her chest. "I left my keys. I have to knock on the door for my sister to let me in. I would prefer she not see you."

His gaze was unreadable as he gazed down at her. "You and I need to talk."

She shifted her feet. "About what?"

"I think that's pretty obvious."

"I must be dense, then."

"We need to discuss this thing that's happening between us."

"Nothing is happening between us."

He arched a dark eyebrow at her. "Really? We can't be alone for five minutes without dry humping each other."

Heat scored her face. She shook her head rapidly. "Nothing is happening. I'm not about to get involved with the likes of you."

"The *likes* of me? You make it sound like I'm some meth addict."

She sniffed and shrugged. "Don't get offended. We're not exactly a good match."

"I'm not talking about a relationship."

She sucked in a breath, trying not to look as offended as she felt. Of course he wouldn't want a relationship with her. "Of course not. Because that would be crazy. You just want to fuck me."

He lifted one big shoulder. "Is that so wrong? You can't deny you're attracted to me."

"Well, I don't do *that*."

"You don't do what?" He peered at her closely like she was some strange species he was trying to understand. "You don't have sex with guys you're not in a relationship with? Is that it?"

I don't have sex with guys. Period.

"Yeah," she agreed.

He stared at her, weighing her words, probably wondering how rude it would look if he turned and walked away right then. Instead, he surprised her by stepping closer. She backed away, but he followed, caging her in, his hands coming up on either side of her head. "Then we've hit a road-block. I don't do relationships and you don't do no-strings sex. One of us is going to have to bend, Walsh."

She opened her mouth on a tiny gasp. She had no idea what to say to that. She only knew his proximity was killing her and sending her libido into hyperdrive.

"Or neither of us bends," she offered in a weak voice.

"No. That's not going to work. You'll be in my bed, Piper. Or I'll be in yours. It's just a matter of time."

Holy cow. Who talked like that? And why did it turn her to mush? Instantly, all she could imagine was Hale naked, coming over her with that beautiful cock aimed directly at her.

"I'm man enough to admit I was wrong about you."

It was her turn to blink. She felt dazed. No one had *ever* said that to her before. It was basically an apology and she didn't remember ever being on the receiving end of one of those. "What was it you thought about me?"

"I thought you were a lost cause."

She flinched. A lost cause. Yeah. He wasn't wrong. She felt like that plenty of times. On the nights she skipped a meal just to make sure Malia ate. When she waitressed and endured grabby hands and disgusting suggestions for only a measly twenty dollars in tips. When she woke up in a cold sweat because she dreamed she was back in high school, trapped in that house with Shelley Rae again.

Lost cause was a fair estimation.

"You weren't wrong about me." She held his gaze.

His features twisted with anger, eyes glinting. "Don't ever say that. Maybe you're *my* cause," he countered.

"You can't save me." She was lost a long time ago. Nothing could change that. "You would do better to forget me."

"Too late for that," he pronounced. "You're something good, Piper Walsh. Beautiful and strong and frustrating as hell, and when we're together it's so fucking hot. You want me as much as I want you. Don't deny it. You want to feel me moving deep inside you. And not just once. Again and again until we're both so spent we fall asleep. And then we'll wake up and start all over again. We'll do it hard and fast. We'll do it slow and easy. It will take days, maybe weeks, until we've had our fill of each other. I won't need food because I'll have your body to sustain me. I'll have this." He cupped her sex through her dress and she gasped.

God, yes.

"Your pussy is so hot right now. It burns for me."

He leaned in, still cupping her, his fingers singeing through her clothes, and she knew he was right. She felt her own heat radiating into his palm. Their breaths panted heavily between them as his erection swelled against her belly.

He continued in his deep voice that embodied sex. "Say yes. Let yourself have this."

His words were compelling and seductive, but they were dangerous, too. They gave her forbidden desires and hope for things she could never have. Especially not with this man.

He's not offering forever. He just wants to have sex with you.

But sex with him would feel like something that was forever to her. She knew that already. It would shatter her.

She seized his wrist and lifted his hand off her. He obliged, letting go.

"Look," she began, relieved at how firm her voice rang when her body was shaking. "Let's end this before we get any more carried away. Besides." She swallowed against the lump in her throat. "I'm moving."

"Moving?" He blinked. "As of when? Where?"

"As of tonight. I lost my job. Remember? There's nothing here for me. I have to leave if I want to support my sister and myself. I don't have a choice. You yourself suggested it."

"Yeah." He blinked again. "But . . . *moving*?" he repeated as if he couldn't wrap his head around that sudden information. He might have thrown that at her as a suggestion, but clearly he didn't think she would go through with it.

"Like you said, I probably should have done it years before, but I wanted to stay close to my brother. So I could visit him. Now I don't have a choice though. I can find a decent job in another city where no one has ever heard the name Walsh."

He opened his mouth as though he wanted to say something more, but right then the door to her apartment opened. "Piper? What are you doing here?"

Malia stood framed in the doorway, Claire beside her.

"Hey," Piper greeted in an overly bright voice, taking a huge step away from Hale. Hopefully the girls hadn't noticed how close they had been standing. "I, uh, had some car trouble so Sheriff Walters brought me home."

Malia's wide eyes drifted to the sheriff. "Oh, hello, Sheriff." Wariness tinged her voice. Clearly she hadn't forgotten the last time she saw him and the discomfort of that encounter.

"Malia," he greeted with a nod.

Claire giggled and fingered a lock of her hair,

curling it around the tip. "Hi, Sheriff Walters," she chirped, eyes moving up and down over Hale. Hussy. When did she become such a flirt?

Hale nodded at the other teenager and then returned his attention to Piper. "We'll talk later."

She cocked her head and gave him a look, unable to say right then and there that she saw no purpose in that as they had nothing more to say to each other. It would be too weird in front of the girls. Malia would pester her for an explanation about that. "Thank you for the help," she said, determined to make his presence here look utterly normal.

He looked between her and the two girls. She got the distinct impression that he wanted to pull her aside to continue their discussion, but no way was that happening. If he even attempted it, Malia and Claire would probably follow them and insert themselves. There was nothing nosier than teenage girls.

"Any time," he said, his eyes intent on her.

She stepped forward into her apartment, forcing the girls to step back.

Turning, she gripped the edge of the door and looked out at him, glad that the girls were behind her now and could not see her face as sudden awareness washed over it. This was it. The last time she would see him. It mattered in a way that she could not have anticipated. Her chest constricted. The closest she had ever come to feeling this way was when her brother had entered prison.

"Good night." She pasted a smile on her face that felt fragile. She quickly closed the door before it failed her and he saw just how close to breaking she was under the surface.

HALE STOOD OUTSIDE her door for several moments before turning and heading for his truck.

She was going to move.

The thought left him reeling. It was the last thing he had expected her to say tonight despite the fact that he had suggested she do that very thing. That suggestion seemed so long ago. Before he felt so desperate and hungry to have her.

Damn it. He'd done this. He'd played a part in getting her fired tonight. When he'd left Annabelle's and drove to Sweet Hill, his single pushing thought had been how he could get her away from Joe's Cabaret for good. He didn't want her working there. He didn't want her in that back room. He didn't want any other man looking at her or touching or having her.

The moment he'd been in conversation with Joe

and sensed the opportunity, he'd pounced. *You should just let her go. She's never going to be right for this job.*

Yeah. He'd said the words. Put them out there and watched in satisfaction as resignation came over Joe's face. He got her fired.

And now she was going to move.

Because of him.

His mind rebelled against the idea and he knew he had to make it right. Somehow.

He refused to consider that it might be the best thing for her to move. Piper Walsh belonged in Sweet Hill. She belonged in his bed.

He had to make her realize that, too.

FIFTEEN

PIPER GAVE HER bed up to the girls, which was just as well. She didn't feel like dealing with her sister's kicking and stealing of the covers.

Alone on the couch, she stared into the dark, her thoughts full of Hale. *Hale.* Her hands slipped under the blanket, wandering, traveling over her breasts, which still felt tender and raw from his ministrations. After years of neglect, they were awake and alive and hungry for more attention. She couldn't stop herself. Her palms skimmed over her nipples, marveling at how erect they were just at the memory of him.

The things he had said. Her cheeks burned as his deep voice echoed through her. *You want to feel me moving deep inside you.*

He wasn't offering her any false promises. She

had to give him points for honesty. He just wanted to sleep with her. He only wanted sex. A part of her was actually tempted. If only it could be as uncomplicated as that.

She hadn't planned on staying a virgin forever. She'd come close before. She'd been a horny teenager. But then life got in the way and put things like sexual exploration and gratification on the back burner. Why not surrender to this thing that was blazing between them? The foreplay had been amazing. She was confident it would be good.

Except then she would have to walk away from him. She worried how she would feel after that. Would meaningless sex make her feel . . . meaningless?

She remembered his eyes then. Heard his voice in her head. That deep voice that embodied everything she desired. She didn't want to give herself to him and then later, when it was all over, feel empty inside. That just might be the final thing to break her.

Her phone, on the floor beside the couch, vibrated, its light glowing in the dark. She picked it up, wondering who could be texting so late.

You can't move.

Butterflies erupted in her stomach. She read the short sentence and then read it again as if she had somehow misread. Even though she knew, she typed: Who is this?

She waited breathlessly.

You know who.

She supposed she did know. Her fingers hurried with a response. How did you get this number? Again, she could hardly breathe as she awaited his reply, thinking about him thinking about her somewhere on the other side of town.

Really. You think I can't get your number?

Of course. She shook her head, feeling silly for even asking. He was the sheriff. He had access to pretty much any information he wanted. She shot back another text. I think this is what you call an abuse of power.

His reply came swiftly. So file a complaint.

She snorted and typed back. Funny.

Tiny dots appeared as he typed. What about your sister? You just want to uproot her?

Piper huffed an indignant breath and fired a reply. She's part of the reason I'm doing this.

What's the other part?

She sighed before responding. I need a fresh start. Just like he had suggested. So why was he changing his tune now?

You can have that here.

She shook her head, bewildered. Why was he trying so hard to convince her to stay? She couldn't believe this was all to sleep with her. Why should he care so much? Her fingers typed back a reply. I've never had that here.

I think you're running away.

She growled in annoyance, her fingers moving rapidly over her phone as her indignation burned hotter. Why would I be running?

He didn't respond. She stared at his words, feeling vaguely panicked, worried that he had seen something she didn't want him to see. Outside the club she had almost admitted to him he was special to her. That he meant something to her. She'd almost told him he was the only man she would let do the things to her that he had done. The only man who gave her all the feels.

Yeah, letting him know all that would be very bad. Baring herself to the sheriff of Sweet Hill could never happen. It could open the door to other things. Things she could never, ever confess.

Finally she saw the dancing dots and knew he was replying. She held her breath, waiting.

You're running from me.

She rolled her eyes. Arrogant. Egotistical. Her fingers sailed over her phone. Don't flatter yourself.

You're scared. You have your no-sex rules,
but that doesn't stop us from mauling each
other every time we're together, so you want
to run away.

Oh! The arrogance. Did he really think himself so irresistible? Two times hardly makes it chronic behavior. I can control myself around you.

Care to be alone with me again so we can
test that theory?

Alone with him? Not a good idea. Even though he was wrong. Most definitely wrong. Her fingers were starting to get a cramp from typing so quickly. That's okay. I'll be long gone before we can test your theory.

There. She reminded him of that. And reminded herself, too. Because it had to happen. She'd resisted it for years but now she had no choice.

He didn't reply. Her screen went dark.

She waited long moments in her lightless living room, holding her phone in her hand, waiting to see if he would reply.

He never did.

Eventually she fell asleep, her phone clasped in her hand.

HALE COULDN'T THINK of a reply to her text so he let his phone go dark. He could still see those words she'd typed though. *I'll be long gone* . . .

Damn it.

He sighed and flung his arm across his forehead, staring into the shadows of his bedroom. Silence hummed around him. She was still determined to move. He understood the logic. He'd taken away the one job she had. Shitty as it was, it paid the bills so she could support herself and her sister. He should be glad for her. She would be moving on to a better life somewhere else.

If he didn't like it, well . . . then he needed to think of a solution that kept her here.

He curled his fingers around his scalp and idly gripped his hair. He'd rather be touching her. Her hair, her skin, her *everything*.

Suddenly sleeping alone in this bed felt . . . lonely. He'd never brought a woman home to this bed before. Never wanted to. But now it felt lonely. Now he could only think about Piper on these sheets beneath him. His grip tightened.

She needed a job to stay here.

She needed a job, but no one in this town would give her one.

He released a gust of breath and rubbed his forehead where it was starting to ache.

He needed to quit thinking with his dick and find her work. Work would keep her here. That's all that mattered. That was the most important thing.

Suddenly he knew what he needed to do . . . even if that meant forgetting about ever having sex with Piper Walsh.

Doing the right thing meant he was going to have to let go of that particular fantasy forever.

THE FOLLOWING MORNING, Piper hunkered over a bowl at her kitchen table, eating cereal and debating how to get her car back. Despite her late night, she woke early. She'd had a restless time on the couch.

Not surprising. She'd almost been arrested. Lost her job. Decided to move. And was propositioned by the town sheriff. Busy night.

The girls were still asleep. She had heard them giggling in bed late into the night. They had the day off from soccer so she imagined they would sleep late.

She straightened when a solid rap rattled her door. Someday she would have a house with a doorbell. She hurried to the door before whoever was on the other side could knock again and wake them.

She stood on her tiptoes to look through the peephole. Hale was the last person she expected to see. After he didn't text her back, she figured he'd given up.

She opened the door and stepped outside, closing it behind her so they could have some privacy.

She crossed her arms. They stared at each other for a long moment. The keys jangled in his hand as he adjusted them in his grip.

"Been thinking about what you said last night."

"I said a lot of things last night." They both did, but yeah, he especially.

He inhaled. "You don't have to move."

"I think I related my situation pretty well to you."

He nodded. "You can't get a job in this town. I understand that."

"So what else is there to say?"

"What if you *could* get a job?"

She angled her head. "How do you mean?"

"I'll hire you."

"You'll hire me?" She felt the incredulity in her face as she stared at him. He had to be joking. "What? Looking for a housekeeper?"

"No." He stared at her in exasperation. "We're looking to hire someone to train as a new dispatch. Doris would like to retire. We'd need someone to take her place. We actually probably need to grow our staff by two or three more. This is a legitimate offer."

She studied him, still not sure if he was serious. A sheriff's dispatch? She didn't have a clue what that entailed, but he mentioned training.

"I don't know . . ."

"You can come in Monday. Work with Doris. See if it might be something you'd be interested in doing. The pay is solid. You'd get benefits. Insurance."

Her heart started pounding in her chest. It sounded too good to be true. And she knew from experience if it sounded too good, it usually was.

She narrowed her eyes on him. "What's the catch?"

His expression turned puzzled. "Catch?"

"What do I have to do in exchange for this job?"

The puzzled look vanished and he just looked pissed, a muscle ticking high in his cheek. "I'm not extorting you for sex. We'd have a purely working relationship. We'd have to forget about everything that's transpired between us and move forward in a professional capacity only."

Forget? How on earth could she do that?

He continued. "Which is what you wanted anyway. Right? You said you don't do sex outside of a relationship."

She lifted her chin. "That's true."

"Well, I don't do relationships so this should work out fine for the both of us. You get a job and don't have to move. Doris gets to start training someone to take her place, which gets her off my back."

She studied him a moment longer, searching for any hint of duplicity on his face. "You're serious about this?"

He looked exasperated again. "You need to learn a little trust, Piper."

"Trust isn't something that comes easily for me." She only needed to think of Rex or Shelley Rae to remember that.

"Well, you're going to have to work on that. Will you come in tomorrow or not?"

Several beats passed before she nodded. "Yes."

"Good." He extended his hand for her to shake.

She stared at it for a moment as though she expected it to turn into a serpent and leap out and bite her. Finally, she took it. His warm fingers wrapped around her smaller hand. Instantly, heat traveled up her arm and she was reminded of the way his hand felt on her body and all the intimate places he had touched her.

She snatched her hand back and pressed it to her side, palm rubbing into her thigh.

He backed off her tiny porch. "See you at 8 a.m. tomorrow."

"I'll be there."

She remained where she was, watching as he got into his Bronco and drove away. She stood on the porch in her bare feet, staring blindly into the parking lot long after Hale had driven away, her thoughts spinning. She'd actually gotten a job.

Gradually her gaze refocused and then she noticed another car with a person sitting inside it. The car was backed into a spot so it could face the buildings. The figure behind the steering wheel was a dark outline. Simply a faceless figure, unmoving. It was his very stillness that unnerved her. She had the sense that he was looking right at her. Yeah, she also had the sense it was a *he*. His shape was too large, too tall, to be a woman.

A shiver broke out on her skin despite the growing warmth of the day. She squinted as though she could make out his features, but it was no use. The window was tinted too darkly.

She suddenly felt very vulnerable standing on her porch, so she ducked back inside her apartment, her fingers trembling as she bolted all the locks in place. She inched away from the door, feeling silly for her reaction. It was probably someone waiting to pick someone else up.

She moved to the table and collected her bowl and spoon. She took them to the sink and washed them, setting them in the rack to drain.

Drying her hands on a dishtowel, she moved to the window and peered out between the blinds, checking to see if the car was still there. The parking spot was empty. Shaking her head, she let the blinds drop back in place.

SIXTEEN

PIPER WORE THE same outfit she wore to job interviews. Sure, the blouse and skirt never brought her luck before, but she hoped that would change today.

Malia had been excited when Piper informed her that the sheriff had offered her a job. At fifteen, she knew enough to know what kind of place Joe's was. And even though Piper told her she was only a waitress there, she knew her sister had never liked it.

Doris came around the oversized counter to greet her when she arrived, treating her to a warm hug. While maybe not the most professional behavior, it was so welcoming that Piper had to blink back tears.

"Now Hale told me to introduce you around and get you set up. I'll start showing you the ropes today. There are three other dispatchers—Yolanda, Becky and Tom. I'll go over the shift schedule with you. You only have to work one night a week. I usually take Thursdays. Yolanda and Tom split the rest of the nights." Piper blinked, letting that sink in. So she would actually be home in the evenings. She would sit down and have dinner with her sister. Almost like a normal family. For the second time that morning, tears threatened.

Doris continued. "When I retire, the four of you will coordinate your shifts. You could just keep my schedule if that works for you." Piper nodded in understanding. "Someone has to be here at all times."

Piper nodded and had to bite her tongue to stop from asking where Hale was. He was her boss now. It was none of her business. Not that it had been her business before, but where he spent his time now only mattered as it impacted her duties.

Even though she didn't ask for his location, Doris eventually volunteered that Hale was out on a run. Apparently the local hardware store had been vandalized. "He's not one to sit on his laurels. He takes a lot of calls personally. He's the face of the department and believes in being visible within the community."

"Sounds like a politician."

Doris shrugged. "It is an elected office, so I suppose he is. Not that he needs to worry about reelection. He won by a landslide last time and the Walters name is gold in these parts."

That must be nice. To be born to a family so beloved that you're instantly accepted. Even lauded.

Everyone was civil toward her as Doris moved around the department and introduced her. She might have read a little stiffness in the demeanor of Sharon in payroll, but Molly, a young female deputy, welcomed her with a warm smile. Deputy Briggs might have been a little *too* warm in his welcome.

He touched her arm as he spoke to her. "If you need anything, let me know. The sheriff can be a bit of a hard-ass." He leaned in close to her ear to volunteer that last bit. "He runs a tight ship and it can be overwhelming when you first come on board. Don't let him intimidate you." Briggs winked, and in that simple gesture she guessed that he thought pretty highly of himself. And most of the female population of Sweet Hill probably agreed with his assessment. He was young and in good shape, if not a little too put together. He was overly tan with teeth so white she was sure he had them professionally bleached.

Piper nodded stiffly, for some reason feeling a little defensive of his assessment of Hale. She imagined the role of county sheriff could be stressful.

Hale probably only wanted to surround himself with the best staff possible to make sure the people in their county were protected and well served.

Wow. Had she just defended a member of law enforcement?

She was clearly suffering from a serious crush and needed to get a handle on it because she absolutely would not be one of those women who slept with her boss. Hale insisted theirs would be a professional relationship and she believed he meant that. He wasn't the kind of man to say things he didn't mean. Now she couldn't be so weak as to try and tempt him away from his promise of self-restraint.

As the morning drifted into afternoon and Doris took her through the paces, modeling how to answer the calls that came in and where to direct them, Piper realized her work here could be meaningful. For the first time in her life, she felt like she might have a purpose beyond that of parenting Malia. Not to minimize her role as her sister's guardian, but someday her sister would grow up and go to college and Piper would be on her own. Suddenly her future felt less bleak.

She would not screw this up.

HALE MANAGED TO stay out of Piper's way until her Thursday night shift.

He knew from Doris she was doing a good job. She was a quick study and picked up everything Doris showed her. From how to take calls from even the most difficult personalities, to filing reports, to interfacing with the public. He had worried about that a little. Piper could be prickly and, historically, people often gave her a reason to be. She had not been treated well by this town.

According to Doris, it turned out he had nothing to worry about. When people needed help and she was their one lifeline, they weren't inclined to spit in the face of the person offering to help them.

The first half of the week he came into the office before her shift started and after it ended, assuring himself she was gone and they would not have to come face-to-face. Cowardly, he supposed, but a little distance was in order after their most recent interactions. He needed to be able to look at her without his first impulse being to jump her bones.

Thursday night she was on from 8 p.m. until 5 a.m. There was no way around it. When he entered the department a little after nine, it was quiet. He didn't see her at the front desk and assumed she was in the break room, maybe getting a cup of coffee. Late shifts required coffee.

Molly Brewster looked up from her desk where she worked on her computer. "Hey, boss."

"Brewster," he greeted. "How are things?"

"Good. Quiet."

"Quiet is always good." Even as he spoke the words, his gaze scanned the main lobby, hungry for a glimpse of Piper. It had been four days and it was like he was starved.

The soft rumble of voices reached his ears. He followed the sound to the break room to come upon Deputy Briggs leaning in close to Piper as she took a steaming mug out of the microwave and added a tea bag to it.

Briggs had several nicknames. Casanova was the kindest. STD was probably the most factual. The guy stuck his dick in every female he could. Hale had warned him the minute his activities impacted the job he was gone. So far Briggs had kept his on-the-job flirting to a minimum and kept his dick in his pants while working.

Hale didn't know what he was saying but whatever it was made Piper laugh, and that hit him like a sucker punch. She'd never laughed for him like that.

Hell, he didn't think he had ever seen her laugh. At least not in scorn or mockery.

Fuck that. He strode into the room. "Briggs,"

he barked. "I didn't know the County of Sweet Hill was paying to flirt with the staff and crack jokes. Don't you have work to do?"

Briggs straightened, a bit of red flushing his cheeks. "Sure, boss." With a quick, regretful glance at Piper, he hightailed it out of the break room.

He turned his gaze on Piper only to find her glaring at him. "Did you have to do that?"

"Do what?"

"I'm trying to fit in here."

He took a step toward her, his hand coming to rest casually on his gun belt. "Fitting in doesn't mean you need to fuck that guy."

He didn't know why he said it. It was mean and unfair and he knew it the moment it shot out of his mouth. But he felt like being mean. Seeing Briggs standing over her and looking at her like she was his next meal brought out the mean in him.

A nerve ticked madly near her eye. "You're an asshole."

"Is that how you talk to your boss?"

She nodded, lifting her chin defiantly. "Apparently."

Hell, he'd missed this. He missed *her*. His gaze dropped to her mouth and he remembered her taste. He was so screwed. How was he going to deal with having her this close all the time and not be able to do anything about it? He could only take so many cold showers and jack off.

It beats losing her all together. Never seeing her again.

That thought jarred him because she wasn't his to lose. She never would be.

"What I said about us keeping it professional extends to other employees, too, you know."

She sputtered. "W-what are you—"

He closed the distance between them, backing her against the refrigerator door, rasping close to her face. "I'm saying you're not going to fuck him or anyone else in this building. Understand?"

"You're unbelievable. Is this how it's going to be? You see me talking to any guy that works here and I'm sleeping with him?"

He jerked his head in the direction Briggs had departed. "I know that guy. Women like him. Just wanted to make sure you didn't fall under his spell."

"Well, you can rest easy. He's not my type." She slid out from between him and the fridge. "And as for me and anyone else in this building . . ." Her voice faded away and she shrugged, the action belying the fire still snapping in her dark eyes. "You might be my boss, but you don't own me . . . or my vagina."

That said, she turned, swaying that ass in a very deliberate manner that had him biting back a groan. *This woman is going to be the death of me.*

He could do this. He'd always been a man of restraint. She would not be his undoing.

Stalking out of the break room, he strode into his office and grabbed the ten-inch stack of reports waiting to be filed. He'd intended to divide them up equally among his deputies to spread out the workload.

He carried the hefty pile out and dropped them on Briggs's desk with a satisfying slam. "Here you go, Briggs. Something to keep you busy since you seem to have so much time on your hands."

Briggs's eyes widened as he took in the stack. Slack-jawed, he looked up at Hale. "All of it? Tonight?"

"I've got faith in you."

Briggs stared at him one beat longer and then turned his head, his gaze landing on Piper where she had resumed her seat at the front desk. Already she talked on the phone, a pen in her hand as she was jotting down notes.

Understanding washed over the big lummox's face. Hale hadn't said the words, but he didn't need to. Briggs heard them loud and clear. *Piper Walsh is mine.*

Hale might not be able to have her, but as far as he was concerned no other man in this department could either. She was off-limits and best to let everyone know that now . . . starting with Briggs.

Nodding morosely, Briggs slipped the first report off the top and opened it. Lesson learned.

SEVENTEEN

$\mathcal{F}$RIDAY WAS BUSY. A school bus took a corner too close and knocked out a fire hydrant. All the kids had to be shuttled into a second bus to get them to school, but before that could happen, all forty plus panicked parents converged on the intersection. It took half the department to manage the fiasco.

It was almost lunch before Hale made it back to the department. Piper hung up on a phone call and looked up to find him in front of her desk. "Hello," she greeted, cursing the sudden increased thump of her heart.

"Here." He thrust a white paper bag toward her. He held two bags actually, but he shoved only one of them at her.

She eyed the bag and him with uncertainty. "What is this?"

"Lunch."

"Lunch?" she echoed.

Doris emerged from the break room then, one of her ever present celery sticks in her hand. It was amazing that the woman carried any extra weight. Every time Piper saw her she was eating celery and drinking water.

"Yes." He nodded. "You need to eat. You're too thin."

Doris made a snorting sound and rolled her eyes, taking a crunching bite. "Some people have the best problems."

"Thank you . . . Hale," Piper murmured, her hands flexing around the bag and crinkling the paper.

She pulled her lightweight cardigan tighter around her body, feeling suddenly self-conscious.

He muttered something that sounded like a profanity. "That's not what I meant. You're not *too* thin. You don't always seem to eat enough . . . or properly. You look . . . fine. You look—" He stopped and scowled.

"What do I owe you?"

"Don't worry about it."

She shook her head. "No, I insist. What—"

"Just take the damn food, Piper, and leave it at that."

She pressed her lips into a mutinous line. He stared down at her. A moment passed before he let loose a curse and stalked away.

She watched his retreating back until he disappeared into his office and then she dropped her gaze to the bag in her hands.

"Interesting." Doris made a humming sound and Piper could only imagine what that meant. She arched both eyebrows and smiled with an encouraging nod at Piper. "That was nice of him. What'd he bring you?"

Piper shrugged lightly, feeling a need to explain what just happened—even if she wasn't so sure. "I'm sure he just grabbed me something because he was getting something for himself."

"Mm-hm." Doris settled into her chair and fished a new celery stick out of her baggie. "He didn't get *me* anything."

"With all the celery you eat, he probably knows you're watching what you eat."

As though proving her point, Doris lifted her celery stick to her mouth and took a healthy bite. She picked up her coffee cup and chased it with a sip. Piper couldn't imagine a worse combination.

"Well? What did our fine sheriff get you?"

Shaking her head, Piper rummaged through

the bag, pulling out a fat sliced brisket sandwich wrapped in cellophane. A pickle. A side of potato salad in addition to a bag of potato chips. The savory aroma filled her nostrils and made her stomach rumble. "How am I going to eat all this?"

"Enjoy it. Take home what you don't finish." Doris shuffled across the room.

Piper unwrapped the cellophane and took a large bite from the overstuffed sandwich, moaning as the flavor of beef and tangy barbecue sauce hit her tongue. She couldn't remember the last time she had eaten anything so good or hearty or decadent. She felt a little guilty that she was enjoying it without her sister. She managed to eat only half the sandwich and the small container of potato salad. Wrapping what was left of her sandwich, she returned it to its bag and walked into the break room so she could stow the leftovers in the fridge.

Turning around, she exited the break room. The phone started ringing and she hurried to her desk, her shoulders squaring back and her chest swelling slightly with something she had never felt before. Something that felt like purpose.

She'd always felt driven when it came to her sister. Purpose and determination had always been there, motivating her to take care of Malia. But waitressing at Joe's had never fueled her with any great sense of personal fulfillment. She had that now though. Doris training her to answer these calls, talking to people on the other side of the line and being the one person that stood between them and whatever danger was threatening to pull them under. She'd never had anything like that before.

And it was all because of Hale. Damn it.

She didn't want him doing nice things like bringing her lunch.

She didn't want to like him. She'd never wanted to like him, so what was she supposed to do with all these new emotions she felt toward him? How was she supposed to deal with working with him every day when she couldn't look at him without remembering what had happened between them at the club? What *she* had instigated?

Dropping onto her chair, she picked up the phone midring and answered slightly out of breath. "Sweet Hill Sheriff's Department. How may I help you?"

PIPER HAD THE weekend off. She couldn't remember the last time she didn't work a weekend. Maybe not since high school . . . not since her brother was arrested. Definitely not in the year she had worked at Joe's.

She slept in late on Saturday and then drove Malia to her afternoon game. She parked her lawn chair on the sidelines thirty minutes early and watched the girls warm up. Like a normal parent who worked normal hours and did normal things.

Amanda, Claire's mom, was there. "Hey, stranger," she greeted with a hug. "Nice to see you."

"Yeah, hopefully you'll be seeing more of me at these games."

Even as short as Piper was, Amanda was smaller. She shielded her eyes with her hand to look up at Piper curiously. "No kidding?"

Piper nodded, eager to share her change in circumstances. "I have a new job."

Amanda lifted her eyebrows. "You quit Joe's?"

"Yep." It was easier than explaining that she had *technically* been fired. "And I've got a new job working as a dispatch at the Sheriff's Department."

Amanda gave a small happy clap. "That's terrific! I know you've been trying to find another job forever. So happy for you! You deserve this."

Amanda was one of the few people who didn't judge Piper for her past. She didn't know how she would have handled getting Malia to and from soccer without Amanda's help. "Thanks, Amanda."

"Now you have no excuse. You'll have to make it to one of our weekend barbecues."

"And finally get to try the fajitas your husband is so famous for grilling? It's all Malia talks about."

Amanda nodded proudly. "That's right. My man can grill some meat." She leaned forward conspiratorially. "And speaking of meat . . . we'll have to make sure to invite his sexy cousin." She waggled her eyebrows. "He's single."

Piper laughed and shook her head. "No thanks."

"Did I mention he prefers brunettes?"

"No matchmaking, please."

"C'mon, girl. You deserve a good man in your life. Now that you'll be keeping more normal work hours you can actually go out on a date."

Except Piper couldn't do that. She didn't even want to. An image of Hale filled her mind. She quickly shoved it away. He was *not* the reason she didn't want to date.

"I will let you know when I'm ready to date," she promised Amanda.

Amanda huffed and crossed her arms, seemingly appeased.

They turned their attention to the game and

spent the next hour cheering themselves hoarse as they watched the girls run back and forth across the field.

After the game, Malia and Piper joined the other players and their families at a local pizza place. She sat at a table with the parents and drank a glass of wine and ate pizza and bemoaned the ref's bad calls and talked about the upcoming soccer tournament.

It felt right. It felt *good*. Normal. She felt like a well-adjusted person raising a happy, well-adjusted kid.

And she owed it to Hale Walters. That was a difficult thing to accept. Especially considering how much he had infuriated her on Thursday with his remarks and his little display of . . . well, she didn't know what that was. She almost suspected jealousy except she knew that wasn't possible. A man who didn't do relationships didn't get possessive or territorial about a woman he wasn't even sleeping with. And not only were they not sleeping together, they weren't even grinding all over each other like two horny teenagers anymore.

A week had almost passed since that madness. Those two nights when they had made out like two sex-crazed monkeys felt like a lifetime ago. As though it happened to someone else. Or as though it happened in a dream. Certainly the memory of those nights had been relegated to her dreams. She actually woke up several times, panting and achy, her hand pressed between her legs in a desperate attempt to assuage the throbbing twinges. Sex dreams. She was having sex dreams. She knew it beat the nightmares that at times plagued her. Maybe.

Whatever the case, she was done fooling around with Hale. It wasn't happening again.

"Today might have been the best day ever," Malia declared in the seat beside her. "You never get to go to any of the team dinners with us."

Piper smiled as she pulled onto the narrow road leading up to their apartment complex. Soon, with her current salary, they'd be able to move out of this dump and get a better place. "I know. And I should get to go to all of them now."

Malia grinned. "I think I'm in love with Sheriff Walters."

Piper's smile slipped. "W-what?"

"For giving you a job."

"Oh." She laughed awkwardly, her heart steadying back into a normal pace. "Yeah. Of course."

Malia gave her a funny look as they pulled into the Sunset Views parking lot. "What did you think I meant? That I looooved him?"

Piper continued laughing nervously. "No. Course not."

"He's so old."

"Old? He's thirty-one." She pulled into the parking spot in front of their building.

"Yeah. Practically ancient. But not too old for you. You should go for him. Old or not, he is hot. And he's got a great body. He must work out." With that remark, Malia climbed out of the car.

It took her a moment to refocus and follow her out of the car. "I can't believe you said that."

"What? He's a total DILF."

"A DILF?"

"Yeah. That's what Claire calls him. You know, like a MILF? Except a DILF."

Mortification washed through her to think her sister was having this kind of conversation about Hale with Claire. "Yeah, yeah, I get it. You don't need to explain. I know what it means." *Dads I'd Like to Fuck*. "The question is, how do *you* know what it means? It's not exactly appropriate."

Malia rolled her eyes. "I'm fifteen. I watch TV and go to high school." High school. The corrupter of all innocence.

Piper stopped and stared at her sister's back before her feet remembered how to walk again. She resumed her pace and caught up with her.

Malia cocked her head and sent her a glance. "Although I guess the sheriff's technically not a dad." Her eyes brightened. "But he could be. You should totally marry him! Oh!" She gave Piper a nudge that nearly knocked her off the path. "You would make the cutest babies! And then I'd be an aunt."

She sputtered, "Malia! Stop it!" *Please. She didn't need any unrealistic aspirations.* "I'm not marrying the sheriff."

But suddenly she couldn't stop considering the idea.

What would it be like to be married to Hale? To live in a house together? To eat meals across from each other? To spend nights snuggling on the couch watching TV? And then her mind drifted to other things a married couple would do.

All kinds of inappropriate things.

All kinds of naughty things.

These things flashed through her mind, making her breasts grow heavy and achy inside her bra. She envisioned his big cock sliding deep inside her as she rocked on top of him, riding him until an orgasm ripped through her shuddering body. His wife would always have that. *Him*. Whenever she wanted it.

"Piper? You okay? You're breathing hard and you have this funny look on your face."

"Yes, yes. I'm fine," she said too quickly as she fished her keys out of her purse with a trembling hand.

Reaching her door, she pulled up hard as she realized it was ajar. The additional lock she had installed on the door had been cut. "Malia," she murmured over her shoulder. "Go to the car and wait there."

"What is it?" Her taller sister peered around her.

If she had to guess, management had ruled against her installing an additional door lock on her own.

"I'm not sure. I think someone's in our apartment."

Malia gasped, her grip tightening on Piper's arm. "Piper . . ."

"Go on. I'll take care of it." She already had a pretty good idea who was there. Her blood burned to think of him walking through their home as though he had every right. It wasn't that late. Only a little after eight. He wasn't even concerned with being discovered.

Leaving her sister behind, she entered the apartment, walking slowly, easing her steps as though concerned about alerting the intruder of her presence. Almost instantly, she identified sounds that told her someone else was in fact inside her home.

She inched carefully forward through the main room, casting a glance into the tiny kitchen and living room space and verifying the rooms were empty.

She hardly breathed as she hovered in the threshold of the bedroom she shared with Malia. The room was small. She'd tried to make it nice for them, covering the bed with a soft teal comforter she got on clearance at Wal-Mart. The plastered ceiling was cracked in multiple places. The wall a dingy white in desperate need of repainting. But it had always been their sanctuary. In that bed at night, with her sister snoring softly beside her, she would imagine a better world for herself and Malia.

But now that room had been invaded. She spotted him immediately in his dingy wife-beater, tufts of back hair peeking out around the edges of cotton fabric as he riffled through the drawers of their dresser.

Speech abandoned her for several moments as she stared in mute revulsion. He was going through her underwear drawer. Bile rose up in her throat as she watched him lift a pair of her panties to his nose and inhale long and deep.

"What are you doing?" she demanded.

Raymond whirled around. For a brief moment, his expression looked almost guilty, and then that sentiment was gone.

"I came over with those rat traps for ya." Now he was suddenly interested in handling her vermin problem?

She'd asked management to do something about that long ago, but she'd mostly been thinking along the lines of an actual exterminator. Not Raymond. "And you needed to look through my underwear drawer for that?"

He smiled slowly, lifting a hand to scratch at the patchy scruff covering the rolling flesh of his jaw. "Well, I was just being thorough." He still clutched her underwear in his other hand. She knew the only thing she would be able to do with those panties after this was throw them in the trash.

"I don't see any traps," she accused.

"I left them on the counter in the kitchen."

"And so why are you in my bedroom?"

Several beats passed before he answered. She could almost see him searching his little mind for an excuse. "I thought I would investigate and see if the rats had spread to any other places in your unit besides the kitchen." He took a few steps in her direction. "They like sweet things, you know." He glanced down at her panties and grinned.

Pervert.

She nodded to her underwear clutched in his hand. "You can put that down." Not that she would wear them again, but it was unnerving as hell to see him holding them.

He pushed the black, thick-framed glasses higher atop his nose with the same hand that gripped her underwear. He wasn't even bothering to hide his creepiness anymore.

He thought he could do this. Corner her and intimidate her. He turned his gaze on her, looking her over in her sleeveless blouse and shorts, taking his time on her legs. She had thought her shorts totally modest, but now she felt indecent with his gaze crawling over her legs.

She inhaled a bracing breath. "I think you need to leave."

"Now don't be rude, missy." His voice sharpened to a scold. "You could be more mannerly. Specially after I went out of my way for you."

"This isn't appropriate."

"Appropriate?" he scoffed. "You think you are

so much better than me? So high and mighty? I know who you are. Who your family is." He fluttered his fingers in the air. "I'm just doing right by you and I don't like the disrespect you're treating me to—"

"Either you leave or I will. And I *will* be taking this up with management."

He laughed harshly. "Think they're going to listen to a bit of trash like you? They put me in charge and they've already got you pegged as trouble." She winced, having no doubt he was the reason they made that judgment about her.

He glanced around the space with a sneer. "You pay three hundred a month to live in this shit hole. They'd just as soon toss you out on that tasty ass of yours than listen to any more of your complaints. I'm the only reason you're still even living here." He stabbed a sausage finger in her direction. "You better start treating me better, you hear me?"

A deep voice rolled over the air: "I hear you."

Piper's chest squeezed at the sudden sound of Hale's voice. She would know it anywhere. She'd heard it in her dreams now for so many nights.

She whirled around to find him directly behind her. He was wearing his uniform and looking as stern and imposing and beautiful as ever in the dark blue.

"O-Officer," Raymond sputtered.

Hale studied him stonily, his gray eyes as cold as a snake's. "I received a call that someone had broken into this residence."

Someone had called him? Just then Piper caught a movement beyond him. A wide-eyed Malia stood there, her cell phone in her hand, and something else in her other hand. A little white rectangle. *Hale's business card.* The one that he had given to Malia that night he hauled her into the department. He'd given it to her with the understanding being that she should call him if she was ever in trouble. Of course, at the time he had thought that Piper was likely the source of all trouble in Malia's life.

Her sister had kept it. She'd used it at the first hint of trouble.

Relief coursed through Piper even as much as she wanted to reject it. She liked to think she didn't need him or any man. She liked to think she could have handled Raymond by herself. Even if he did outweigh her by two hundred pounds and his mind was foul and twisted.

But she wasn't a fool either. Better than anyone she knew how easy it was to become a victim. It didn't mean you were weak or stupid. It didn't mean you had done anything wrong. More often than not it meant you were unlucky enough to run smack into a giant douchebag bent on all manner of assholery.

"Everything's all right, Officer." Raymond patted both hands on the air in a placating manner. "I'm the manager of this facility. We got this under control."

Piper snorted and opened her mouth to protest when Hale broke in. "No, *I* got this," he said sharply, his gaze cutting. "And it's Sheriff. Sheriff Walters."

Hale turned his attention to Piper. "What's going on?"

She exhaled. "We came home to find him in our apartment—"

Raymond interrupted. "I came inside to set up some rat traps—"

"Rats?" Hale scowled and looked around, assessing the room.

With a start, she realized he had never been inside her home before. She experienced a flash of embarrassment. "We had rats getting into the kitchen pantry," she quickly explained. As though living with rats was a normal thing. "I found him in *here* going through my underwear drawer."

"As the manager of this complex, I have every right to enter the unit—"

"You were going through her underwear drawer?" Hale asked, his voice lethally soft.

Raymond laughed uneasily. "C'mon. I'm harmless."

"Sounds like you're a sick fuck," Hale pronounced.

Raymond's eyes bulged. "Hey. You can't talk to me like that." He stepped forward, puffing out his chest.

Hale flexed his hand on his gun belt. "If I were you, I wouldn't come at me."

Raymond halted, his eyes wide. For the first time, she read fear there.

Hale continued. "I'm going to put in a call to the management of this complex and make certain they're aware that they've placed their trust in a predator. I expect that they're going to fire you—"

"You can't do that!"

"I serve the County of Sweet Hill. It's my duty to protect the public from men like you. I would tread carefully. My officers are going to keep a close eye on you. Whatever hole you crawl into, just know that someone will always be around watching you."

"Just because I put a hand in her underwear drawer?" Raymond blustered.

Hale stepped forward, closing the distance between him and her landlord. His deep voice reached her ears, but not the words. She couldn't hear what he uttered. Piper moved to stand beside her sister. Whatever Hale said, the color bled from Raymond's face. The man nodded jerkily and then scrambled past Hale. He didn't even look at her or her sister as he exited the door of her bedroom.

She whipped her head to stare at Hale. "What did you say?"

"Nothing."

"I'm pretty sure I want to be a cop when I grow up," Malia announced in an awe-tinged voice.

Piper looked at her quickly. "I thought you wanted to be a vet."

"That, too." She shrugged.

"Be a vet," Hale said, his voice distracted.

Piper looked back at Hale only to catch him assessing her room again, a frown pulling his lips. The stab of embarrassment returned. She ignored it and lifted her chin. "Thank you, Hale."

"You're lucky I was close by when Malia called. What if I got here half an hour later?"

She couldn't help but shiver at that.

"You can't live here," he announced.

"I don't think Raymond will be bothering us anymore."

"You don't know that. I think he got the message, but people can be unpredictable. You both need to move out of here."

"I was planning on that, but I thought I'd get a few paychecks first so we could cover the deposit and—"

"Pack up your stuff now. It's not safe here."

She bristled at his high-handedness. She knew he was right regarding safety. This place had never been safe. Even before finding Raymond going through her underwear she knew that. That's why she had the additional lock installed . . . to give her some sense of security. But it was humiliating to be told that. He held her gaze, looking utterly calm and unflappable. Like her arguments mattered not at all and he was going to get his way in this.

He might have helped them out tonight and he might be her boss, but that didn't give him the right to boss her around outside of work. "Malia, can you wait outside?"

Her sister looked between them, clearly torn. She did not want to miss any of their discussion. "Malia," Piper said in a sharper voice. "Please."

Malia nodded and reluctantly stepped out.

Piper squared her shoulders, hating the heat of mortification creeping up her throat in a burning

tingle. "I can't just pack us up. We don't have anywhere to go. It will take me a week at least to find
another place—"

"You can stay with me until you find a new place."

Hale didn't even flinch as he made the offer.
No. Not offer. Statement of fact.

She released a snort of laughter. "I can't do
that. I can't just move in with you." Did her heart
have to flutter a little at the thought of that?

"You're not staying here." He glanced around
her place again.

She followed his gaze, seeing it through his eyes
and feeling a fresh stab of shame. He probably
had a great place. He'd probably only ever lived
in great places.

"You and your sister can stay with me until you
find your own place. Someplace nice and safe."

Safe. Her throat thickened. She already felt
safer just because of him. It was dangerous, letting herself look at him like some sort of savior.
Saving people was his job. She shouldn't kid herself into thinking he did it for her because she
meant anything to him.

"I'm responsible for that girl out there." She
pointed to the door. "I'm not moving in with you."

He motioned around them. "You can't stay here.
It's a slum—"

"What happened to your decision to keep things professional between us?" She cut him off before he made her feel any worse about her living conditions.

"I have three bedrooms." His mouth quirked as he studied her. "What? You think I was expecting you to share my bed? Haven't I kept my word since you started work? Have I touched you? Hit on you?"

She frowned, feeling only slightly silly. "No. You haven't, but moving in with you is still inappropriate. You're my boss."

"What's inappropriate is you and Malia staying in a place where your landlord breaks in so he can rummage through your underwear. What if it was just your sister here when he entered the unit?"

She pursed her lips and crossed her arms.

"It's only temporary. You said it will take you a week to find a new place," he reminded. "No one even has to know."

She crossed her arms over her chest, feeling herself relenting. The fact of the matter was . . . she didn't want to stay another night in this place. She wouldn't sleep a wink. How could she? She'd never get over the sight of that man, a foot from her bed, pilfering through her panties.

He stared at her steadily. "Piper," he said her name softly. "It's just a safe place for you and your sister."

And isn't that what she had always and foremost wanted for her sister? Her safety?

She smiled at him, the curve of her lips a brittle thing on her face. "First you give me a job. Now a place to crash. It's like Christmas." She was grateful . . . but she was also resenting him for it.

"You've earned the job. Doris said you're a natural at it. Has it occurred to you that you're providing a service and being compensated? I'm not giving you anything."

It was precisely what she needed to hear right then. He didn't make her feel like such a parasite, dependent on him.

"Temporary," she finally agreed. "And I'd like to pay rent for the week we stay with you. You can deduct it from my salary."

"Piper—"

"Just agree that I can pay for the week or forget about it."

"You're a stubborn woman."

"Agree," she pressed.

"Fine." He looked around again, his nostrils flaring slightly. "Now can we get out of here?"

Crossing her arms, she called for her sister.

Malia hurried back inside the apartment, all puppylike eagerness. "Yes?"

"Pack your things. We're leaving this place."

"For real?"

She looked back at Hale. "Yes. For real."

EIGHTEEN

*H*IS HOUSE WAS incredible. He lived on the outside of Sweet Hill on several acres. The property was sprawling. The house was spacious. She instantly fell in love with the open-concept kitchen and living room with its hardwood floors and great big windows that stared out at the desert hills spotted with sparse foliage. A big screen was positioned over the stone fireplace and she couldn't help remembering that image she had about Hale with a wife . . . snuggling on the couch and watching movies together. Now she could add a crackling fireplace to that vision.

A porch wrapped around his house, stretching into a wide covered deck in the back that overlooked a well-tended garden. In the distance she could hear the gurgle of a creek. She stood there now, looking out into the night.

Inside, Malia was running through every room, investigating the house like they might be staying longer than one week. Like this might be something permanent. And that was a dangerous thought. Neither one of them could get too comfortable here. That would be bad for everyone.

Tomorrow, she would start looking for a new place.

"Can I get you anything?" Hale's steps sounded behind her on the deck.

She tore her gaze from the star-studded night and looked over her shoulder. "I'm fine, thank you. And please don't think you need to wait on me. Or Malia."

"All right. I won't." His gaze held hers and she felt the familiar warmth steal over her. How did he do that with a look? It wasn't even one of his *I-want-to-tear-your-clothes-off-with-my-teeth* looks, and she remembered those. She'd been on the receiving end of those before. This was just Hale. Looking at her. And it made her chest tighten. "I'll treat you like you've been living here forever."

He couldn't mean that, but she merely smiled.

She'd already dropped her stuff in the bedroom next door to Hale's room. Malia's things were in the smaller bedroom that doubled as an office/

bedroom. She would have offered her sister the bigger guest room, but once Malia spotted the TV in that room with its gaming system, she called dibs.

"This really is kind of you," she said.

"You've already said that, Piper."

She nodded. Several moments of silence passed. She was acutely aware of his bigger body beside her, radiating warmth. She stood there for as long as she could. "I think we'll call it a night, then."

"All right. See you in the morning."

"Good night." She left him standing on the deck and moved through his house, trying not to feel too comfortable or at home here.

Because it couldn't last.

IT WAS A tricky thing, not falling in love with living with Hale. Heavy emphasis on the "living with" part. She was *not* in love with the man.

Just because he was hot and had an honorable streak running through him did not mean she was in love with him. Not at all. Her heart wasn't free to love. She'd known that ever since her brother entered prison. Devil's Rock was his cage, but she had her own cage, too . . . even if it wasn't visible to the world.

Sunday morning he treated them to breakfast:

scrambled eggs, bacon, toast and pan-fried potatoes. They sat on the back deck, a fan whirring
overhead, keeping them cool. Morning sunlight
bathed the rugged hills behind his property. Only
patchy grass and scrub brush and cacti covered
the terrain. They spotted a coyote trotting along a
distant ridge. Malia pointed it out in delight.

For a moment, Piper found herself reveling in
being there. Until she realized she shouldn't. Her
brother would shake her senseless if he knew she
was playing house with Sheriff Hale Walters . . .
and she would deserve that.

"You eat like this all the time?" Malia asked
around a mouthful of ketchup-drowned potatoes,
her eyes taking in the impressive spread of food
on the table.

"I like to treat myself to big breakfasts on the
weekends. There's nothing better than breakfast,"
he declared, lifting his coffee cup to his lips. His
cup stalled halfway there as his eyes met Piper's.
Heat crept over her face because she felt sure he
was thinking that there actually was something
else better than big breakfasts. Something they
weren't doing.

Hale continued a moment later. "When I was a
teenager my mom had to cook twice this much for
me and my brother."

"Growing boys eat a lot," Piper murmured as she smeared strawberry jam onto her toast.

"And we played sports. She would have to make a tower of pancakes for each of us on top of what you see here." He motioned with his fork to the table of food.

"Wow," Malia said, swallowing her bite and stabbing at some potatoes with her fork. "I usually just eat Pop-Tarts."

He tsked and shook his head . . . and yeah, Piper felt like the worst parent right then. Not that she could have afforded to feed Malia breakfasts like this before she got her new job. *But things are going to be different now.*

After breakfast, she and Malia helped with the dishes and then spent most of the day looking at apartments around town. Hale offered to go with them, but she declined, determined to keep what boundaries she could. However, after spending the night at Hale's she was wondering if maybe she should find a house to rent. Something with a yard and in a good neighborhood. It wouldn't be as big or nearly as nice as Hale's house, but it would give them their first home with real space. Maybe they could even get a pet. A cat that wouldn't mind being left alone while they were at school and work.

Hale got called away to a multiple-car pileup right before dinner that required almost every uniform on staff. Piper and Malia fed themselves. After dinner, Malia finished her homework and went to bed while Piper looked at online listings for rental houses. She emailed a few queries and then went to bed herself, surprisingly tired even though it wasn't even 10 p.m. yet. Already her body had adjusted to the life of a normal person. Someone who worked normal hours and had weekends off. The moment her head hit the pillow, she was out.

IT WAS AFTER midnight when Hale got home. He hated nights like this. The odor of burnt tires and chemicals clung to his uniform. Once in his bedroom, he stripped out of his clothes and tossed them in the hamper.

Two dead and six hospitalized. Such senseless loss. One guy had a few too many, got behind the wheel and lives were changed forever—at least for those lucky enough to have survived. It happened far too often.

He took a shower, lifting his face to the warm spray of water, letting it wash away the sweet metallic aroma of blood that filled his nostrils.

Knotting a towel around his waist, he walked through the house and double-checked that all the doors were locked. He had Piper and Malia to consider now. The thought made his chest expand a little, made this night feel a little less awful. A little less bleak.

Normally, he came home to an empty house. This was only their second night here with him and it already felt good to come home to a place that felt like . . . a home.

He knew he needed to be careful. They weren't staying. This wasn't permanent. Piper had made that very clear, and, of course, he didn't want her to stay. He'd never lived with a woman and there was a reason for that. He liked being on his own. He just needed to keep remembering that.

He was returning from the kitchen and passing Piper's door when he heard her cry out. He backed up a step and stopped right outside of it, every muscle suddenly wire-tight. He stood close, listening for several silent moments. Nothing. He was about to move on to his room when he heard her short scream.

He burst in the room to find her sitting up in bed, her chest lifting with heavy pants as though she had just run a marathon. She stared straight ahead, gazing blindly with glassy eyes.

He sank down beside her and gave her a small shake. "Piper! Piper, what is it?"

She immediately fought him, slapping at his hands and arms.

"Piper!" He locked his arms around her and hauled her against him.

She stilled, her glassy eyes gradually coming into focus. "Hale?" she whispered.

"Yeah, sweetheart. It's me," he whispered back, their faces so close he could taste her breath. And that's not all he noticed.

She was only wearing a thin T-shirt. And he wasn't wearing anything except a towel. He had no problem feeling the tight little buds of her nipples beading through her shirt into his chest. His body instantly reacted. He throbbed for her, remembering her silken channel, the clinging warmth, the way she'd milked his finger like it was his cock. His dick rose swiftly in response, tenting his towel.

He forgot all promises of professionalism. He forgot that she was a guest under his roof and the right thing to do would be to keep his hands off her. There was only hunger. Need.

He ducked his head, going for her mouth, his hands on her arms tightening, readying to pull her under him.

"Piper! Are you okay?" Malia called from the hall.

He launched himself back as though burned—away from Piper, away from temptation. His hand flew to his towel, making sure it remained in place. At the sound of Piper's teenage sister, his erection subsided.

"Malia," she said breathlessly as her sister entered the room, bright color staining her cheeks as she looked between them. "It was nothing. Just a nightmare."

"Again?" Malia hurried deeper into the room and circled the bed, climbing in beside her sister. "Maybe I should sleep with you." The girl looked solemnly at Hale. "She's not used to sleeping alone."

I'd be happy to sleep with her.

He shook off the wicked thought.

Then something else Malia said clicked. *Again.* Piper had a nightmare *again*. This was a chronic thing for her? His chest tightened. He didn't like that idea.

He looked at her where she sat on the bed, pulling the sheets higher to cover her T-shirt in an attempt for modesty. Like he hadn't seen those breasts and tasted them before. Like he still didn't see and taste them when he closed his eyes.

"You have nightmares a lot?" he asked.

"Not really—"

"Pretty often—"

The sisters spoke simultaneously, but he was inclined to believe Malia, especially after the death glare Piper shot her.

Piper looked back at him. "It's been an eventful weekend. I'm sure that's all it is."

He nodded, not believing her. There was more to it than that. More to Piper Walsh. He'd known that for a while now. She had her secrets and she kept them close. Hell, everyone did.

But for some reason, he wanted to know every one of hers.

NINETEEN

PIPER STOOD ON her tiptoes and peered through the peephole only to feel her chest sink. She backed away from the front door as though Death itself hovered on the other side. Damn. She was hoping to avoid this.

"Who is it?" Malia asked from behind her.

"Um, Faith and North."

Malia hopped a little in place and then lunged around Piper to open the door with a happy squeal. "Hey, guys!" she greeted warmly.

North and Faith stepped inside and hugged Malia. They made a striking couple with their dark hair and tall bodies. It was like they were created for each other. Piper felt like a little gnat beside them.

Faith wasted no time zeroing her laser-beam eyes on Piper. "Heyyyy, there. I didn't know you moved. Had to find that out from Doris." There was no dodging the accusation in her voice or the way her eyes drilled into her.

Doris, the only person at the department who knew she was temporarily living with Hale and only because Doris had stopped by yesterday to drop off the leaf blower she had borrowed.

At Doris's shocked expression, Piper had explained she had to move out suddenly from her apartment and Hale had offered them somewhere to live until they got a new place. She had stressed it was temporary, but that didn't stop the look that came over Doris's face once the surprise ebbed away. Smug, knowing and even a touch calculating. She had definite ideas forming behind those blinged-out glasses of hers.

"Ohh, what did you bring us?" Malia rubbed her hands together as she eyed the box in North's hands. She was far too accustomed to gifts from these two whenever they visited.

"A butter cake." Faith was still staring at Piper. "My brother's favorite." She paused a beat. "I'll get you the recipe if you like, Piper."

Piper blinked, feeling targeted at that not-so-veiled offer. As though Piper might have a reason for wanting the recipe for Hale's favorite cake.

As though there was a reason she would want to master any of Hale's favorite recipes.

Of course there wasn't a reason, but that didn't stop his sister from looking at her as though she was sizing her up for a bridal gown.

North set the box on the counter. Malia immediately peeled back the lid to eye inside it.

"Where's Hale?" Faith asked, setting her handbag down.

"He's outside grilling some steaks."

North nodded and headed toward the back door as though that information had been an invitation for him to head outside.

Piper watched him for a moment, feeling a stab of nervousness at the intent look she had observed on his face. She knew the two men could hardly be called friends, but they had reached a peace of sorts. She'd hate that to end because of her.

North considered himself a guardian to her and Malia. Never mind that she was an adult and didn't require a guardian. He was going to have something to say on the subject of her staying here. She had no doubt of that. She hoped he didn't mention it to her brother. She was hoping that Cruz never had to know.

She turned after North and started to follow. Her intervention might be necessary. Faith grabbed her arm and pulled her down into a chair. "Oh, no, you don't. Let the guys talk. And it will give us a chance to catch up."

Catch up? Why did that ring so ominously? Why did it feel like she was about to suffer an interrogation? As Faith grilled her, North would be outside conducting his own cross-examination. It was mortifying, really.

"So. How long are you staying with Hale?" To the point.

"I'm looking for a place now." She glanced at her sister, who was already cutting into the cake without even an invitation to do so. "It shouldn't take long."

"I hope we never leave," Malia proclaimed, licking glaze off her fingers. "I like it here. Hale is a great cook. He's making rib eyes."

Piper frowned at her sister. This was exactly what she didn't want to happen. Malia getting too comfortable and liking it here too much. And when had she started calling him Hale instead of Sheriff Walters?

"So what made you decide to move?" Faith asked, her voice far too innocent. "Last time we talked you were adamant that you couldn't afford any place else."

"Well . . . your brother offered me a job."

Faith stared at her, her unblinking gaze looking closely. To resist fidgeting beneath that scrutiny, Piper turned and went back to work on the salad she was prepping to go with the steaks Hale was grilling. God, even in her head that sounded hopelessly domestic and her heart gave a stupid little pang of longing.

"Yes. I heard that. I didn't know that Hale had officially opened Doris's position for applicants."

Piper smiled at her noncommittally. From conversations with Doris, she definitely didn't think he'd interviewed other candidates. Clearly he had done her a favor by offering her the job without even knowing if she could do it.

He'd stepped in like some kind of savior, giving her a job and then pulling them out of that hellhole where they'd been living and giving them a place to stay. Even if he had been responsible for getting her fired, he'd gone above and beyond to repair the damage.

Malia's phone started to ring. She glanced at it and dropped her cake, hurrying out of the kitchen. She could be heard diving into high-pitched chatter as she vanished into her room.

The instant her sister was out of sight, Faith wasted no time. "What is going on with you and my brother?"

Piper winced, tempted to call Malia back into the kitchen just to spare her. She cleared her throat. "It's not what it looks like."

Faith waved airily. "Well . . . it *looks* like y'all are shacking up and playing house."

Piper glanced at the half-assembled salad before her. "Yes, but we're not *shacking* up. It's not like that." At least, not since she moved in here. They had been perfectly respectable in their interaction with each other.

"It's not?" Faith looked skeptical.

She jerked her head back to where her sister had disappeared. "I have a sister. I wouldn't do that . . ."

"Please." Faith rolled her eyes. "I'm not suggesting you and my brother are being inappropriate around Malia. But I know the power of attraction. The minute North moved next door to me, it was inevitable. I can see that now. He and I were destined to hit the sheets."

Piper gaped.

Faith nodded and continued. "Maybe you can't see it yet. Maybe my brother can't."

Was Faith telling her she should sleep with her brother? Her mouth sagged open momentarily before she recovered herself. Really, it wasn't like she was some miss-ish female. "I—I . . ." she stammered, at a complete loss.

"And you're a good sister, Piper, but you deserve your own life and happiness."

She inwardly cringed. No. No, she didn't.

Faith went on, her tone emphatic and resolute. "What goes on behind closed doors has nothing to do with Malia. Don't pass up a chance for happiness, Piper. I think you and Hale could be good for each other."

She shook her head, almost wishing that were true . . . that it could be that easy. "We are not you and North."

"Well, maybe you're not committed to each other yet . . . my brother has his hang-ups about relationships, but I wouldn't be surprised if he forgot all about that. He just needs the right woman." She looked meaningfully at Piper.

"Well, *I* would be surprised." Piper shook her head. He'd been very clear that he didn't do relationships.

"I'm just saying it wouldn't be a bad thing if I was your sister-in-law."

Piper chuckled and then killed the sound. She didn't need to encourage Faith's outrageous ideas.

"As tempting as that is, I think you shouldn't get any ideas. I'm not marrying your brother."

A slight sound caught her attention. Turning, her gaze collided with Hale's. He stood in the opening to the kitchen, holding a tray of steaks. North stood beside him wearing a decidedly unamused expression.

"Ah . . ." She didn't know what to say. She wanted to crawl under the table and hide.

"Steaks are ready," he volunteered.

"Well, we won't keep you from your dinner." Faith hopped off the bar stool where she sat and picked up her purse.

"Would you like to stay?" Piper invited.

"No, no. We didn't mean to crash your dinner. You didn't plan on two extra people. Enjoy your steaks. Just save room for butter cake." She motioned to the cake Malia had already helped herself to.

"Thank you for the cake. It's my favorite," Hale commented.

"I know, bubbie." She grinned. "That's why I made it."

"What inspired this?" Suspicion gleamed in his eyes. "It's not my birthday."

"Can't a sister just bake her brother a cake?"

He stared at her for a long beat, those gray eyes missing nothing. "Doris told you Piper was here." Statement of fact, not a question.

Faith sniffed. "I'm glad I have someone to keep me apprised of what's going on. My friend here doesn't tell me anything." She cut an accusing look to Piper. "And neither do you, Hale."

"If there was anything you needed to know, I promise I would tell you."

An awkward silence fell. North didn't look too happy and she imagined his protectiveness was warring with the fact that these two were siblings and naturally adversarial and he knew he should probably take a step back when they were sparring.

"Don't let your dinner get cold," Faith declared cheerfully, and came at Piper for a hug.

North followed suit, murmuring near her ear, "You call me if you need anything. Don't feel like you have to stay here. You can crash with me and Faith anytime." He pulled back with his hands still on her shoulders, staring down at her with deliberation, letting his words sink in.

She nodded and sent a quick glance to Hale as he received a hug from Faith. He watched her and North without expression.

"Sure," she agreed even though the last thing she would ever do was move in with North and Faith. She couldn't even imagine it. They were on the verge of getting married. She wouldn't dream of invading their little love nest.

There was a brief handshake between the two guys, still as awkward as ever. Just because they tolerated each other didn't mean they would ever be good friends.

Then they were gone and it was just Hale and Piper, alone in the kitchen.

She released a breath, glad Faith and North were gone. She knew they were well meaning, but it was a little overwhelming with Faith's assumptions and prying.

Hale set the tray of steaks on the counter. Curls of savory steam drifted up from the meat. "So you're not interested in marrying me, huh?"

She blinked in mortification even though she detected humor in his voice. "I know that must be a relief to you," she said wryly. "To know that I have no designs on you. You don't need to lock your bedroom door at nights."

He chuckled lightly. "That *is* a comforting reassurance."

The mood lightened and she felt herself smiling.

She stepped to the side, reaching for the drawer that held the salad forks just as he moved in for the same drawer.

His chest collided with her back and they both stilled as though burned at the contact. It was their first close contact since she'd started to work for him and it gave her heart palpitations. Did he feel it, too, or was she the only one who suddenly couldn't drag air into her lungs?

Stupid, stupid, stupid. Of course he wasn't affected the way she was. He was a grown man with plenty of experience.

She tried to act normal, opening the drawer and taking out the forks. She gripped them tightly and rested her clenched hands on the counter.

Hale didn't step away and she felt his breath rustling her hair.

"Excuse me," she murmured, turning her face sideways, glimpsing him from one eye. Even that partial view did nothing to disguise the breadth of him, the wall of masculinity at her back.

He didn't budge. Not even an inch.

"Hale," she whispered. She didn't know what she was saying in that utterance. She didn't know what she wanted. For him to stay put and touch her? Kiss her? Or back away and leave her alone?

His hand came down on the back of her head,

his fingers dragging through her loosened hair, sliding down the long strands. "Like silk," he whispered. "All of you . . ."

A sigh escaped her. It shouldn't have felt so erotic—God knew he had touched her far more intimately—but it did. It felt erotic and tender. Like he was branding her with that stroke of his hand. A shiver rolled through her and she started to lean back into him—

"Hey, guys! Is dinner ready? It smells amazing."

At Malia's words, they quickly moved apart, Piper dipping the forks into the salad and tossing them as he slid open the drawer and removed a knife.

"Yes, can you set some plates on the table?" Thankfully her voice gave nothing away. It reflected none of her turmoil.

None of her longing for the impossible.

TWENTY

*P*IPER PULLED UP in front of the sheriff's department five minutes before eight. Hale had left before her this morning, but not before making a pot of coffee and leaving eggs warming on the stove for them. She expelled a heavy breath. This wasn't good. For God's sake, he cooked as well as he kissed. Who knew he could be so domestic? That living with him could feel so very right?

It was dangerous. She could get used to this kind of life. She snorted and glanced at herself in the rearview mirror, staring at herself skeptically. Who she was kidding? She had never lived like this. Of course she could get used to it. He was spoiling her. And she had to get away. She had to get away while she still could.

She planned on using her lunch hour to go view

a rental house nearby. The owner had already emailed her back and said she was available any time today to show the property. The sooner Piper got her own place, the better. The sooner she would stop wanting things she could never have.

She climbed out of her car and headed across the parking lot. The tiny hairs on her nape prickled and she paused, looking around. She didn't see anyone out of the ordinary. Hale's Bronco was already here, sitting in his designated spot in the parking lot. There were several cars occupying the lot and the shopping center across the street was busy, a steady flow of people entering both the doughnut shop and coffeehouse. There were a lot of people around. Any one of them could be watching her. It didn't have to mean anything.

Growing up the way she had left her with a particularly keen sense of awareness. When there were always questionable people around, people who would just as soon hurt you as look at you, you needed to say on guard. You needed to duck before the blow came. If at all possible, you wanted a head start if you had to run. It could be the difference between life and death . . . or at the minimum, the difference between a busted lip or black eye.

Situational awareness was everything, and right now hers was going off with a vengeance.

Shaking off the feeling, she entered the building and took her place behind the desk. Doris was still working alongside her. She planned to go another month. Molly warned Piper this was her way of giving Piper plenty of time to plan a grand retirement celebration.

"We have people in the holding cells already. Apparently there was a big party last night that didn't finish until this morning." Doris leaned in to share, her eyes wide with delight behind the lenses of her glasses. The woman might have worked the majority of her life in this department, but that didn't mean she didn't enjoy gossiping about the antics of those unlucky enough to land themselves on the wrong side of the law. "And this is only because the neighbors called when a fight broke out that spilled into the yard and woke up the entire neighborhood. At 4 a.m."

"Wow. Sunday night parties." Piper shook her head. She supposed her mom and dad partied on Sunday nights, too. Her earliest memories were always of a house full of people, drinking and laughing and fighting. It had seemed fairly ongoing. But it had been a long time since she was exposed to that type of life. Working here, she would once again witness evidence of all manner of vice.

Doris shook her head. "Sundays are for church, football and pot roast."

Piper watched as Briggs led a young guy out from the holding cell, guiding him into the vacant chair positioned by his desk. He'd been beat to hell and back. One eye was so badly swollen that you could hardly see his eyeball. Dried blood trailed from his nose down his chin, staining his shirt. That nose looked horribly misshapen and enlarged. Clearly it was broken. She wondered if maybe he shouldn't be at a hospital.

Her gaze lifted toward Hale's office, wondering if he had seen these new arrivals.

A woman walked in just then carrying a delicious-looking Bundt cake, beautifully iced beneath a glass dome. The only thing prettier than the cake might be the woman herself. She was wearing a very vintage-style dress. Tight bodice and flared skirt with a tiny belt that gleamed blue against the back gingham pattern. Her blond hair was swept into a tight ponytail that bobbed as she walked.

"Good morning, Doris." Her voice had a sing-song quality to it.

She set the cake on the counter with a flourish. "This is for Hale."

Well, okay, then. Hale. Not Sheriff Walters.

"I'll be sure he gets it, Hannah."

The blonde scanned the office area beyond Doris and Piper. "Is he busy right now?"

"He's in a meeting."

"Oh." She pushed out her bottom lip in a pout. "You'll be sure to tell him I made this for him." She stroked the glass dome in lazy circles with her perfectly manicured nails. Pink just like her lipstick.

"Of course, dear. Tell your mama I said hello."

"Will do." Her gaze shifted and settled on Piper. "And who is this?" The question was put out mildly, but there was something there. A decided chill that wasn't present when she spoke to Doris.

"This is Piper, our new dispatcher."

"Oh." She looked Piper up and down, her gaze lingering on her solid white button-down blouse. Circa Target $6.99. She wore a pair of teal blue pants, also from Target, to match. "I didn't realize Hale was hiring. Maybe I should apply?"

"Maybe," Doris said brightly. "Are you looking for work?"

She trailed a pink-nailed finger along her pearl

necklace. "Well, no, I don't need to work. Daddy wouldn't hear of it, but if Hale needs help, I'd be willing to do anything for him."

"I'm sure you would."

Hannah laughed and then fluttered her fingers. "Well, I have to run. I'm having coffee with friends."

"Toodles," Doris called after. Turning to Piper, she said with a frown, "Did I also mention you're the gatekeeper between Hale and the women of this town?" She nodded in the direction the blonde had just departed.

"What?"

"They drop in all the time. Cakes, muffins, scones, cookies, brownies . . ." She waved accusingly at the cake. "I've gained thirty pounds since he took over after his daddy."

Women brought him *baked goods*? Piper glared at the cake, wanting nothing more than to chuck it in the trash. "What do they hope to gain—"

"Hale. In their beds. Even better if they can get a ring out of him. That's the grand prize. Well, besides the obvious . . ." Her hand gestured to somewhere below the waist.

"Doris!"

"What? I'm not blind? He's a fine-looking man. The best to offer in this town and every woman under the age of ninety wants to see what he's packing under that uniform." She sniffed. "Not me, mind you. Once you change someone's diapers that tends to take the edge off that curiosity for good."

Piper laughed and shook her head. "Doris. You're too much."

"That's what people say."

Still chuckling, Piper sat up a little straighter as a big barrel of a man entered the building and walked with hard strides toward the desk. He slid his thumbs inside his suspenders as he addressed her. "I'm here to pick up my daughter. She was at a party y'all raided."

"What's her name?" The question had barely left her mouth when the father lifted his gaze and spied something over her head. "YOU!"

He charged around the counter.

"Sir!" she exclaimed. "You can't come back here." She rose and tried to cut him off, looking over her shoulder at whatever had him so distressed.

The guy sitting at Briggs's desk glared with his one functioning eye across the distance at the angry father. Clearly they had beef. Maybe it wasn't such a good idea to have them within spitting distance of each other.

"Deputy Briggs," Piper called, hoping to alert him to the situation while also attempting to stall the irate man's progress.

Briggs looked up. "Oh, hey, Piper. Need something?"

She shot him an exasperated look as she tried to push the barrel-chested man back. Couldn't he see what she needed?

"Piper!" Doris cried out, her voice sharp with warning.

She glanced at Doris. The older woman waved her over with an agitated motion. *Get over here*, she mouthed.

"You want something, Halpen?" The younger man pushed up from his chair to address the older man. He was slighter of build and banged up from the previous fight, but that didn't lessen his bravado—or stupidity—as he swaggered forward.

"You got my baby girl arrested!"

"Hey. Can't help it that she can't stay away from me. Guess she likes what I give her." He shrugged brashly.

"You bastard!" Halpen sidestepped around her and the two of them ran headlong into each other, fists swinging, striking each other wherever they could reach. They crashed into a desk, breaking it.

"Mr. Halpen," she cried out, hovering over them as they rolled on the floor.

Briggs watched, slack-jawed. Awesome. So much for lightning-fast reflexes.

The two men wrestled their way back to their feet and she grabbed hold of Mr. Halpen's brawny arm, hoping to stop them before they destroyed any other property. "Please, stop!"

Halpen flung back his arm and the force sent her flying. She landed hard, her teeth jarring from the fall. She heard Doris shout her name . . . and then suddenly there was an unfamiliar sound. A staccato clicking sound followed by the heavy thud of a body hitting the floor.

She came up on her elbows, gaping at the sight of Mr. Halpen's big body convulsing on the floor, wires stretching from his big belly to a Taser gun gripped in Hale's hands.

The younger man froze, holding his hands up in the air. "Don't Tase me!"

"Briggs! Why don't you make yourself useful?" Hale snapped, his expression tight with fury. Briggs dove to action, cuffing the younger man.

Piper remained where she was, watching as Hale made quick work of cuffing the immobilized Halpen.

Suddenly Doris was there, helping Piper to her feet. "You shouldn't have gotten involved," she clucked.

She brushed at her slacks. "I'm fine. I've got lots of padding." She rubbed her backside.

"You hit the floor hard, honey."

"Piper." Hale barked her name. She looked at him. Another deputy had joined him and was helping him with the stunned-looking Halpen.

"Wait for me in my office," he directed as he guided Halpen into a sitting position.

"Uh-oh," Doris said under her breath, and that was hardly heartening given she had known him all his life.

She motioned to the front desk. "Um, Doris and I have a lot of work to—"

"Now, Piper." A muscle ticked high in his cheek. "I'll be with you in a few moments."

She nodded stiffly, fighting against the giant lump suddenly clogging her throat. She walked evenly to his office, hoping she looked composed and not like a scolded child—which was how she felt.

She sat on the couch, knees pressed together, hands knotted in her lap, feeling very much like she was waiting for her sentence.

So she had messed up. So she should have let the actual law enforcement officers do what they had been trained to do and handle the situation. She got caught up in the moment. It had seemed like the right thing to do at the time.

"Damn it," she muttered under her breath. She had just wanted to do good and here she was. Only a week in the job and she was already in trouble.

Several minutes passed and her palms grew sweaty. Surely he wouldn't fire her? Right? How awkward would that be now that he had given them a temporary place to stay?

Finally the door opened and Hale walked in, looking even more intimidating than usual. That very official uniform covering his big body always gave him an added edge, but the scowl on his face certainly didn't help.

He closed the door behind him. Her pulse jumped at the click of the lock. He advanced on her, stopping directly in front of her with his legs braced apart. She pressed her knees even tighter together and squirmed slightly, as if that might alleviate the sudden throb between her legs. She was so bad. He simply walked into the room and her girl parts woke up. *Wrong, wrong, wrong.*

"What the hell were you thinking?"

He was pissed. Angrier than she'd ever seen him. Body tense as steel. Gray eyes snapping. Jaw clenched. She was ashamed to admit that looking at him this way turned her on.

She'd been around anger all her life. She'd witnessed it lead to violence. She should be alarmed and backing away . . . not thinking how incredibly hot he looked right now.

She attempted to explain. "I was only trying to help."

"You work the fucking desk and answer the phone. You don't get in the middle of brawls, Piper. You see that kind of shit going down and you back away. Don't run into it."

She flinched and nodded.

"What if you'd gotten hurt?" A nerve ticked madly near his eye. Still furious.

And she was still turned on.

"I'm fine." She flattened her palms on the couch and shifted her weight. For the briefest moment, her gaze dropped to his crotch. It was eye level, after all. Mortified, her gaze shot back to his face.

He didn't appear to notice. He blew out a breath and dragged his hand through his hair. "If you're going to continue working here, you're going to have to know your place."

A thread of resentment flickered inside her. Her

place? Her chin lifted a notch. "And what's my place?"

He stared down at her, still as furious as ever. In fact, he looked even angrier. Like she had somehow disappointed him with her lack of deference.

She moistened her lips and his eyes dropped to her mouth, catching the movement. She couldn't help herself. She licked her lips again.

His breathing fell harder.

She looked away again, her eyes lowering, and this time she noted there was a significant bulge in his pants. Her breath caught. The sight of it lit her every nerve on fire. She fidgeted again on the couch. Crackling moments passed. She could only gaze at that bulge as it continued to grow, her belly clenching and twisting.

Her gaze flew to his face, shock rippling through her, and something else. Something primal that made all her soft parts melt and quiver in submission. He was hard for her. Here. Now. Like this.

His gray eyes fixed on her, molten hot. He wanted her.

She glanced around his office, eyeing the locked door, the closed blinds. Yes. She was considering it—she wanted to. She wanted him so badly the ache was killing her.

"Piper." His voice was thick, and there was a promise of punishment in the grain of it. She knew she should rebel against it. The core feminist in her should be offended—the part of her that had worked so hard to guarantee that no person ever took advantage of her.

And yet her hands reached for him. Pulled down his zipper by slow degrees. She ventured inside, glancing at his face as she wrapped her fingers around his thick erection.

She pulled him free with a sigh of gratification. She stroked the beautiful length of him, so hard and pulsing. Her thumb rolled over the head, delighting as the skin deepened to near purple. Her stomach clenched as pre-cum beaded his slit. With a moan, she dipped her head and licked it up.

He groaned and buried his hand in her hair.

The taste of him undid her. She slid her lips around the crown of him and swallowed as much of him as she could, sucking as she went down.

He cursed and pushed up his hips, feeding her hungry mouth. His reaction gave her a heady sense of power that only stoked her arousal. Her sex clenched in near pain, desperate to be filled. One of her hands pressed between her legs and rubbed hard, grinding down on the clit, seeking out her own pleasure. Her hands were well familiar with how to do it. They were her only recourse these many years.

"No, you don't. You don't deserve to get off." He pulled her hand out from between her legs and then hauled her to her feet. "Take off your pants."

He sat on the couch, one of his big hands taking the place of her mouth and fisting himself.

She hesitated.

"Now."

She hurried to action, kicking off her ballet flats and unbuttoning her pants and shimmying out of them. She straightened in front of him.

His eyes glittered at her as he worked his cock in slow pumps.

"Panties," he said, the single word conveying exactly what he expected of her.

Her thumbs went to the waistband of her white cotton panties and then hesitated as sudden self-consciousness seized her.

His gaze snapped to her face. With a growl, he grabbed her by the waist and yanked her underwear down for her, prompting her to step out of them. Then, before she knew what he intended, he had her bent over his lap.

She squeaked and pushed both palms down on the couch, arching herself up. She was unprepared for the first spank. Her mouth parted in shock at the delicious sting.

Then he did it again and her core went from warm to pulsing, burning need.

"You don't get to put yourself in danger. You're mine," he rasped as his hand covered her cheek and massaged where he had struck.

She dropped her forehead to the couch with a keening moan as his big hand kneaded her. Moisture rushed between her legs and she couldn't stop herself from lifting her ass higher and parting her thighs slightly, hoping, praying, that he would lower those rubbing fingers and offer her some relief.

His fingers followed her unspoken plea, traveling over her wet lips and brushing at her opening. "This is mine." Then he delved a finger inside her.

She bit the side of her palm to keep from crying out as he drove his finger deep. He explored her in steady strokes, finding that little spot and then pushing on it until she started to shake. Suddenly he stopped.

"Please," she begged.

He resumed until he was only giving her slow and easy strokes again.

"Do you deserve it?" he growled.

Oh, he was cruel. How could he stand it? He hadn't gotten off on any of their previous encounters. Didn't he need his own release? He'd been all about giving her pleasure, but now he was tormenting both of them.

She wouldn't have it. Not anymore.

She looked over her shoulder at his hard face and practically snarled. "Why don't you just fuck me already?"

She didn't know who she was anymore. She'd turned into a creature that would say anything . . . *do* anything to have this man inside her.

Something cracked in his expression. He grabbed her by the waist and flipped her over to straddle him.

The last of his control broke.

It should terrify her. This big sexy beast of a man was about to take her virginity. She should maybe mention that to him. She should backpedal and retract the invitation. Invitation? Hell, she'd taunted him into it.

Instead, she looked down, watching as he poised the crown of himself directly at her opening. He pushed inside her, just the head at first, and she gasped. Woah. That was way bigger than his finger.

Her hands flew to his shoulders.

His eyes trained on her face and she felt pinned beneath that stare, unable to look away.

"You feel . . . perfect, Piper," he growled, and then let go, lunging up and pulling her down hard at the same time.

It was surreal. The sensation of him wedged deep, pulsing and so foreign inside her. She opened her mouth on a silent cry, overwhelmed at the fullness of him, at the burn of her inner muscles clamping around him.

He groaned softly and then moved again. He looked down at where they were joined and then all of him went still. "You're bleeding." His voice sounded stricken. "What—"

She followed his gaze, seeing the evidence with her own eyes. "That's normal. For the first time." At least that's what she had always heard.

His gaze shot back to her face. "What the f—"

"It's done," she quickly said.

"You've never done this before?"

She wiggled her hips slightly, enjoying his sudden hiss and the pleasure it sent vibrating along her nerves. "It had to happen eventually."

She kissed him, not wanting any more words

between them to ruin this now. He was tense beneath her and she felt him waffling, undecided.

Clearly she was going to have to do some persuading.

"Hale," she said against his mouth. "Come on." She worked her hips over him, carefully testing out the way their bodies fit together and delighted that nothing seemed to hurt anymore.

"Piper," he husked against her lips. "You should have told me. I would have made it better than this."

"You can make it good. Just . . . don't stop," she panted as she rocked her hips, gasping at the friction and focusing on her pleasure.

His gray eyes fired and suddenly he lifted her up without dislodging himself from inside her. He flipped her onto her back on the couch, his eyes still holding hers. "Does it . . . hurt?"

She shook her head.

Then he began stroking her in steady thrusts. Her head fell back and she swallowed her cries, dimly aware there were people on the other side of the door.

He took one of her legs and propped it along the back of the couch and the angle just brought him deeper. The friction built and she felt herself tumbling. Her orgasm crashed over her in waves, but he didn't let up. He rode through the tremors, increasing his pace. It was unending. A raging current without ebb.

She couldn't stay silent anymore. A rattling cry rose up and his hand quickly came down, covering her mouth as he drove into her, sliding her along the couch with the force of his body. His fingers splayed over her cheek, his palm against her lips. She kissed the callused flesh there, reveling in this, in him, in the fierceness of their joining.

Just when she thought it couldn't get better, something broke loose inside her and she screamed into his hand, arching her head and neck off the couch. The muffled noise gradually faded and she went limp, her body quivering in the aftershocks as she drifted back down.

He continued to move. One of his hands clamped down on her bare hip as he thrust, anchoring her, branding her. Suddenly he held himself still, a hoarse sound escaping his lips.

She felt his release, the pulse and twitch of him buried deep inside her. She watched his face in awe, the expression of bliss like nothing she had ever seen. Only something she had felt. Just now. With him.

He dropped his head into the crook of her neck and held himself still for several moments.

Gradually sounds returned. The birds outside the window. Voices carrying from inside the station. A metal drawer slamming. Footsteps passing the door.

Oh. God. What did she just do?

He climbed off her and moved to his desk. He grabbed several tissues from a box and then handed her the box.

A whisper shook out from her lips. "Th-thank you."

She took the Kleenex and sat up slowly. Her legs trembled like a newborn colt's. She turned sideways and cleaned between her legs, heat scalding her face.

She heard his slight movements and guessed he was cleaning himself as well. Still keeping her back to him, she reached for her underwear. Slipping them on, she quickly slipped into her pants, attempting to wrap her brain around the fact that they'd just had sex. *Unprotected* sex. Her mind couldn't even dwell on the possible consequences of that right now.

"Piper."

Dressed again, she turned slowly and faced him. Even though she didn't want to. Even though she wanted to turn and run out the door without looking at him. Why couldn't she be one of those sophisticated woman that slept with a man, patted him on the cheek, thanked him for a good time and strolled out of the room?

Because that's not you. Because you've never done that.

Because you care about this man.

The last thought brought her up hard. Oh, crap. She did care about him. More than she had any right to. That's why she had let this happen.

"I think you should take the rest of the day off."

She stiffened. She didn't know what she expected him to say, but it wasn't that.

He must have read the bewilderment in her face—and yes, the hurt, too. He continued. "You can't walk out there and act like nothing just happened."

She nodded slowly. He was right, of course. She wasn't that good of an actress. She just lost her virginity to her boss on a couch in his office. She doubted she could return to work for the day and act like her normal self.

"O-okay."

"I'll tell everyone you were shaken up after what happened."

"They'll think I'm some delicate little flower—"

"They'll have seen or heard what you did. That will be the last thing they think."

She released a breath, somewhat mollified.

He went on. "Go home. Relax."

Home. He meant *his* home. It wasn't her home. It was dangerous to think of his home as her own.

"All right." She moved for the door.

"Piper." She stopped and glanced back, suddenly eager to be away from this room that smelled of sex and sin and never-going-back. "We will talk about this when I get home."

Talk.

She could already imagine how that conversation would go.

This was a mistake.

It can never happen again.

Maybe he would even throw in an apology. Like this was something he had done *to* her and she hadn't been a willing participant. That would be very like him. The honorable sheriff/town golden boy taking responsibility. Saving the day. Holding the door open for everything with a uterus. It couldn't have been her fault. She couldn't have wanted it as much as he did. Forget that she had goaded him into it.

His expression revealed nothing. Once again,

he was the stoic, stiff-lipped lawman she had first seen at Joe's months ago.

He no longer looked like the man from moments earlier, so entirely shattered and undone with his need for her. He looked in control and unfeeling as hell.

Wrong or not, she missed the other him.

"I'll see you back at your house." Turning, she walked out of his office.

TWENTY-ONE

PIPER WENT HOME and showered, washing away all evidence of what happened between her and Hale. Well, all visible evidence anyway. What happened today would forever bear a mark on her. She couldn't take a breath without feeling him. Aside of the acute tenderness between her legs, her skin ached with the memory of him. And her heart . . . Well, she didn't know what her heart felt, but it *felt* something. It felt a great deal and that was a problem she didn't want or need.

After her shower, she decided to keep her appointment to view the house. She met with the Realtor and walked through the small three-bedroom located within walking distance from the high school. A definite perk for Malia. It also had a garage and backyard with a small covered patio. It was more than anything they'd ever had for themselves. They could make a home here. It could be something good—great, even—for Malia. For Piper, it was more than she deserved.

Unfortunately, she couldn't move in for another two weeks. Knowing she might not find anything better or available, she filled out the lease application before leaving. Somehow she would deal with living with Hale for two more weeks. Or maybe not. Maybe they would check into a motel. After what happened between them, she couldn't imagine living under his roof for even one more day. How could she manage it?

It was just after one when she finished up with the Realtor, so she decided to stop at the store for groceries to make dinner. It wasn't that she was feeling particularly domestic or that she wanted to play house with Hale. The man had been cooking for them, and it was time she did her share of the work and returned the favor. She knew how to make a few dishes and chicken enchiladas happened to be one of them.

She bought the necessary ingredients, including food for a few lunches for her and Malia. She even bought chocolate chip cookie dough. It had been a while since she had baked cookies. It felt good to have money in her bank account so that buying cookie dough didn't feel like such a splurge.

She was loading groceries into her trunk when she thought she heard someone calling her name. Looking up, she scanned the parking lot. There were just the regular shoppers on a Monday afternoon. Mostly stay-at-home moms with their toddlers and retirees. No one paid her any mind.

Shrugging, she slammed her trunk shut and got into her car. She strapped on her seat belt and started the car. Looking up, she gasped at the man standing directly in front of her bumper.

At first it was his sudden presence that surprised her. And then it was *him*. She knew him. Oh. God.

It had been several years but she had never forgotten the face of any one of her high school tormenters. Limned in sunlight, he stared at her intently through her dirt-smudged windshield. One of his hands was tucked into the pocket of his jeans; the other hand he lifted in a wave that was chilling in its casualness. Because there was nothing casual about the way he had terrorized her in high school.

What was he doing here? Did he think to pick up where he left off in high school?

Her adrenaline raced as she slammed the gear into reverse and backed out of the spot, nearly colliding into another vehicle in the process. The other driver laid on the horn, but she didn't care. Her flight instinct kicked in and all she could think was: *get away get away get away*.

And she did. As fast as she could drive, she whipped through the parking lot and left the grocery store behind.

Once on the highway, she relaxed her grip on the steering wheel and expelled her breath. Her adrenaline wasn't nearly as easy to calm. She hadn't seen Colby Mathers since graduation. Since he went away to college. He was one of *those* kids. The ones destined for better things like college. After all these years, she never expected to see him again.

By the time she got back to the house, she was still shaking. She brought her groceries inside and started unloading them, telling herself it was no big deal. The guy had probably been back for years and this was the first time she came face-to-face with him. It was probably pure chance. And even if it wasn't, it didn't matter. He wasn't going to do anything to her. Years had passed. He wasn't her bully. She wasn't his victim. Not anymore.

When she heard the front door open, she snatched a knife from the dish rack and whirled around. She wasn't expecting anyone home this time of day.

Hale stepped inside the house and raised both hands up in the air at the sight of her with the knife. He arched an eyebrow and said teasingly, "Don't stab me."

"Hale." She lowered the would-be weapon.

"Should I have rung the doorbell?"

"Of course not. It's your house. You just startled me." She put the knife back in the rack and resumed putting away the last of the groceries.

"You went shopping?" He looked over the bags on the counter.

"Yes. And I met with a Realtor and looked at a rental house." Turning, she put a carton of juice in the fridge.

"Today? Already?"

She nodded, grateful that she had something to do with her hands and somewhere else to look. "I signed a lease."

"That fast?"

"Yes. The bad news is we can't move in for two more weeks." She glanced at him.

"That's not a problem." His expression gave nothing away and she couldn't tell if he did mind or didn't.

"I was thinking we might check into a motel until we can move in."

"That's not necessary. Save your money."

She removed a bunch of bananas and set it on the counter. "Hale, this is . . . awkward."

He cocked his head as he studied her. "I'd think after what happened between us nothing could be awkward."

Her gaze strayed from his. "I guess this is where we have the talk."

"What kind of talk?" She heard him shift and looked up. He leaned against the counter, arms crossed over his broad chest, his expression mild.

"The . . . after-sex talk," she supplied.

He released a breath that sounded suspiciously like a chuckle. "Because you've had so many of those talks."

She huffed at his reminder that she had been a virgin. "Are you complaining about that fact?"

His gray eyes seemed to heat as they stared at her. "Not at all. For a novice, you were spectacular."

Her cheeks caught fire right along with other parts of her anatomy. He had been spectacular, too.

She reached inside a bag and took out a jar of peanut butter. Anything to avoid that searing gaze.

He resumed talking. "I think, in this conversation, we begin with the obvious."

"Which is what?"

"Are you on the pill? Or anything else?"

"Excuse me?"

"Typically it's a before-sex conversation, but since we skipped it we should probably cover it now. I know you weren't actively having sex, but some women take it for other reasons."

"I—I'm not on the pill or anything else."

He nodded morosely. "I'll use protection from now on, but you need to get on the pill right away."

She gaped. Was he so confident they would continue sleeping together?

He closed the distance between them, dropping his hands on the counter on either side of her as his deep voice rumbled out from his chest. "Because now that I've been inside you without anything between us, I'm not going to want you any other way."

If possible, her mouth sagged open wider.

"You look surprised."

She forced her mouth shut and nodded. "What about keeping things professional between us?"

"Little late for that. In fact, it was too late for that the moment I took that lap dance in the back room." He closed the distance between them until their bodies were pressed perfectly together, their mouths almost touching. "I'm done deluding myself. How about you?"

She swallowed but the lump didn't go away. It remained fully stuck in her throat. No, the only thing she felt slipping away was her resolve.

"This might be the dumbest thing I've ever done," she whispered. The air thickened between them, charged and electric.

"What time does your sister get home?"

"I have to pick her up from practice at four-thirty."

"Good."

"Why?"

"We have two hours." Wrapping his arms around her waist, he kissed her as he lifted her off her feet. She wrapped her legs around him, instinctively knowing what to do. He held her like she weighed nothing at all and carried her down the hall toward his bedroom.

Once in his room, he tossed her on his bed. She scooted back on her elbows and watched him as he removed his uniform one piece at a time.

"Why are you grinning?" he asked in a growly voice.

"I'm just thinking how every woman in Sweet Hill would kill for this striptease."

Fully naked, he reached down, yanked off her sandals and tossed them over his shoulder. "These days I only perform for you."

Those words shot a thrill straight to her heart. She squeaked as his hands went to the waistband of her leggings and pulled them down in one move.

Once he'd gotten rid of all her clothes, he came over her, aligning his naked body with hers. She fanned her hands over his chest, her nails scoring his hard chest.

Staring into his eyes, she had never felt more vulnerable and exposed in her life. He clasped her head with his hands, his big palms rasping her cheeks as he kissed her long and deep . . . until she felt as though she had melted in the bed. It was shocking and delicious and the most erotic thing she had ever experienced.

She couldn't help herself. She parted her thighs, welcoming him in. His hips settled in the inviting vee of her legs, his erection lining up along the seam of her.

"God, you're already wet down there," he spoke hoarsely into her mouth.

She undulated her hips, grinding against him,

gasping every time he bumped her swollen clit. He nudged at her opening and she cried out, so ready for him, desperate for penetration.

"How am I supposed to stop and put on a condom when you feel like this?"

She made a mewling sound of disappointment when he didn't just take the plunge and fill her where she most ached.

He was right. She needed to get on the pill because she didn't foresee a future without more of this. She didn't *want* one. At least for a while. Until she got him out of her system or he got her out of his.

Forcing herself to lie perfectly still and not pull him close in complete disregard to sanity—she had already committed enough insanity for one day—she bit out through clenched teeth, "Hurry. Get it on, then."

With a dark chuckle, he flung himself from the bed and rummaged in his bedside drawer. While he was gone, she couldn't help herself. She slid one hand between her thighs while her other hand fondled her breast.

When he came back over her, he paused as his hot gaze slid over her. "Now that's fucking hot, baby." Wearing the condom now, he stroked himself as he watched her play with herself.

"Hale," she begged, rubbing her clit in hard little circles. "Please. Now."

He positioned himself between her thighs, impaling her with a hard thrust. Again and again, he pushed his cock into her until she was arching her back and screaming. Moisture rushed between her legs, slicking the way for him. Their bodies came together in loud smacks.

Bending his head, he consumed her breast, his tongue and teeth attacking one nipple vigorously. "Taste . . . so sweet," he gasped as she ran fingers through his hair, tugging on the strands and moving him to her other neglected breast.

His hands latched on to her waist and he came up with a groan, hammering into her as though his life depended on it. "I told myself I'd go slow . . . gentle this time."

She raked her nails down his chest. "Harder," she gasped.

His eyes dilated and he did as she commanded. Flipping her over onto all fours, he gave her exactly what she craved, taking her from behind. His cock hit her impossibly deeper, stroking all the nerves in her sex in a new and astonishing way. The edges of her vision blurred as he launched her into an orgasm. She grabbed the headboard with one hand as she rode it out, not coming down from the crest yet before he reached around and started rubbing her oversensitized clit.

"Too . . . much," she gasped.

He lowered his broad chest until his body aligned with hers. "Just fall into it, sweetheart," he growled into her ear.

Somehow understanding, or trusting him enough to try, she relented, relaxing and melting into the firm massaging stroke of his fingers. And she came in an intense burst, tears springing to her eyes. She convulsed and shuddered violently.

"Oh, I feel that, baby. So tight . . . wet . . . you're squeezing me." He shot up, giving her one final thrust before he shouted his own release.

They both froze, locked together as their climaxes overwhelmed them. After an endless moment, he pulled out from her. Lifting away from the bed, he disappeared to toss the condom into a small trash can. Then he was back, pulling her against his side.

She couldn't move, too dazed and overcome.

After a moment, she found her breath to ask, "Is that what I've been missing all these years?"

He laughed lightly. "This is where I say it will never be this good with anyone else."

She giggled, her fingers splaying over his impressive chest. Privately, she acknowledged the truth in that. They laughed, but she worried he was right. How could it ever be this good with anyone else?

Bleakness filled her. Because this—*him*—could never be hers. This was fleeting. There was no place for him in her life. The sheriff of Sweet Hill could never find happiness with the likes of her. The irony was almost too much. She already felt like a fool for taking things this far. He was a good man. Any number of women deserved to be here in his bed instead of her. Any number of women deserved his heart.

Just not her.

THE NEXT TWO days passed in a crawl and Piper knew it was because she and Hale never managed to be alone together. There were no more trysts at home or work. One thing or another kept them apart, but every time their eyes met there was the memory and the heat and the want. The ache never went away. It was a constant pulse inside her. A living, breathing thing that pumped inside her blood. She was certain everyone around them could hear it—or look at her face and read her absolute longing there. Her coworkers, her sister. And yet no one seemed to notice. They carried on with life as though hers had not been torn off its axis.

ON WEDNESDAY SHE left at lunchtime and drove across town to drop off her deposit check to her new landlord. She was still moving forward and planning to get her own place. Just because she and Hale were . . . well, she didn't know what they were, but they were *something* and whatever that something was didn't change anything. She wasn't shacking up with her boss, the *sheriff.* She wasn't that dumb. Okay, she was dumb enough to have sex with him twice but she had her limits and living with him was one of them.

She was back at work in less than thirty minutes. As she stuffed her keys into her purse and hurried across the parking lot, she was calculating how long it would take to warm up a cup of soup and eat it before she needed to relieve Doris.

"Piper."

She froze at the sound of her name. She knew the voice. Even all these years later she could still hear it in her ear. *Trash. Hoe. A girl like you belongs on her knees. Why don't you meet me in the bathroom during lunch and we'll see how those lips of yours look around my dick.*

Clutching her keys in her hand as though they

could serve as some kind of weapon, she turned slowly and faced her high school tormentor.

"What do you want, Colby?"

Looking at his face, she knew he could have hurt her even worse than all those ugly words and taunts. They had felt bad enough at the time, but if he'd had his way and the opportunity presented itself, this guy would have broken her.

"I've been trying to get up the nerve to talk to you for weeks now." The worn tip of his shoe scuffed the ground.

She glanced toward the door of the building, gauging the distance if she needed to run for it. And yet she was also oddly compelled to face him. It had been seven years. She was a different person now. Not nearly as trusting, but neither was she anyone's victim. She liked to think she could handle him and anything he threw at her. She *needed* to know that.

"Why do you want to talk to me?" Even as she asked the question, she braced herself, expecting the old insults.

He buried his hands in an old army-green jacket that swallowed him. He'd been heavier in high school. A muscle-bound jock who overloaded his tray with multiple hamburgers at lunch. Now he looked strung-out. Like he hadn't had a good meal in ages. His cheeks were sunken and his skin had a sickly pallor. "The way I treated you was wrong. *I* was wrong."

She snorted in disgust. "Is this some kind of joke?"

"My life went to shit since high school . . . since Shelley Rae died."

She jerked a little at the name. She always tried so hard not to think about her. She couldn't stop the nightmares from coming when they would, but she made a valiant effort to keep Shelley Rae out of her waking thoughts.

"I didn't realize you were that close." She knew they ran in the same circles. All the popular kids did—and the kids whose parents had money. She eyed Colby up and down. He didn't look like he had two nickels to rub together now.

He removed a hand from his pocket and scrubbed the back of his neck with it. "We had a . . . thing. She wanted it to be more."

Piper nodded slowly, processing that. "It was you," she whispered. "You were the one that was supposed to come over that night to her house."

"Yeah. It was me."

Warped as it was, she guessed it explained a

little bit more about the night Shelley Rae had died. She was infatuated with Colby, so she wanted to *give* him Piper—all doped up and wrapped up in a bow. "She thought drugging me so you could rape me would win you over for her?"

He nodded, his expression grim. "Yeah. I guess she did."

"You would have raped me," she accused, feeling so oddly detached right then. Not even afraid. Only enraged.

"Yes. That was the idea. I—I'm sorry."

"You're sorry? You sick . . ." Her voice faded. There were no words.

He nodded again, looking miserable. "I spent the first couple years after she died trying to act normal. Trying to *be* normal. I did what my family expected. Went to college. Majored in business. Then I just couldn't anymore." He took a deep breath. "Well, you don't want to hear all about me and my sad shit." He shook his head like a dog after a bath. "I've been clean for the last six months, but my sponsor says I won't ever feel right if I didn't make amends—"

"Is that what this is? Why you've been stalking me all around town? I'm some fucking number on your AA list?"

"Uh, yeah. I can't live like this anymore. The guilt has been eating at me. Shelley Rae would still be alive if it weren't for me—"

"You didn't kill her."

He stared at her intently, his eyes so bloodshot she wondered if he was actually clean or still high. "I've got my guilt to bear. I played my part that night."

She nodded. "Yeah. You did." And her family—her brother and sister—were suffering for that.

"Well, this is my apology in all sincerity to you. For everything I did to you in high school . . . for what I wanted to do to you that night."

Several beats passed. "Do you feel better?" she finally asked. Because she didn't.

Facing Colby right now dredged up all the awfulness from her past, which was never far from the surface anyway. It didn't make her feel any better. Maybe it gave him peace, but not her. Her burden wasn't lifted. He was going down the list of people he had screwed over and working toward lifting *his* burden, but she would never have that relief. Her soul was as heavy as ever.

"Well, that's awesome for you. I'm glad *you* feel better."

He stared at her for a long moment and it was like this man—her would-be rapist—was seeing directly inside her mind. "You'll never feel better. Not until you unburden yourself of everything that bothers you."

"Yeah? Thanks for the great advice, Yoda. Go to hell." Without giving him a chance to say anything else, she turned and stalked away, pushing through the doors to the building.

Of course the first face she would see would be Hale's. He was emerging from his office in the company of the local county prosecutor. Fortunately, she wasn't familiar with the prosecutor. Her brother had been prosecuted through the City of Sweet Hill and not the county.

His gaze met hers and lit up even as he shook hands with the prosecutor. And it was like a punch to the solar plexus because after facing Colby she could only think how he wouldn't look at her the same way if he knew everything about her. If he knew the truth.

This was exactly why she should never have gotten tangled up with Hale—among other reasons. Cruz would be furious to know she was involved with him and he would have every right to be. He'd given up his freedom so that she could take care of Malia. So he could protect both of them.

Every moment with Hale, she risked everything and it had to stop. She had to stop this selfish behavior. She had to end it.

TWENTY-TWO

*T*HEY MIGHT HAVE cast aside all attempts to keep their relationship professional, but Hale couldn't seem to get Piper alone. Alone where he could get her naked. He was like a teenage boy desperate to be alone with the first girl who let him see her tits. It was rather extraordinary. He had never been that teenage boy even when he was a teenage boy.

And yet living under the same roof and getting her alone wasn't as easy a task as one would think—as *he* would *hope*. Workplace sex was out of the question. Even if he couldn't stop staring at the couch every time he was inside his office and remembering how sweet it had been between them. He would never regret it, but it was a bad idea to repeat the behavior. If she continued to visit him in his office with the door shut, people would talk. She was gaining the respect of the others in the department. The last thing he wanted was people thinking ill of her. She'd been unfairly judged for so much of her life already. He wouldn't perpetuate that cycle.

But it wasn't any easier to get her alone after work.

Tuesday night Malia had a soccer game, so it was after nine before Piper got home with her and then Malia stayed up late working on homework while Piper went to bed. He could hardly sneak into her room while her sister was working on her geometry at the kitchen table.

Then Wednesday night he got called into work and didn't return home until well after 2 a.m.

By the time Thursday rolled around he'd suffered enough cold showers and decided he was done torturing himself. He waited a full two hours after Malia went to bed, which put it at midnight when he was creeping out of his bedroom and skulking through the hallway like some kind of thief in his own house. Or maybe a teenager. He was carrying a condom in his hand, after all. Until she was on the pill, he wouldn't be as reckless as that first time.

It dawned on him that he might be far gone over this girl. As he crept into her bedroom and shut the door quietly behind him, gently turning the lock, he realized that he might be *more* than far gone.

He might feel for her more than he'd ever felt for any woman. God knew he *wanted* her more than any woman. As he eased the sheets down her lush little body, he knew he was treading in new territory. This desire for her was all-consuming. He liked her. He liked her under his roof. The only thing he would like more was Piper in his bed every night.

She was wearing a T-shirt, but it might as well have been sexy lingerie. Just the sight of her, even in the gloom of her room, gave him an instant erection.

He reached under her shirt, hooked his thumbs around her panties and slid them down her silken legs, acknowledging that he really didn't care how far gone he might be anymore. This was all he cared about it. These moments with her.

He stared at her face. She looked so young and relaxed in slumber, and he wondered if she knew what she was doing to him. Did she have any clue how much power she wielded over him?

He ran his hands over her legs and she sighed, parting for him. Even asleep, she seduced him. He splayed his hands on the insides of her thighs and spread her wider. How could he have gone this long without tasting her the other times they had been together?

Unable to wait any longer, he dipped his head and took his first taste, tonguing her long and deep. She moaned in her sleep, bending her knees and pushing her sweet pussy into his questing mouth. He lapped her up, drinking deep. He never thought a woman could taste so sweet. He found her clit and worried it gently with his teeth before sucking it deep and sending her gasping awake.

"Hale," she cried.

"Shhh," he whispered against her quivering flesh.

"What are you doing to me?" she moaned, and fell back on the bed, her hands tangling in his hair.

"First," he said, his tongue still playing on her, "I'm fucking you with my mouth." He spent a few more moments proving just that, sucking and nipping and then spreading her wide and spearing his tongue deep into her opening, until she was writhing on the bed under him.

Then he sat up, ripped open the condom, rolled it on and eased into her slowly. "Now I'm fucking you like this."

She came on his second stroke, vibrating and milking his cock, pushing him closer toward his own release.

He loved how responsive she was. It was like she was his instrument, made only to react to his hands. It had never been like this with anyone before her and it terrified him. Because he couldn't imagine having this with anyone else. Because with her, he didn't want anyone else.

He came hard and swift, dropping over her with ragged pants. "We went entirely too long without doing that. I need you every day."

Her hand came up to caress his face. She didn't speak, but he knew something was wrong. His Piper was never at a loss for words.

His Piper? Was that true?

Yes, it was true. He'd been barreling toward this moment since she poured a pitcher of water in his lap. Other women brought him muffins and cakes, but this woman brought him joy and challenge.

"What is it?" he asked.

"This can't . . . We can't keep doing this."

"Hold that thought. I'll be right back to tell you why you're wrong."

He got up from the bed and disposed of the condom, returning to her side, his heart hammering. If this was the beginning of a breakup conversation, he had never felt this sense of panic before. This desperate sense of *I-can't-lose-her*.

"You were saying . . ."

"I'm moving out next week. I just think we can stop this before it goes any further and gets more complicated. We work together and you don't do relationships—"

"I would do it for you," he heard himself saying without thought . . . and then he realized it was true. He would. He wanted a relationship with her.

"Oh God." She buried her face in her hands. "I can't believe this is happening. This wasn't supposed to happen. You weren't supposed to make this so difficult."

He pulled her hands away from her face. "What are you talking about?"

"You weren't supposed to be like this. You weren't supposed to actually want me—"

"But I do want you. And don't tell me you don't want me either. You'd be lying."

"Of course I want you." Her voice grew choked. "But there are things about me that you don't know."

"Then tell me."

She stared at him in the near dark, her eyes liquid pools of light. "All right. It will change everything though."

"Not the way I feel about you," he insisted, and meant it.

For some reason, however, he felt a sinking sensation in his gut. He didn't believe there could be anything that could change how he felt about her, but the way her face looked right now, he knew he wasn't going to like what he heard, and he knew putting it out there would change things for her if nothing else.

That was the most alarming thought of all.

SHE HAD TO tell him.

Since Colby's confession, she could hardly sleep. Living a lie wasn't nearly so hard when she didn't have to look at Hale every day. When her heart didn't beat faster every time he walked in the room. When she didn't care about him and want him so damn much her chest ached.

When she didn't love him.

She'd gone and fallen for him and she couldn't help wishing for more . . . for everything, for the life she'd told herself she could never have. The life other women got to have. She wanted him to be hers forever, but she'd always told herself she could never have that. It had never been a particular challenge denying herself a storybook forever because she'd never had anyone like him in her life. But here he was, being beautiful and so very enticing.

She had to come clean with him. And not just with him. She had to confess to the world or she would never feel free and deserving of anything.

She couldn't live her life with this hanging over her anymore.

"I have to tell you something. I did this . . . thing." She stifled a snort and cleared her throat. That was putting it mildly.

"I don't care."

She gave him a pained smile. "Hear what it is before you say that." She took a careful breath. "When I was eighteen, a girl in my high school invited me to spend the night at her house. Shelley Rae Kramer." She winced. She couldn't really remember the last time she had said her name out loud.

"The girl your brother murdered."

Of course he would know the details of her brother's case. She held Hale's gaze, neither agreeing nor disagreeing. "Shelley Rae and I never really got along," she explained, hesitating at that admission. It was a gentle euphemism.

Now that Shelley Rae was dead, it felt . . . wrong to speak ill of her. It was like Piper was trying to shift blame. But Shelley Rae had been a bully. There was no other description for her. Cruel and devious, she had tormented Piper since elementary school.

She continued. "I thought she wanted to be friends. She claimed she did. She apologized for the years she had bullied me. We were supposed to have a genuine girl's night. I was a fool."

"No, you weren't," he argued. "You wanted it to be true."

"Her parents were out of town. We were watching movies, eating pizza, popcorn. It was fun. The kind of thing I never got to do. And then suddenly I got . . . dizzy. It was like I was moving through a fog." She fluttered a hand. "I remember spilling my drink on the carpet."

She stopped. That night existed in fragments for her. She'd struggled to remember it in its entirety over the years, but she only dreamed of it in snatches. Sometimes new bits would appear. "I told her I was going to be sick . . . and she laughed at me. Called me trash. All of sudden she was that mean girl again."

"What did she do to you?" His voice was hard and she risked a quick glance at his face. He looked angry, but she knew he wasn't angry with her. Not yet. That moment was yet to come. He was angry right now at what she was describing and that's because he cared about her. He still thought she was an innocent victim of a high school bully. She swallowed painfully. If only that was the end of it.

She took a careful breath. "She roofied me. And, oh, she delighted in telling me that." A broken laugh tore from her lips. "She relished it . . ."

He cursed.

Flashes of that night punched through her memory. Staggering through Shelley Rae's media room, her world spinning, the bile rising in her throat. Her hands stretched out in front of her, straining to reach for the perky cheerleader who kept laughing and hopping out of reach as she flung cruel taunts at Piper. Even in her glee, Shelley Rae's face twisted with a hate that Piper couldn't understand.

Piper bumped into a side table and knocked over a lamp. It struck the hardwood and shattered to pieces.

"She told me she still hated me. She didn't want to be my friend. She called me trash." She winced. "All kinds of awful names. Inviting me over, acting like she was my friend, was a setup. She said someone was coming over and they were going to show me a good time."

"Someone as in a guy?"

"Yeah. She had arranged everything." Bitterness crept into her voice. "One of the guys from school was coming over to rape me."

He cursed again and reached for her. She scooted back on the bed, holding out her hands to ward him off. "No. I might have started out the victim in that scenario, but it didn't end that way."

"What happened?"

"I managed to grab her. We fell to the floor." She shook her head. "We fought . . ." She remembered the struggle. The shards of lamp all around them. She remembered Shelley Rae slapping her and calling her names. She remembered lifting her arms, heavy as bricks, to hit her back.

Then she remembered nothing more. Just a big wall of blackness.

She woke much later. Sunlight streamed into the room . . . and she was lying in a pool of blood. Blood that wasn't hers.

"I killed her. We broke a lamp when we were fighting." She motioned to her neck. "I jabbed a piece of glass right into her throat."

She was crying now, her words drowning in great sobs. In her telling, the tears had started to fall and now they ran unchecked down her face. Hale pulled her into his arms. She tried to resist, but she was weak. She wanted it too much. She wanted it almost from the start with him. She wanted him to love her despite this. Despite everything.

"But your brother . . . he's in prison for killing

the Kramer girl—" He stopped and pulled back to look at her. "Piper, no . . ."

Her words fell in a torrent. "I called Cruz. He took the blame. He said I had to let him. He insisted." The tears were coming fast now and her voice was practically indecipherable. "Cruz had custody of Malia, but he was about to lose it because he got into trouble . . . some petty theft charges. We weren't worried because I was eighteen. I was going to get custody of her. If I went to prison, then Malia would go to foster care. Cruz said that couldn't happen. She was only eight and she'd already been through so much. She couldn't lose both of us."

Hale let go of her and swung his legs over the side of the bed, propping his elbows on his knees, and buried his face in his hands. "Piper," he groaned. "You should have told the police. You couldn't have been found responsible for—"

"Oh, really? You're so sure of that?"

He stared at her bleakly and she knew even he wasn't sure.

"No one would believe a couple of Walshes." She shook her head. "Especially back then. It was just a couple years after my mother's accident. But you're right." She nodded resolutely. "I did a terrible thing. I killed a girl and let my brother take the rap. He's been in jail seven years because of me, but I can't live with this anymore. Malia is fifteen now. Maybe Claire's family could take her in for the next three years. You're a sheriff. You have influence. You could help make that happen. Please, will you do it for Malia?"

He lifted his head and leveled a suddenly alert stare on her; his lips worked as though searching for the right words. "What are you saying, Piper?"

"I'm going to confess. I—I'm going to the police tomorrow." Even though her voice trembled, she had never felt so certain of anything in her life. Just stating her intention lifted a weight off her chest. "I'm going to tell them everything—"

"Like hell you are," he growled. And suddenly he was over her, pinning her down on the bed, his expression fierce. "I'm not losing you because you defended yourself against some psychotic girl. It was self-defense," he said, his voice still hard, vibrating with fury. "What she did to you was fucked up. Any jury—"

"No." She shook her head. "I don't remember any of it. And any jury in this town will look at me now like they would have looked at me seven years ago. A no-good Walsh, jealous of the perfect rich girl. And what are they going to think of me for letting my brother rot in prison all these years?"

"He doesn't have that much time left on his sentence—"

"One more day in there is too much." Her tears fell harder. "How do you think I feel? How can I live with myself out here . . . loving you while he's stuck in there? It was one thing when I was miserable, living my own hell and working at Joe's, but you make me happy and I don't deserve that. I don't deserve to be free. I don't deserve you—"

His mouth crushed into hers, silencing her. She melted against him, her mouth wet from the fall of her tears. Their teeth and tongues collided.

His hand skimmed down her naked form, grabbing hold of her backside as he devoured her. His cock swelled between them as he growled against her lips, "You're not telling anyone."

"I have to." She gasped as he widened her thighs apart with his hips. "I can't ever be happy . . . we can't be happy . . . with this hanging over us."

"No." He ground his cock into her, tormenting her and making her writhe beneath him.

"I'm confessing."

"You can't." He kissed her deeper, both hands

under her now, his hands massaging her ass as he rocked his erection against her sex, sliding against the slippery folds.

"Hale," she moaned. "Please . . ."

He pushed inside her, but then stopped, holding just the crown of himself at her entrance.

She arched, pushing and pulling at his shoulders. "Please, give it to me. I need you." It might be the last time and she was desperate to claim it for herself. It would be something to take with her, to cherish and keep close when she was alone in a cell.

He inched in, just an incremental amount, and then pulled back out. "Promise me you won't tell anyone. You won't go to the police."

She writhed under him. "This isn't fair."

"Promise me, Piper," he commanded, his voice hard and eyes glittering.

She bit her lip, rolling her hips, trying to bring him inside her body.

He eased his hand between them and gently, delicately, teasingly, stroked her clit.

"Hale," she wept.

"Say. It."

"Yes, I promise."

He plunged inside her, thrusting without relief.

He pounded into her as if he could exorcise the demons from her past.

"Mine," he panted. She had a sense he was punishing her for keeping her secrets, for thinking that she could ruin this thing between them.

She reveled in his body movements, in his pulsing shaft gliding in and out of her throbbing sex. She lifted her hips for him, sealing this in her memory.

She gripped the slick skin of his massive shoulders and clung to him. Animallike sounds tore from his lips. Her orgasm hit her in a blinding flash. She lowered her hands and scored her nails over his taut backside, breaking his rhythm and forcing him deeper.

He groaned and jerked out of her, spilling his seed over her belly.

He fell beside her, breathing harshly. They both gazed at the ceiling. His voice rumbled over the air. "You're not leaving me, Piper Walsh. You can get that thought right out of your head."

Gradually his breathing evened and she realized he had fallen asleep.

She rose from the bed and slipped into the bathroom to clean herself up. She paused when she caught sight of her reflection in the mirror. Her eyes were huge and luminous. The weight was still there. The burden.

Tomorrow she would lift that burden and hope that he didn't hate her for breaking her promise to him. She was going to have to add lying to the man she loved to her many sins.

TWENTY-THREE

*I*T WASN'T THE first time Hale visited Devil's Rock Penitentiary. Work had brought him here plenty of times, but this was the first visit of a personal nature.

Cruz Walsh lowered himself in the chair across from him. There was no hiding the wariness in his expression. "Last time I checked, I never committed a crime in the County of Sweet Hill."

"I'm not here on county business."

He lifted a dark brow that was bisected with a scar. A scar that hadn't been present in his mug shot so he could only guess this was courtesy of his time in prison. "Why are you here, then?"

"I'm in love with your sister."

A tic went wild in his cheek but otherwise he didn't react. Several moments passed before he leaned forward and rested his arms on the table. His hands curled into white-knuckled fists. "You leave her the fuck alone."

"I'm going to marry her."

Cruz's dark eyes roamed his face, assessing, probing. Bewilderment gleamed in there, but also fear. Hale knew precisely why he was scared.

"I'm here for your blessing." He paused at Cruz's snort. "You have my promise that no harm will ever come to her. I don't care about what happened in the past . . ." He let his words hang meaningfully. "I will always protect her. *Always*."

Cruz leaned back in his chair, letting his arms drop in his lap again. "Yeah?"

"Yeah."

A long silence ensued as the two stared at each other. Finally Cruz leaned forward again, bringing his face close to the glass. "You hurt her and I don't know how, but I'll find a way out of this cage and I'll come for you."

Hale smiled. "Fair enough."

AFTER SHE DROPPED Malia off at school, hugging her extralong and telling her how much she loved her, she drove straight to the Sweet Hill Police Department. She knew the building well. She'd been there several times with her mother, and of course the night Shelley Rae died and Cruz was arrested.

The lead detective still worked there. She asked for Detective Sorenson and he came out right away to greet her. He'd always been decent to her. She was glad he hadn't retired yet and he would be the one to take her confession.

He led her to a conference room. Another detective joined them. A camera sat in the corner. It wasn't in operation, but she nodded at it. "You might want to record this."

The two men exchanged looks and the younger man moved to the camera.

"Piper, what brings you here?" Sorenson asked in a mild voice.

She rubbed her sweaty palms over her thighs. She couldn't help it, but she thought of Hale. She hoped he could forgive her for this, but it didn't matter. It had to be done.

"I'm here to confess to a crime." Deep breath. "Seven years ago, I killed Shelley Rae Kramer."

Sorenson's eyes widened. She rushed into the details of that night. Sorenson followed along, occasionally jotting down notes. When she was done, the detective released a breath and looked at his colleague again.

She glanced at the young man and did a double take. He wore the most curious expression. His forehead knitted together in wonder. He didn't look at her like she was a horrible person. No, he looked at her like she was crazy.

"Ms. Walsh," he said. "All these years . . . you thought *you* had killed Shelley Rae Kramer?"

She nodded. "I did. It wasn't my brother. I swear it. I'll take a lie detector."

Sorenson uncrossed his legs and scooted his chair around to face her. "Listen carefully. You didn't kill Shelley Rae."

Fear bloomed in her chest. It had never occurred to her they might not believe her. "I'm telling the truth."

"I believe that's what you think, but you're innocent of this crime."

"My brother didn't do this!"

"Yes, I know that. Colby Mathers came in late last night and confessed to killing Shelley Rae. We were about to leave this morning to bring you in to corroborate his story, although that was really only a formality. He gave us the shirt he was wearing that night. He's kept it all these years. It's covered in blood. We've sent it to the lab, but we're pretty convinced that it will return positive for Shelley Rae's blood."

"Colby? Why?" She shook her head. They were friends. Shelley Rae was giving Piper to him that night as some sort of warped present. Why would he kill her?

"Apparently when he showed up she was attacking you."

He studied her closely. "Do you remember anything about that night?"

She shook her head. "I remember we were struggling. She drugged me . . . I was so weak. And then nothing. I passed out."

He nodded. "Colby said she drugged you. He shoved her off you and she fell into a broken portion of the lamp. A shard went straight through her jugular. He claims it was an accident. He ran though. He didn't call an ambulance. He didn't call the police."

"Felony manslaughter at the minimum," the other detective surmised.

"I didn't do it," she said, more to herself than them, staring blindly ahead. All these years she thought she'd killed Shelley Rae.

Her soul had suffered the weight of that sin. She thought every awful thing to befall her deserving . . . God or karma seeing to her penance. Her brother went to jail for her murder.

Her gaze snapped to Sorenson. "My brother!"

He nodded. "I already have an appointment set up with the DA."

Tears choked her. "He's gonna get out?"

"I can't imagine he'll have to be in there much longer. Now there are formalities to . . ."

She dropped her face into her hands and broke into sobs, not hearing another word he said, too overcome. She was innocent. And Cruz would be coming home.

Suddenly there was a commotion outside the room and the door burst open. Hale stepped into the room. Sorenson stood. "Sheriff Walters—"

"Piper." Hale's gaze fell on her and the agonized look on his face made her heart seize in her too-tight chest.

"Hale, what are you doing here?"

His gaze skipped to the two bewildered detectives, then darted to the rolling camera in the corner. "This interview is over," he said in a steel voice. "You're not arresting her. She's going home—"

"Of course we're not arresting her." Sorenson looked affronted.

Hale paused.

"Hale, it wasn't me. Someone else did it. Someone else killed Shelley Rae. I didn't do it and my brother is going to get to come home."

Instead of looking relieved he looked furious. "But you came here and confessed?"

"Um . . ."

He looked at both detectives. "I'm taking her home now."

Sorenson held up both hands as if illustrating that they had no intention of detaining her.

With a stiff nod, Hale grabbed her hand and hauled her out of the police department. "My car is over—"

"We'll get it later," he growled, depositing her in the passenger seat. For a moment, she had a flash of déjà vu to the time he hauled her out of the club.

He drove them home—much too fast, she couldn't help noting. "How did you know where I was?"

"You didn't go to work this morning. Didn't take much to figure where you went." He slid her a resentful look. "You promised me."

"Under duress," she shot back.

"I didn't have a gun to your head."

"You seduced me with sex. Baiting me with the promise of my orgasm wasn't exactly fair. I would have said anything. You knew what you were doing."

She crossed her arms and stared out the window,

angry with him. This was a dream come true. She'd never imagined this turn of events . . . and he was ruining it. She was free. Soon Cruz would be free.

They pulled in the driveway and she was out before he could come around to her door. In fact, she had her keys out and the front door unlocked ahead of him. She stalked back to her bedroom, but he followed like a tenacious bulldog, looking big and intimidating and sexy as hell in his uniform. It was distracting. But at least he was dressed. Naked was worse. Better but worse.

"You walked in there and confessed. You gave up on me."

She whirled around. "Is that what this is? You didn't get to save me? I wounded your ego."

"No!" he exploded. "I fucking love you and you tried to take yourself away from me. How could you have done that? You were willing to give up on us. It would have broken me, Piper."

She stared at him in shock. "But . . . you don't do relationships . . ."

He laughed humorlessly, holding his arms wide. "What do you think this is? Casual?"

"Well . . . no."

"We've been in a relationship for some time now whether either one of us put a name on it." His chest lifted on a ragged breath. "I'm in love with you, Piper Walsh. And I don't want you to move out. I don't want you in this bedroom down the hall from me either."

"Hale—"

"I want you in my bed. Every night." He stopped and their gazes held. "You said you loved me last night."

"You heard that?" she whispered.

His response was succinct. "Yes, I heard. And I love you. I *need* you, Piper."

She gasped.

In two strides he lifted her against him. "Are you really so surprised? You confessed to murder last night and I didn't give a shit. I'm a lawman and I would have done everything to protect you and cover it up."

She cupped his face. "I know. I just thought you were being heroic. I didn't think you could really love—"

He kissed her. Inhaled her. Devoured her until her head spun. She clung to his shoulders and wrapped her dangling legs around his waist.

He broke away to mutter against her mouth, "For years you've been beating yourself up and blaming yourself for a crime you didn't commit. For blaming yourself for your brother's imprisonment when you did the only thing you could do at the time to protect Malia. I get it. I doubt I could have been as strong. You haven't been dealt the best hand in this life, Piper, but I want you to live the rest of your life with me and we'll make it amazing. Together."

She was crying then and kissing him, raining feverish kisses all over his face. "Yes. Yes. Yes."

He dropped her on the bed and stood back, wrangling free of his clothes. She watched him, grinning so widely her cheeks ached.

Suddenly she saw everything ahead of her. This beautiful man and their love, their future full of all the things she only dreamed about. Things other people had. Not Piper Walsh.

This was better than that because she wasn't dreaming it up at all. It was real and it was hers.

EPILOGUE

Five weeks later . . .

*H*ALE WATCHED AS Piper flitted around the house, moving picture frames and then moving them back, adjusting a vase of flowers, critically eyeing the appetizers on the counter, sticking her head in the oven to poke at the brisket that he'd smoked earlier and wrapped in foil to keep warm.

She glanced back at him, worry heavy in her dark eyes. "You don't think it's drying out in there?"

"The oven is off. It's just keeping it warm. And I've never dried out a brisket in my life."

She nodded but didn't look reassured as she closed the door shut again.

She'd been like this all day. Running to the store multiple times, cooking, cleaning, calling Faith for advice about this or that. She'd changed her dress two times already.

She blew by him again, the loose braid she wore bouncing over her shoulder. She muttered something under her breath and glared down at her second dress of the day. He knew what that meant.

He reached out an arm and caught her by the waist, pulling her back against him.

"Hale!" She pushed halfheartedly at his chest. "Everyone is going to be here any moment."

By *them* she meant their guests: roughly a dozen plus people, close family and friends all assembling to celebrate the release of Cruz, exonerated from the crime he was convicted of seven years ago.

If ever there was time for a celebration this was it. Cruz Walsh was a free man. Even if he didn't act like it.

When he was finally released three weeks ago he wore an expression more fitting for a funeral than a man who had just gained his freedom. Hale knew it disappointed Piper. She wanted her brother to be happy.

"And this place looks perfect," Hale assured

her. "Cleaner than it's ever been. The pillows you got for the couch are a nice touch, too." He couldn't care less about pillows but he knew she cared. That's how his life was now. He cared about the things she cared about.

She nodded distractedly and looked down at her body again. "I just want to change my clothes—"

"*You* look perfect."

She went limp, allowing him to fold her in his arms and pull her close. "I *feel* like a hot mess."

"You're *my* beautiful hot mess though." He pressed a slow, open-mouthed kiss to her throat and nuzzled the sensitive skin there.

She shivered in his arms and her breath caught. "It's your job to say that. You're my boyfriend."

He paused at that. He was definitely her boyfriend and even though he had never rightly been any woman's boyfriend before that designation fell lamely on his ears. It felt small and insignificant. He actually had to fight back a grimace. Piper was more than a girlfriend to him. She was his entire world. Like his father before him, he had fallen totally and deeply and irrevocably in love with a woman and his life was richer and more meaningful for it. Given the situation, he knew what he had to do. He'd known for weeks now.

She brought her hands up and buried her face in them. "What if he hates everything?"

"You mean, the fact that you're throwing him a congrats-you're-out-of-prison surprise party? Yeah. I'm pretty sure he's going to hate it."

"But he just thinks it's dinner," she protested.

Yeah. That's what she had told her brother, but Hale had let Cruz in on the surprise. He didn't do it to be a jerk and ruin things. No. He did it because he had a feeling the guy wasn't going to show up for the dinner party—and that's when Cruz just thought it was a get-together that had nothing to do with him specifically. It would have crushed Piper, so Hale let Cruz know about the party and exactly why he needed to be present for it.

She groaned. "Maybe I should just call everyone and tell them not to come?"

The doorbell suddenly pealed through the house.

His grinned at her panicked expression. "Too late for that."

"Maybe it's just Malia with Claire. I can send them away and still call everyone else." She escaped his arms and darted for the door to peer out the peephole. Pouting with disappointment, she looked back at Hale. "It's your sister and North."

"Well, that does it then. No going back now. You know there's no sending Faith away."

Sighing, she pasted a smile on her face and opened the door, greeting them warmly.

More guests arrived then. North's brother, Knox, and his wife, Briar, with their cute little toddler in tow.

Malia with Claire and her family.

Hale's father. The old man hugged Piper and Malia warmly. His father doted on them from the moment he met them. He made up any excuse to drop by, and he loved going to Malia's soccer games. Sometimes he got warnings from the referees when he got too enthusiastic in his sideline shouting and cheering. Just like when Hale and his brother played sports, he was very vocal of what he deemed bad calls. He might have even gotten worse over the years.

Doris and her husband. There was no keeping her from a party. And Hale knew better than not to invite her to this particular occasion.

The Ruiz family arrived next. They lived next door to Piper when she grew up. Piper told him that Mrs. Ruiz watched after Malia a lot back then. Especially after their mom died. Piper doubted she could have finished high school without her help. According to Piper, Mrs. Ruiz had been devastated when Cruz went to prison. She'd doted on him like a son.

"Everyone's here," he murmured over the chatter filling his house.

Piper smiled tightly. "You think when he pulls up and sees all the cars he's going to come inside or bail?"

Hale shrugged one shoulder even though he knew nothing would keep Cruz from showing up—not after their talk.

"He'll be here, sweetheart." He rubbed a reassuring circle on her back.

To Piper's frustration, Cruz had been rather aloof since his release from prison. They all had dinner together that first night he was released, but he'd declined Piper's subsequent invitations.

Hale had reminded her that it would take him time to adjust after seven years at Devil's Rock. Even North had warned her of that, but knowing didn't stop her from wanting her brother to be happy. Especially because she was so happy. He knew her well enough to know she was still feeling guilty . . . as though she was somehow not entitled to finding her own joy.

The doorbell rang and she practically ran to

answer it. Hale followed at a slower pace, attempting to calm his own sudden nerves. God, he felt like a nervous kid. He rubbed his sweaty palms on his slacks.

The house quieted as she opened the door.

Cruz stood there, his eyes falling on his sister. He was big and intimidating . . . especially with that thin scar running down the side of his face. That didn't stop Piper though. She stood on her tiptoes and flung her arms around his neck. Walsh hesitated a moment and then his big arms wrapped around her and hugged her back, lifting her off her feet.

Malia came forward then and hugged him, too.

"I didn't think you would come. Thought the cars outside might have spooked you." Piper stood back, watching with delight shining in her eyes as her siblings hugged.

"I wasn't going to," he announced with a grimace.

"What changed your mind?" Malia asked.

Cruz looked over their heads and found Hale's gaze. He nodded at him. "The sheriff came to see me and said I better be here."

"Hale?" Piper blinked and looked between the two of them, stiffening. "He made you come?"

"I wouldn't say he made me." A smile creased

Cruz's face. It actually looked awkward on him. Clearly he was a man unaccustomed to smiling. Probably not much to smile about in prison. "Let's just say he provided me with motivation. I wouldn't miss tonight for anything in the world."

Piper shook her head, clearly bewildered. Her gaze fixed on Cruz. "You came even though you knew it was a surprise party for you . . ."

"No, I decided to come when I found out it was going to be a *double* celebration."

Hale reached into his pocket.

"Double?" she echoed, her forehead wrinkling in confusion.

Several gasps filled the room as Hale lowered to the ground.

Piper swung around to see why everyone was reacting that way. Her eyes landed on Hale: down on one knee before her, a jeweler's box open in his hands.

It was her turn to gasp.

Malia shrieked but he kept his attention riveted on the woman he loved. "Piper Walsh, will you spend the rest of your life with me . . . as my wife?"

Her hands flew to her mouth but that didn't muffle her sobs. She nodded, not looking away from him as he took her hand and slid the diamond solitaire on her shaking ring finger. It fit easily. As though it was destined for her hand. "Yes," she finally managed to get out in a hoarse croak. "Yes, yes, yes, yes."

Rising to his feet, he kissed her, indifferent to their applauding audience. They kissed for what felt like forever but it still wasn't nearly enough, He doubted he'd ever have enough of her.

As much as he had wanted their family and friends present, he could only see her. Could only absorb this moment with her. Her face. Her blinding smile. The happy tears shining in her dark eyes. The world faded away as he etched it all into his memory, into his soul. The moment she agreed to bind her life with his.

It was amazing that he had thought he never wanted this: love, a wife, happily-ever-after. Amazing that he had found this . . . found *her*.

It truly was a beautiful life.

And don't miss the rest of Sophie Jordan's unforgettable Devil's Rock novels!

ALL CHAINED UP

Some men come with a built-in warning label. Knox Callaghan is one of them. Danger radiates from every lean, muscled inch of him, and his deep blue eyes seem to see right through to Briar Davis's most secret fantasies. But there's one major problem: Briar is a nurse volunteering at the local prison, and Knox is an inmate who should be off-limits in every way.

HELL BREAKS LOOSE

Shy and awkward, First Daughter Grace Reeves has always done what she's told. Tired of taking orders, she escapes her security detail for a rare moment of peace. Except her worst nightmare comes to life when a ruthless gang of criminals abducts her. Her only choice is to place her trust in Reid Allister, an escaped convict whose piercing gaze awakens something deep inside her.

FURY ON FIRE

After years in prison, North Callaghan is finally free. But the demons haunting him still make him feel like a caged beast. He loses himself in work and hard living, coming up for air only to bed any willing woman to cross his path. So when his new neighbor snares his interest, he decides to add another notch to his bedpost. The only problem? Faith Walters is a white picket fence kind of girl.

At Avon Books, we know your passion for romance—once you finish one of our novels, you find yourself wanting more.

May we tempt you with . . .

- **Excerpts** from our upcoming releases.
- Entertaining **extras**, including authors' personal photo albums and book lists.
- Behind-the-scenes **scoop** on your favorite characters and series.
- **Sweepstakes** for the chance to win free books, romantic getaways, and other fun prizes.
- Writing **tips** from our authors and editors.
- **Blog** with our authors and find out why they love to write romance.
- **Exclusive content** that's not contained within the pages of our novels.

Join us at
www.avonbooks.com

AVON *An Imprint of* HarperCollins*Publishers*
www.avonromance.com

Available wherever books are sold or please call 1-800-331-3761 to order.

FTH 1013